THE RED PEARL EFFECT

A Sam Quick Adventure

SCOTT CORLETT

THE RED PEARL EFFECT

Second Edition
LCCN: 2019909281

ISBN: 978-0-9905364-6-8 (Hardcover)
ISBN: 978-0-9905364-7-5 (Softcover)
ISBN: 978-0-9905364-8-2 (EPUB)
ISBN: 978-0-9905364-9-9 (Mobi)

Contact: scottcorlett.com

Editing by Zenuscript
Cover design by Zenuscript
Interior design by Zenuscript
Author photo by John Nieto

For Peter

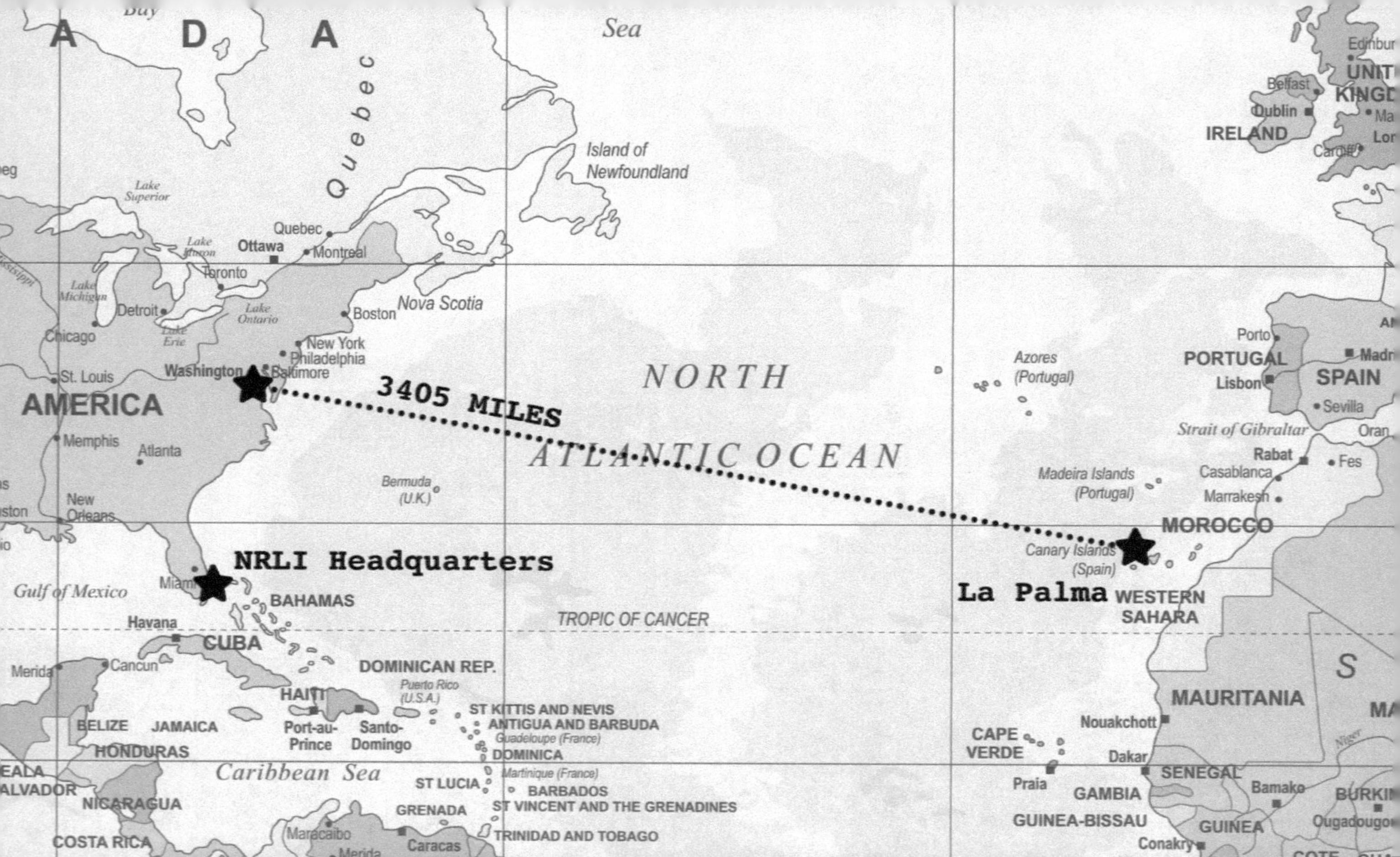

ADA
Bay
Sea
Quebec
Island of Newfoundland
Lake Superior
Lake Michigan
Lake Huron
Lake Erie
Lake Ontario
Mississippi
Quebec
Ottawa
Montreal
Toronto
Boston
Nova Scotia
New York
Philadelphia
Baltimore
Washington
AMERICA
St. Louis
Chicago
Detroit
Memphis
Atlanta
New Orleans
ston
NORTH
ATLANTIC OCEAN
3405 MILES
Azores (Portugal)
PORTUGAL
Lisbon
SPAIN
Sevilla
Madrid
Strait of Gibraltar
Oran
Rabat
Fes
Casablanca
Marrakesh
Madeira Islands (Portugal)
MOROCCO
Canary Islands (Spain)
La Palma
WESTERN SAHARA
Bermuda (U.K.)
NRLI Headquarters
Miami
Gulf of Mexico
BAHAMAS
Havana
CUBA
TROPIC OF CANCER
Merida
Cancun
DOMINICAN REP.
HAITI
Port-au-Prince
Santo-Domingo
Puerto Rico (U.S.A.)
ST KITTIS AND NEVIS
ANTIGUA AND BARBUDA
Guadeloupe (France)
DOMINICA
Martinique (France)
ST LUCIA
BARBADOS
ST VINCENT AND THE GRENADINES
GRENADA
TRINIDAD AND TOBAGO
BELIZE
JAMAICA
HONDURAS
EALA
ALVADOR
NICARAGUA
COSTA RICA
Maracaibo
Merida
Caracas
Caribbean Sea
S
MAURITANIA
Nouakchott
CAPE VERDE
Dakar
Praia
Niger
SENEGAL
Bamako
GAMBIA
GUINEA-BISSAU
GUINEA
Conakry
COTE
BURKIN
Ougadougou
MA
Edinbur
Belfast
Dublin
Cardi
UNIT
KINGD
IRELAND
Ma
Lor

THE
RED
PEARL
EFFECT

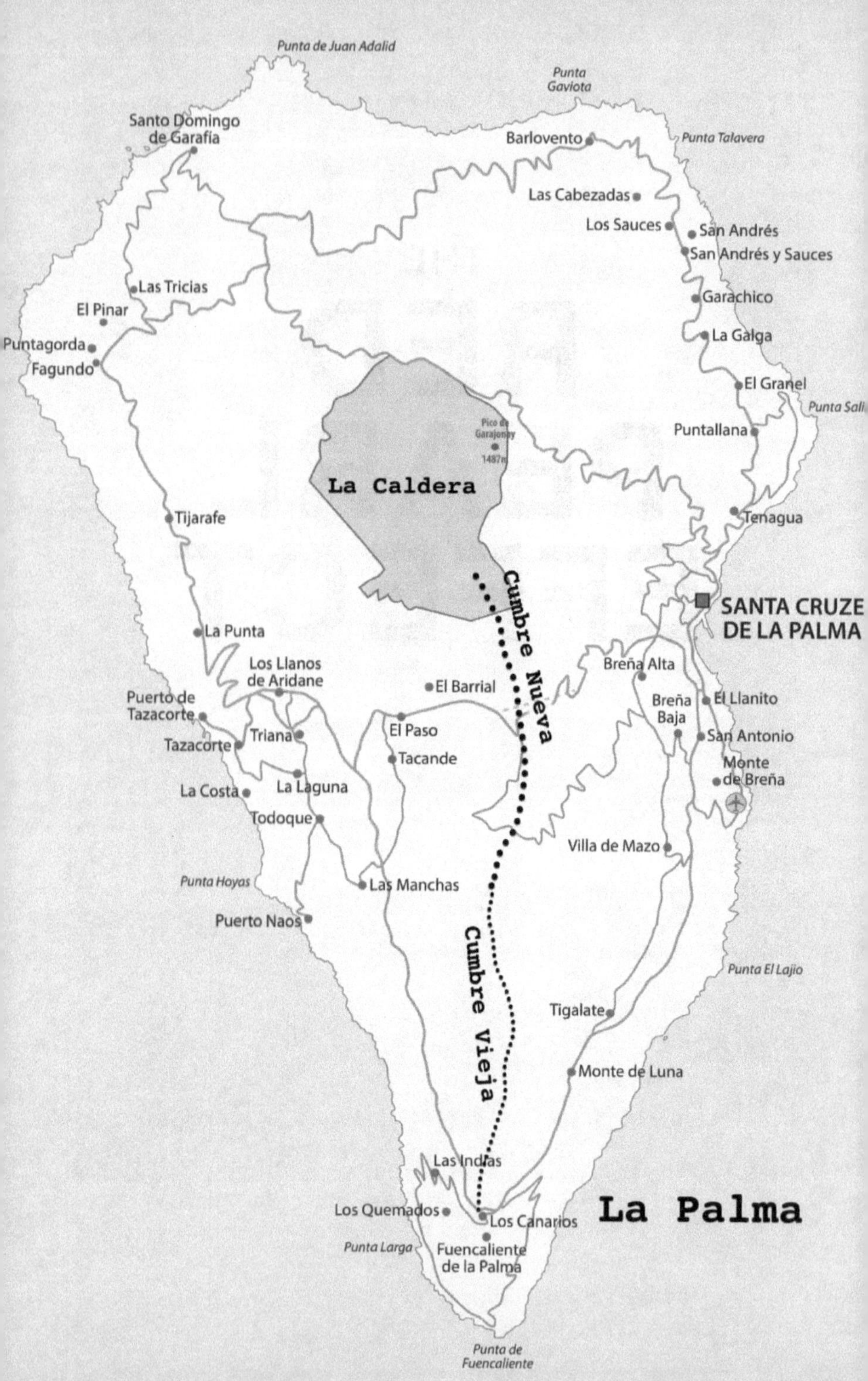

Punta de Juan Adalid
Punta Gaviota
Punta Talavera
Santo Domingo de Garafía
Barlovento
Las Cabezadas
Los Sauces
San Andrés
San Andrés y Sauces
Las Tricias
El Pinar
Garachico
Puntagorda
La Galga
Fagundo
El Granel
Punta Sali
Puntallana
Pico de Garajonay
1487m
La Caldera
Tijarafe
Tenagua
Cumbre Nueva
SANTA CRUZE DE LA PALMA
La Punta
Los Llanos de Aridane
El Barrial
Breña Alta
Puerto de Tazacorte
Breña Baja
El Llanito
Triana
El Paso
San Antonio
Tazacorte
Tacande
Monte de Breña
La Costa
La Laguna
Todoque
Villa de Mazo
Punta Hoyas
Las Manchas
Cumbre vieja
Puerto Naos
Punta El Lajio
Tigalate
Monte de Luna
Las Indias
Los Quemados
Los Canarios
La Palma
Punta Larga
Fuencaliente de la Palma
Punta de Fuencaliente

PROLOGUE

JUNE 1949
La Garganta del Diablo Mine
Island of La Palma, the Eastern Atlantic

Today would decide if he lived or died.

But for a few moments longer, Poncio Díaz could believe the day would be just like any other he had spent chasing the red ore deep into the old volcano: his bones echoing with the constant crash of metal against rock, his face and torso caked in red dirt, and his hair and dungarees drenched with sweat as if he had walked into the ocean.

Díaz slammed his pickax into the rock. Stone and soil collapsed to the ground. By the time the metal claw broke free of the dirt, Díaz realized today was nothing like any other before.

Not anything at all.

Nada.

First, the delicate hairs in his ears vibrated. Then the reverberations washed down his body, slid into his gut and spread out to his extremities, onto his ax and boots, and the surrounding timber and rock, until everything in the mineshaft was shaking in unison.

Men shouted.

The massive support timbers groaned and whined under the pressure of the quaking earth.

Then the first stone fell from the tunnel ceiling.

Díaz threw down his ax, grabbed the two young miners working beside him, and shoved them up the shaft, all the while praying to San Gabriel to keep watch over his family at home in the village.

Ahead of Díaz, men slid left and right, as they madly grabbed for any handhold to propel themselves up the tunnel, their boots slipping in the red muck as if it were ice.

Rock and dirt rained down.

The noise was deafening.

Then the rock wall exploded. Steam blasted from the breach into the face of the young miner directly ahead of Díaz. The man was dead before he could even scream.

A jet of boiling water chased the initial steam flash, shot straight across the tunnel, and started scouring away the opposite rock like a hydraulic drill.

Díaz could do nothing but slam himself against the wall, as the torrent of scalding water and dirt roared past him down the shaft. The flood crashed into the tunnel's dead end and formed a roiling, red whirlpool, with the dead miner spinning at its center.

Then just as suddenly as the earth started heaving, it stilled.

But Díaz and the other miners hardly noticed. One thing now transfixed every man present—the water spewing from the rock.

The miners uphill of the breach yelled back at Díaz. Their words were lost to the water's thunder. But Díaz knew exactly what they were shouting: *"¡El agua del Diablo!"*—the miners' name for the water trapped deep in the mountain, superheated by the volcanic forces below, and periodically released into the shafts by either an unlucky miner striking a vein or a shift in the rock.

Díaz looked around. His gaze caught on the dead miner's floating body. He crossed himself. Then he confirmed he was the only man alive caught below the gusher. He immediately waved on his coworkers without hesitation. He would let no one else die for him.

The men watched him for a moment longer. Then the older miners started dragging the younger men up the shaft. The attacking water could collapse the tunnel at any moment. And the miners' creed—safety then rescue—demanded their continued ascent despite their friend's plight.

Díaz watched the last man disappear from sight. He looked from the searing water spraying across the shaft ahead of him to the deadly lake climbing from the tunnel's dead end behind him.

Utterly alone, Díaz now faced only two options, both equally terrifying: hope the flood abated before the rising water boiled him alive—or run through the blistering cascade in a bid for escape.

In Tazacorte, the town on the harbor below the mine, the ground had stopped moving, but the bells of San Gabriel Arcangel, the little church, still wildly tolled as if worn by panicked cows. Villagers poured into the chapel, among them, Ana Díaz, clutching her infant son.

She pushed the child onto a pew, crumpled to her knees, and clasped her hands so tightly in prayer that they turned into a knurled chunk of ice-blue flesh, all blood and life wrung from them.

Despite the tolling bells, Ana Díaz heard only one thing now, the chanting in her head: *Algo está terriblemente mal . . . Algo está terriblemente mal . . . Something is terribly wrong . . . Something is terribly wrong . . .*

In the mine, scalding water roared from the breach. Steam and aerosolized mud choked the air. Poncio Díaz watched the rising lake of boiling water take a first, tentative lick of his boot.

It was now or never.

Díaz crossed himself and pictured his wife and son one last time. He crouched and leveraged as firm a foothold as possible. Then he sprang forward into the spray. The boiling jet blowtorched his right flank. He almost collapsed from shock.

But Díaz staggered onward.

He nearly reached the main tunnel.

Then he heard it.

Fleetingly, he thought the water's roar was multiplying.

Then the mountain violently contorted.

Timbers screamed and cracked like gunfire.

Shaft walls began sliding as if made of sand.

Díaz forgot the fire in his side and scrambled forward, begging God to keep safe his wife and son.

But they were not.

In the village, ceilings crashed down. Walls crumbled. Bells clamored wildly. The church bucked and swayed. Mothers and fathers threw themselves over their children. Ana Díaz screamed for her husband and covered her son.

On the volcano's summit above the mine, a geyser of molten lava shot into the sky like an orange flare deployed by the island in a desperate appeal to the neighboring atolls.

Moments later, not far from the mine, soil and rocks started disappearing into the hillside. At first, the sinkhole was roughly circular. Then it broke along a line running parallel to the mountain ridge, growing faster than the distance between two horses galloping in opposite directions.

In San Gabriel Arcangel, the frescoed ceiling cracked like a breaking mirror. Clumps of plaster rained down. In last desperation, mothers shoved away their clinging children, stuffing them under the heavy pews.

On the mountain, the growing breach ripped from north to south for seven miles, cleaving the island in two. The half-trillion-ton flank supporting Tazacorte began sliding into the ocean.

The village fishing docks sank beneath the waves.

The sea rushed the town's lower reaches.

In the mine, Díaz dragged himself into the main tunnel. He fought to keep moving, but the earth was falling from beneath him. He grabbed an ore cart and went to his knees.

He felt his heart furiously convulse, as it frantically tried to gird his plummeting blood pressure. Shock set in. He fell to the red dirt.

Seconds later, Poncio Díaz was dead, his scalded flesh hanging from his body like strips of wet, ragged paper.

In the old church, stone rained. Support timbers crashed down. But amid the chaos, one figure returned to calm: Ana Díaz, her son tucked beneath the heavy pew, relaxed back against the old polished wood, looked up, and reached out her arms. She saw her Poncio. He was smiling at her, his head cocked, and his eyes as loving as ever.

But instead of reaching for her hands, he gently shook his head and pointed to their son. She saw his lip move: "*Te quiero.*" Then he disappeared, and her soul quaked a thousand times more violently than the crumbling island.

Of course, her husband was right: it must be this way. She forced herself to the stone floor and crawled under the pew, wrapping her body around her son.

A final cacophonous clang of bells drowned out the last dying prayers, as San Gabriel Arcangel, defeated, folded in on itself.

Part I

Reykjavik
Arkhangelsk
Faroe Islands (Denmark)
Shetland Islands (U.K.)
FINLAND
NORWAY
SWEDEN
Oslo
Helsinki
Stockholm
Lake Ladoga
Lake Onega
St. Petersburg
Yaroslavl
Nizhniy Novgorod
Perm
Moscow
Ufa
Tula
Penza
Samara
Orenburg
North Sea
Baltic Sea
ESTONIA
LATVIA
LITHUANIA
Edinburgh
DENMARK
Copenhagen
Minsk
UNITED KINGDOM
Belfast
Dublin
Manchester
London
Cardiff
IRELAND
Hamburg
Amsterdam
Berlin
POLAND
Warsaw
BELARUS
Kiev
Voronezh
Volgograd
Rostov-na-Donu
Astrakhan
NETH.
BEL.
GERMANY
LUX.
CZECH
SLOVAKIA
UKRAINE
MOLDOVA
Paris
FRANCE
Munich
AUSTRIA
SLOV.
HUNGARY
ROMANIA
Lyon
SWITZ
Milan
CROATIA
Belgrad
BOSNIA AND H.
SERBIA
Bucharest
Marseille
Monaco
ITALY
Rome
MONT.
ALBANIA
KOS.
BULGARIA
Sofia
Istanbul
Black Sea
Caspian Sea
GEORGIA
ARMENIA
AZER.
TURK
Porto
AND.
Barcelona
Napoli
Athens
Izmir
Ankara
Ashga
PORTUGAL
Madrid
SPAIN
GREECE
CYPRUS
TURKEY
Lisbon
Sevilla
Algiers
Tunis
MALTA
SYRIA
LEBANON
Tehran
Qom
IRAN
Strait of Gibraltar
Oran
Constantine
TUNISIA
Mediterranean Sea
Damascus
Baghdad
Isfahan
Rabat
Fes
Tripoli
ISRAEL
IRAQ
Madeira Islands (Portugal)
Casablanca
Marrakesh
Alexandria
JORDAN
MOROCCO
Cairo
KUWAIT
Canary Islands (Spain)
ALGERIA
LIBYA
EGYPT
SAUDI ARABIA
BAHRAIN
QATAR
Abu
La Palma
WESTERN SAHARA
Medina
Riyadh
U.A.E.
MAURITANIA
Sahara
Jeddah
Mecca
Arabian Peninsula
Azores (Portugal)
Tigris

- 1 -

NOVEMBER 1989
The Soviet Embassy, East Berlin

The crowd's cheers might crack open the embassy's walls. Good, he thought, let them.

Since morning, Senior Warrant Officer Dmitry Petrov had watched the mob thicken in the street outside. Now, for as far as he could see, people jammed every inch of ground, sharing bottles and hugging in ever-shifting combinations, all as they sang their German songs, celebrating their city's reunification.

Petrov turned from the window and looked into the mirror hanging over the bureau. The face staring back at him was drawn, but the eyes, lively, two blue oases amid the pale skin. He straightened his jacket and brushed the red epaulettes covering each shoulder.

He grabbed his Makarov PM off the dresser and slipped it into its holster. Air picked up speed between his teeth, pulsing and twisting into the tune of "God Bless America."

My chance comes soon. Anything can happen now.

. . .

The crowd's noise died as he descended the stairs. Petrov was alone, still softly whistling, while he climbed down the long flight into the embassy basement.

At the bottom, now silent, he walked a dozen yards along the corridor, until he reached a nondescript door sandwiched by two soldiers, each young man standing in full salute.

Petrov nodded, and one of the guards immediately knocked on the door. It opened. Petrov did not blink at the muzzle aimed at his face. His analog grunted from inside the room and lowered his gun.

Petrov entered the small, windowless chamber. His colleague holstered the weapon and left without saying a word. Petrov turned the lock and then slid onto the wooden chair.

He glanced at the table lying along the opposite wall. Petrov never knew how many he would find sitting there when he reported for duty. Sometimes, ten of the metal suitcases sat aligned in a neat row. Sometimes, none.

No one had ever told him what the suitcases held, only that he must guard them with his life. No words were needed. Petrov knew these were the deadly pawns in the forty-year game of atomic chess between his country and the West, the miniaturized nuclear weapons or so-called suitcase bombs that the Soviet Union freely moved via diplomatic shipments to its embassies deep within the enemy's territory. Bombs that could, without the slightest warning, decapitate the governments based in the cities home to those embassies.

He counted. *Four.*

Petrov wondered what would happen to them when his country finally collapsed. His only concern, he ultimately concluded, was figuring out how he would escape during the coming chaos, first into Western Europe, then to America. He leaned back and closed his eyes.

An hour later, a knock broke his nap. Petrov sighed, stood up, and then grabbed the lock. He leveled his Makarov at the door, as was protocol. He opened the door, prepared to lower his weapon from the scowl of a KGB agent.

Instead, a bullet shattered his front teeth.

Petrov fell to the ground, his eyes wide, a signal in his ravaged brain wildly ricocheting but never quite finding the path to his trigger finger. From where he landed, he could see the guards lying in the corridor and the blood seeping from their throats.

Petrov watched two men wearing Soviet military dress enter. A shoe slammed the Makarov from his hand. The attackers moved directly for the suitcases.

One intruder whistled, as he stopped at the table. "I've never seen one in person."

"Not much to look at," the other man said, patting one of the bombs.

Petrov's eyes widened—they were speaking Russian, but their accents were wrong. *Central Asian maybe.* He struggled to clear his airway, but only foamy blood spilled from his mouth.

One man glanced at Petrov. "No loose ends, remember."

The other man nodded.

Their muzzles swung toward Petrov's chest, and their voices said in perfect unison, "Thank you, comrade, for your exemplary service to Mother Russia."

I was so close—

The bullets tore through his uniform and savagely chewed Petrov's heart. And the shooters grabbed the suitcases.

-2-

PRESENT DAY, JUNE 1
South Florida

The frost-blue Jaguar squealed to a halt an inch from the no-parking sign, and Molly Matson jumped out of the car. A tennis polo and short skirt highlighted a figure good for someone half her age. Her face was naturally smooth and lightly tanned, and only her casually swept-back white hair gave any indication of her true years.

Matson cut though a courtyard surrounded by cement-block buildings on three sides. Ahead, on the quad's fourth side, lay a strip of sand backstopped by blue-white surf.

The small campus was located just south of Miami, wedged between a two-lane highway and a quiet stretch of Atlantic shore. The modest facilities belied the importance of the Naval Research Laboratories and Institute, or *Nar-ly* as staff pronounced the acronym. In fact, NRLI was the U.S. Navy's elite research lab and a crown jewel of the American military establishment.

NRLI's mission was protecting the national security of the United States of America in the broadest sense. Not only did NRLI develop advance weaponry and defensive systems. But its military and civilian scientists researched everything from alternative energy sources to vaccines against bioterror attacks to defenses for the U.S. cyber infrastructure.

At the last building on the right, simply marked B-38, Matson turned and followed wet footprints approaching from the beach. Inside, the tracks led her to the hall's end.

She rapped a half-open door, beside a nameplate that read "Sam Quick, Director, Molecular Biology."

Inside the lab, Dr. Samantha Quick looked up from a laptop. Faint lines deepened around eyes cut from pale sky, as her lips parted in an easy smile. "Hey there, stranger."

Matson marched in, shaking her head in mock disdain at Quick's attire. Her friend and colleague Sam Quick was a distinguished molecular biologist, but the younger scientist looked and dressed more like a lifeguard just coming off duty. As usual, Quick was wearing her tank top and hiking shorts, exposing lightly muscled arms and legs, while flip-flops clad her feet, and the dark, shoulder-length hair framing her face was wet.

"How was the water?" Matson asked, knowing Quick spent her lunch hours swimming laps in the Atlantic.

"Just like those happy hours you keep dragging me to—filled with sharks."

Matson grunted in response, as she stopped beside Quick, at a long counter covered by churning laptops and elongated trays pegged by tiny vials filled with various-hued liquids, like futuristic cribbage boards. Beyond the lab bench stood a wall of windows looking out on the ocean. In a nearby corner, a potted palm sat surrounded by a deep mat of dropped leaves, the room's only sign of personalization.

"Let me guess: ALCHEMY," Quick said.

"ALCHEMY is indeed why I am here. If you would please conjure a map of northwest Africa on this infernal machine," Matson said, pointing at Quick's laptop.

Quick tapped a few keys, and a map filled the screen. Matson's finger pinned some white pixels floating in the Atlantic off Africa's western coast. "Zoom in here."

A boomerang-shaped archipelago expanded and resolved, revealing a small island chain. Matson's finger swept along the arc to the northwestern-most island and tapped twice.

"I was cleaning out my files and ran across a geology journal article describing some zinc deposits in a little volcano on the Spanish island of La Palma, 125 miles off the African coast." Matson looked at Quick, and her brow rose. "Some *unusually concentrated* zinc deposits."

Quick was quiet for a moment. Then she replied with the nonchalance that Matson knew meant her friend was keenly interested, "The rocks sound promising?"

"Fit for a queen."

Matson patted a stack of papers lying beside the laptop. "Given the self-aggrandizing adjectives triple-somersaulting off this top page, these must be the résumés for the summer internships. Why don't you choose a few well-qualified grad students to accompany you out to the island and help with the grunt work?"

Matson started for the door, putting on her sunglasses. "Just feed 'em some cock-and-bull about hunting for the usual bugs, and they'll fall all over themselves to carry Sam Quick's water bottle."

"I'm fairly sure the NRLI handbook, if not various state and federal sexual-harassment statutes, forbid using Molly Matson's definition of 'well qualified,'" Quick called after her.

The older scientist stuck her head back in the doorway and looked over her glasses. "What's this world coming to when you can't pick a research team based on bicep circumference?"

-3-

MONDAY, JULY 9
Island of La Palma

BBC World Service, it's eight o'clock GMT. Concerns grow about radiation detected in central London—

Sam Quick snapped off the radio, leaned back in the driver's seat, and stared at the windshield. These few moments were her first downtime since arriving on the island two days ago and the ensuing dawn-to-dusk mission preparations. But Quick was not looking out at the surrounding picturesque village or beyond at either the lush green mountains to one side or the vividly blue sea to the other.

Rather the molecular biologist was mentally reviewing the day's action plan. Quick knew she had to execute perfectly if she hoped to achieve success on the ALCHEMY project before time ran out. But given what she had seen yesterday at the mine, they were closer than ever. *Three days collecting samples, then back to Florida—*

"*¡Buenos días, Dr. Quick!*"

Quick turned and found Manuelo Alcanzar striding toward the red Jeep. His face, nearly perfectly round, broke into a crackle glaze of a thousand tiny wrinkles, as he raised an arm in greeting.

Quick returned the smile. *"Buenos días,* Manuelo. *¿Estás bien?"*

"Very fine, thank you," Manuelo answered in good English, as he reached inside the topless Jeep and shook the scientist's hand. "And where are the young ones this morning?"

Quick pointed.

Turning, Manuelo raised his arm again. "Ah, good morning, señorita Kalia and señor Eric."

From the hotel steps, a woman and man waved in return, then bounded down the stairs, each with a backpack slung over a shoulder.

They were a mismatched pair, neither of who would be first taken for a graduate student in the hard sciences. Kalia Slater looked like she just shot a Hawaiian tourism commercial, sporting wavy, dark hair, a big aloha smile, and a deep tan consistent with being a volcanology student on Hawaii's Big Island. Eric Hunt was a short, muscular fireplug with a blond crew cut, silver eyebrow ring, and complexion befitting someone who divided his time between his midwestern university's molecular biology lab and the fitness center.

They dumped their packs into the Jeep and then climbed onto the back seat, while Manuelo took the position beside Quick.

Five minutes later, above the village, the red Jeep wound through switchback after switchback, as it climbed the steep volcano. Only a narrow gravel ribbon separated the road from open air. Below, terraced banana farms followed a mountain crease down to the Atlantic's blue water. On a distant curve behind, a speeding orange car looked like a flitting ladybug.

Sam Quick glanced at her passengers. Then her eyes returned to the road. Her foot doubled its pressure on the gas pedal. And the Jeep whipped into the next turn.

. . .

Climbing down from the Jeep, Quick pointed at a rock formation covered with reddish stains lying a hundred yards uphill. "Be sure to grab some pix and samples of those mineral deposits." She patted a walkie-talkie clipped to her belt and looked from Slater to Manuelo. "And you know the drill: any problems, radio me pronto."

Quick nodded at Hunt, and the two headed off.

Manuelo glanced at the back of Hunt's retreating T-shirt. It was emblazoned with red skull and crossbones with the words "Don't Rock It, Sink It" printed underneath. Then he looked at the sign nailed up beside the mine entrance. The faded red paint read, "*¡Peligro! ¡No Entrar!*" And beneath the text, an image mirrored the skull and crossbones of Hunt's T-shirt.

He thought of the villagers' name for the abandoned mine: *La Garganta del Diablo*—the Devil's Throat—and all the miners who had died pursing the red ore, their deaths giving rise to the macabre label. *Esta expedición es un buen dinero, pero me alegraré cuando termine.*

The old Spaniard sighed and shouted, "Be careful, *mis amigos!*"

But Quick and Hunt had already disappeared into the mine.

Inside the shaft, Quick took the lead, with Hunt following closely behind, walking down the center of the rail tracks that had once serviced the mine. Alongside them, bundled wires that the team had tacked up yesterday ran along one wall of the red rock. Glowing lights dangled from one cable. From the other wire, every forty feet, hung the plastic discs that relayed the walkie-talkies' radio signals to the surface.

Quick and Hunt continued walking in silence for the next hundred yards, until they reached a junction with an intersecting shaft. Here, they turned right, following the cabling.

The side tunnel was rougher than the main shaft. The scientists were now sweating, as the air grew progressively hotter as they moved deeper into the mine. Every few yards, they had to climb over rockslides that washed out the tracks. They didn't bother trying to dodge the muddy water dripping from the stone above and instead simply let it splatter on them like red rain.

The tunnel ended at a hexagonal chamber where six shafts converged at a heavy wooden circle bisected by rail track, a rotating platform for redirecting ore cars to any of the tunnels. At the platform's center, the scientists paused beside a pile of fallen stone and broken timbers that spilled from one tunnel, freezing the industrial merry-go-round in place.

Then Quick pointed at one of the open shafts, with its lights strung into the distance.

- 4 -

MONDAY, JULY 9
London

"Earlier today, London Metropolitan Police announced that radiation was detected at an undisclosed location in London SE1." The crisply dressed newsreader smoothed the papers before him, "Metropolitan Police now confirm the detected radiation is due to plutonium of an unknown source found dispersed in a car park.

"Plutonium is a radioactive element commonly found at nuclear power stations and at atomic research and weapons facilities. Metropolitan Police stress that no evidence yet suggests terrorist involvement. Metropolitan Police further say the hazard is now fully contained and no menace to public welfare presently exists. In response, the government has elevated the threat levels for all service branches, and the Prime Minister is scheduled to provide a statement at 6 p.m. GMT. Both Scotland Yard's Hazards Team and MI5 are aiding the inquiry." The reader turned the page. "Manchester United signed—"

A gentle warble interrupted from across the room. Utley sighed and pressed a button on the remote control. Behind him, the television went silent. For a moment longer, through the window, he continued watching the office workers holding their cocked umbrellas trudge through the relentless rain as if they were giant black mushrooms riding an endless conveyor belt.

Despite being at home in his library, Utley was dressed every bit as formally as the slogging business people: a charcoal-gray two-piece suit of Scottish wool and English tailoring, with a tie of cerulean silk. His figure remained trim, while his face was gaunt like that of any mature man of fit build, with a narrow nose, and intense, jadeite eyes. Above it all, his hair persisted preternaturally thick and black.

The ringing continued, and Utley turned from the window, sank into a wingback chair, and grabbed the phone handset.

"Yes?"

For several minutes, the room was nearly silent, broken only by the soft, uneven rasp of Utley's breathing. Finally, Utley said, "I see. Yes, thank you very much."

He put down the handset and lifted a crystal tumbler. He spun the contents into a vortex, as he stared down into the drink. But the whirling amber offered no answers. Utley sighed, took a long draw, and then set down the glass.

This moment was long due. Lately, he had wondered if it would even arrive before his body fully failed him. *And now, just like that, it was here.*

Then Utley did what he had done countless times before in his life—what he had to.

He grabbed the phone and punched in a long series of digits. He returned the handset to his ear and stared at the muted television, at the line jagging inexorably upward across the screen, representing the price of North Sea crude.

"We need to meet."

- 5 -

MONDAY, JULY 9
Island of La Palma

Quick dropped her trowel and then swiped the sweat beading her forehead. "Break time. With this heat, no wonder the islanders call this mine the 'Devil's Throat.' Let's grab lunch topside before we move to the second collection site."

"You're the boss." Hunt capped a small plastic jar filled with bits of dirt and rock. Then he grabbed his smartphone and scanned a barcode on the container's label. A database on the phone recorded a geo-temporal location tag with the soil sample's time and spatial coordinates.

Quick watched this activity, still impressed by the app that the grad student had written seemingly overnight for cataloging their specimens. She grabbed her walkie-talkie and pressed the toggle switch.

"Manuelo . . . Kalia"—Quick's voice echoed along the mineshaft, as the nearest repeater grabbed the radio signal and relayed it topside—"we're heading to the surface."

A low rumble responded. Small stones scurried down the walls. Timbers creaked and groaned. The lights pitched and tossed. Shadows raced over the rock.

After a few seconds, the shaking died.

The scientists looked at each other. "I guess our devil has a touch of indigestion," Quick said. She downed the toggle switch again. "Manuelo? Kalia? That shaking you just felt was Eric's hunger pangs. We'd better get him some lunch ASAP."

She released the button. Static issued from the walkie-talkie's speaker. The toggle went down again. "Hey, amigos—"

A string of fast metallic pops echoed down the shaft, cutting off Quick, and then tapered to silence.

"WTF—," Hunt started.

"Gunfire," Quick said, instantly recognizing the sound that had been as common as dust on the family ranch of her New Mexican childhood. "The only question is how far from here."

She slammed the toggle switch. "Kalia? Manuelo?"

Only static responded.

Then the speaker crackled, and a voice whispered, "Sam . . . two men . . . they—"

Static cut in.

Quick hit the toggle. "Kalia, can you hear me? Kalia?"

"Manuelo is—"

The speaker reverted to hissing.

"Kalia? Kalia?"

Nothing but static issued from the walkie-talkie.

Quick hit transmit button. "Kalia, if you can hear me, immediately get yourself to a safe place. Eric and I are on the way."

Quick surveyed the equipment lying on the ground, mainly plastic sample bottles and small digging implements. Her gaze rested on one tool. She grabbed the small pickax that they had used to smash larger rocks and slid its handle into a loop on her work belt.

Quick looked at Hunt. "Ready?"

The lights answered for the grad student: They all died, leaving the two scientists standing in the pitch black of the abandoned mineshaft, thousands of feet beneath the surface of the volcanic mountain.

. . .

Quick and Hunt chased their flashlight beams, sprinting as fast as the rail ties, red mud, and fallen rock permitted. The only sounds were the crunch of stone or splash of water beneath their pounding boots. The walkie-talkie remained mute, worthless without the energized plastic discs to relay signals to the surface.

Ahead, the shaft curved hard to the right. Quick caught Hunt's arm, slowing them both. She whispered, "We're nearly halfway to the mine's entrance, which means—"

"We're about to meet anyone coming this way," Hunt finished the thought.

Quick nodded, snagged a rock, and tossed it as far ahead as the arcing shaft permitted. The response was instantaneous. Sparks exploded just to their left. Pings of ricocheting bullets filled the tunnel.

The scientists threw themselves against the wall.

Quick whipped her flashlight beam around the tunnel. No side shafts were available to change course. Gunfire continued shattering the air, strafing the tunnel. She pointed behind them, deeper into the mine.

They spun and, Hunt now leading, sprinted back toward the collection site. The shooter continued blasting. All around them, dull thuds and sharp explosions marked bullet strikes on dirt or stone.

They rounded a tight turn. Quick grabbed Hunt's shirt and pulled him to a stop. Ahead lay a long, dead-straight stretch that would offer no cover when their pursuer caught up.

But Quick was not looking ahead. Instead, she was inspecting a pitch-black niche in the tunnel wall, an opening to one of the vertical shafts plunging to the mine's lower levels.

Another set of shots rang out, closer.

Quick sliced her flashlight beam around the opening's perimeter, tracing a line of wooden planks bolted flat around the sides.

"Elevator shaft. The boards mark where the platform stopped." Quick pointed the flashlight downward. But the light pushed back the darkness no more than thirty feet. Quick returned the beam to the planking. "Shimmy out on this board as far as you can."

"Then what?" Hunt slid his foot onto the old wood.

More shots ricocheted throughout the tunnel, now painful to the ears.

Like I said, you're the boss." Hunt started rapidly shimming sideways along the narrow board, with his back against the rock, as he blindly reached for handholds, knocking loose small rocks with each grab, which, after a long count, pounded against something wooden sounding below.

"No worries," he whispered, "sounds like we've some jagged boards to cushion our landing."

Quick followed him onto the plank. Hunt reached the far corner and stopped. He was perched clinging to wet rock on a three-inch precipice, facing a chasm of unknown depth. Quick crept along the wood only far enough that she was no longer visible from the tunnel.

Then she killed her flashlight, leaving them in total blackness.

The tunnel began echoing with the sound of crunching stone.

"The footsteps suggest only one person approaching. When I say 'go,' you draw our visitor's attention. Then stay exactly where you are," Quick whispered from the darkness as coolly as if she were ordering a gene analysis in the air-conditioned comfort of her Florida lab.

"Roger," Hunt whispered back, his teetering boots reconfirming the blind plummet waiting a mere shift in body weight away, as he carefully reached for his pocket.

Another moment, the approaching footfalls now sounded to the scientists as if they were chewing mouthfuls of gritty cereal.

A fan of faint light appeared along the tunnel's opposite wall.

The pickax slipped free of Quick's belt, and the molecular biologist recalled a bit of ranch-life wisdom that her grandfather had passed to her when she was a child, which had seemed quaintly old West at the time, but that she now realized was just as applicable today as it had been in the 1800s: *When gunfire announces a visitor, there's only one polite greeting.*

The wedge of light grew wider, stretching onto the tunnel's floor and ceiling, glinting off the rails and puddled water. The crunching footfalls now sounded like rocks in a blender. Hunt held his breath, just able to make out Quick standing beside him.

The gun muzzle appeared at waist-level, moving steadily forward.

Quick went up on her toes.

The gunman's flashlight emerged.

A hand appeared on the weapon.

The man's profile glided into view.

Quick's "go" sliced the air.

Hunt's smartphone exploded with alternating flashes of patrol-car red and blue. The man's head jerked toward the vertical shaft.

"I'll take that if you don't mind."

Quick dove sideways as if trying to reach a long ball on a tennis court. Except instead of a racket, her pickax was slicing through the air.

The man's finger ripped back the trigger. Bullets sprayed in wild arc across the tunnel and then into the vertical shaft, at head-height, jagging toward Hunt.

Quick hoped to snag the gun with the ax and rip it from the man's hands. But the gunman crouched as he fired the weapon.

There was no way back now.

The spike entered the soft skin on his neck's far side. Quick, her hands cemented on the ax handle, whipped forward and around, transferring her momentum to the gunman.

Locked in a death spiral, the man could only helplessly spin sideways while his body reflexively followed the pickax to prevent his windpipe from being ripped from his neck.

But his finger remained clamped on the trigger.

Gunfire strafed wildly into the vertical shaft, its stroboscopic flashes slowing the action to a crawl.

Keeping one hand locked on the ax handle, Quick reached around the man with her other arm, trying to grab the gun. In a desperate attempt to regain control, the man slammed Quick back into the rock wall. The blow dazed Quick. The man shoved her toward the open shaft.

Hunt jumped from the plank and rammed his shoulder into the assailant. The man fell backward and teetered on the edge of the open shaft. His arms and the firing gun pinwheeled as he fought to regain his balance.

Quick simply released her grip on the ax. The loss of her counterweight flung the gunman over the edge.

Fire flashes lit the shaft for several seconds. Then they died with a loud crash below.

Quick clicked on the flashlight. Both scientists were panting, bent forward, hands on their knees.

Hunt looked at Quick. "How did you know that would work?"

Quick shrugged. "It was the only logical course of action. You, on the other hand, were supposed to stay put—not that I'm ungrateful you lent a shoulder."

"Yeah, lying low's not really my style—you learn that real fast when you're the geeky kid on the playground."

"In any case, you're my first intern to simultaneously disregard my instructions and earn your letter of recommendation."

Sam Quick pointed her beam toward the surface. "Now, let's find Kalia and Manuelo."

- 6 -

The shout echoed throughout the cavernous space, bouncing off the brick walls, the neat rows of metal girders, and the patchwork of old pipes and conduits running near the high ceiling. Once the clatter and strum of massive factory machines had filled the room. Now it was nothing more than a hot, dusty shell, hollowed of its mechanical innards and only smelling faintly of its past labors.

Centered amid this all, three desks formed a semicircle, all topped by shiny aluminum computers, paper-thin monitors, and various devices with flashing lights. The source of the outburst sat before the center screen, staring at an image of London's Big Ben overlaid by a trefoil yellow-and-black radiation symbol.

"That's the signal. Just like they said it would be. Plutonium found in London. That's it," Gabriel said, poking the monitor with enough force to set it rocking on its base.

He was sitting ramrod upright, shirtless, with heavily tattooed shoulders and arms, and white-blond hair floating high above his seatback. An array of metal studs, collars, and rings that looked more appropriate for industrial plumbing lined his ears top to lobe.

He raised his hands. "We're a go."

Sitting at the adjacent desks, a second man and a woman each slapped one of his upheld hands. The man was short and heavyset, with a soft, somehow friendly face, and black, wiry hair. The woman wore dreadlocked hair bundled like a sheaf of thick-stalked, golden wheat. Below this crown, her eyes were brown and large. And like Gabriel, outsized metal weighed down their ears.

"Super excellent, man, I can't believe it's finally going to happen," Jacob said.

"Yeah, super excellent," Amanda repeated, sounding slightly bored.

Gabriel scrolled his screen. "Just like they said: The Brits are already putting all their heat on the Jihadis."

Jacob splayed in his chair and spun around. "It's perfect. When it's all done, the blame goes their way."

Amanda nodded. "Yeah, maybe a little too perfect, I still say."

"We have been over this shit too many times already," Jacob said. "It's happening like they said it would. What, do you think the CIA is gonna spread some scary plutonium shit all over London just to try and set us up? No way. Not happening."

"I'm not saying it is a setup . . . but what if it is?" Amanda said. "The news story—"

"Shut"— a beer bottle exploded against a brick wall—"up." A dark stain spread wide and then ran down the masonry, narrowing to a point like an exclamation mark to the command.

Amanda's mouth snapped closed. She and Jacob glanced at each other, as Gabriel stalked toward the stain, his combat boots crushing the little arcs of freshly broken glass.

He stopped at a window adjacent to the impact, leaned

forward, and pressed his hands flat against the dirty panes. His shirtless back was surrealistic canvas: an American flag lay tattooed just above his waistband, with a mushroom cloud exploding up from its center, and dollar signs raining down like nuclear fallout.

He stared out at the building's surround of crumbling asphalt. His gaze traveled over the razor-wire fence, to the dock and the canal. The mighty Erie Canal, he thought with a snort. *Not even so much as a friggin' rowboat floating by.*

Without turning from the window, he said, "We're in control now. But our opportunity is thin. There are no second chances in this game." A joint and lighter slipped from his pocket. "If the wrong people peg our shit, we'll end up in sweatboxes on Cuba, and our mommies and daddies won't be able to do jack about it."

Still facing the window, he slid the nub between his lips, put the lighter close, and inhaled deeply. All was quiet for several long moments.

Then smoke blasted from his nostrils and bounced off the window glass. "Now, who's going to pick up the pizza?"

-7-

MONDAY, JULY 9
Island of La Palma

The ball of light at the tunnel's end grew larger. Quick and Hunt sprinted forward. Another dozen strides, and they emerged into fresh air.

Quick reached him first.

The old man lay face down by the mine's entrance. His blood pooled in the surrounding dirt. A walkie-talkie hissed inches from his fingertips.

Quick clamped a seeping hole in Manuelo's back. "Check for a pulse," she said, as she looked around the mine yard. She saw no person nor any vehicles other than the expedition's red Jeep, but that didn't mean an associate of their attacker wasn't nearby and armed with the same weaponry as the man in the shaft. And out here in the open, she and Hunt were easy targets.

After what seemed like minutes of pressing the guide's carotid artery, holding his breath the entire time, Hunt finally exhaled. "A pulse, but faint and erratic."

"Get the Jeep," Quick ordered, as blood seeped between her fingers.

Hunt ran for the 4x4.

"Sam! Eric! Manuelo!"

Up the hillside, a jagged line of shaking branches and fleeing birds was rapidly weaving toward them. Then Slater crashed from the bushes and then jumped from the rocks.

"How bad is it?" she said, kneeling beside Quick. She looked as if she had lived a month in the wilderness, covered by dirt and bits of leaves and twigs.

"Just barely a pulse," Quick said. "Did you see who did this?"

"I was uphill collecting samples, when I saw a small orange car pull in and then two guys get out. Then the shots, so I hid. Eventually, I saw one man leave in the car, but I don't know the whereabouts of the second man."

"I don't think we have to worry about him," Quick said.

"But I should have done something to help Manuelo—"

Quick shook her head. "Sometimes you must save yourself first to save someone else. Getting yourself shot would have done nothing to help Manuelo."

The 4x4 squealed to a stop beside them.

"Kalia, take over for me. We need to get him in the Jeep."

"Please be OK," Slater whispered, as her hands slid into Quick's place.

Quick grabbed Manuelo's legs. Hunt wrapped his arms under the guide's chest. Moving in unison, they lifted the Spaniard into the Jeep, as Slater's hands remained locked on the wound.

"Kalia, maintain pressure. Eric, monitor vitals," Quick said, jumping on the driver's seat.

The engine roared. Dirt and gravel flew from under the tires, setting the birds screeching. Hunt grabbed the roll bar with one arm to steady himself and Manuelo, while Slater's hands stayed tight on the wound, as the Jeep hurdled down the rutted two-track lane.

Quick cranked the wheel. The Devil's Throat disappeared behind them. And the mountain dropped steeply ahead.

If not for the day's events, Sam Quick, Eric Hunt, and Kalia Slater would have enjoyed the stunning view from 6500 feet high, west over the Atlantic, a dead-straight line to the United States, 3405 miles away.

- 8 -

The slap reverberated throughout the elegant salon like a gunshot.

"The plan is in motion," the enormous man said in Russian, as he pulled his reddened palm from the desktop that he had just hit with all his considerable might. Like the remains of a fossil dig, the man's facial bones hinted at a former vitality. But now, his face was rocky and cratered, flesh piling up in pallid, irregular mounds beneath his eyes and around his chin and jowls as if bull-dozed from the hollows at the centers of his cheeks.

Sergei Sokolov stomped from behind the desk and over to a credenza. "The British dogs and their American masters will search London and all the UK high and low for their precious plutonium, soiling themselves with fear of a deadly snowstorm. While tomorrow, the shipment will quietly leave Baku."

A mother-of-pearl scope plunged into a pyramid of Grade 000 Royal Beluga caviar. Sokolov tilted his head back, and roe spilled from the spoon into his mouth.

A woman stepped beside Sokolov. "Yes, my darling, all is as it should be." Beside his dour mountain of gray flesh, Nin Zanin appeared a bright toy: she was clad in a tight, red blouse and a matching miniskirt. Shiny, dark hair, a large beauty mark high on her right cheek, and eyes the shape of unshelled almonds adorned her face.

Sokolov looked down at her. A black line of caviar juice dribbled from his lower lip to an inky drop gathering in his chin's rough cleft. "Everything is up to us now, Nin. We cannot fail. Russia's greatness must no longer remain hobbled by small men clawing for rubles. NATO flanks us to the west, and the Chinese press us from the east. Russia's supremacy depends on our success."

"To be sure, under your hand, Sergei, Mother Russia shall soon rise again." Nin reached up and transferred the caviar juice from Sokolov's chin to her fingertip.

Then she moved to a wall covered by a huge world map. Her finger slashed at the chart.

"But first we must destroy the one true enemy." Nin stepped back from the wall. The black juice formed a pirate's X on the map. Directly atop Washington D.C.

"One step at a time, my lovely Nin. Are you sure no one will discover the bodies in London until it is too late?"

"Do not worry, Sergei." Nin returned to the credenza. "All the intermediaries are, shall we say, under such a heavy workload they won't have time to speak with the authorities."

Sokolov snorted and scooped another load of fish eggs. Staring into Nin's eyes, he raised the spoon and dribbled the caviar into her mouth.

Nin's tongue swept her lips clean. "Now, Sergei, we must celebrate the beginning. And to help us do that, this morning, some very nice Ukrainian girls arrived."

Sokolov took her hand. "You are an angel, my Nin."

-9-

The vise gripping his head tightened another notch. Inspector Juan Reyes stared at his office doorway, sighed, and then said in good English, "You must be Mr. Davies. Please come in and join your compatriots."

Quick, Hunt, and Slater turned and studied the man standing behind them. The visitor looked like a former pro athlete early into his second act as a confident business executive, sporting a solid build, salt-and-pepper hair, and island business attire of a polo shirt and linen pants.

Zach Davies stepped forward and offered his hand around to the Americans, his brow wrinkling as he read the print on Hunt's shirtfront: "The Revolution Won't Be Tweeted."

Then Davies turned to Reyes and reached out his hand, *"Encantado de conocerte, Inspector. Por favor, llámeme 'Zach.'"*

Reyes ignored the gesture. "Mr. Davies is, I understand, an attaché from your American embassy in Madrid. He has come to"—his face contorted—"assist with our investigation."

The skin around his eyes relaxed a bit, as he added, "Fortunately, Dr. Quick, finishing your official statements will conclude your involvement in this matter. Now perhaps, you can enlighten Mr. Davies as to the reason for your visit our lovely island?"

For a moment, Quick stared at the dark eyes intently watching her from below the salt-and-pepper hair. *Is he really some embassy drone sent by NRLI? Or is he CIA?* In her line of work, these visits were routine but rarely ever welcomed, and certainly never by Sam Quick.

The scientist kept her tone neutral. "The goal of my expedition is acquiring soil samples containing bacteria of interest from La Garganta del Diablo, La Palma's zinc mine. We chose the Devil's Throat because some of its resident bacteria should prove resistant to high zinc concentrations."

Davies looked at Quick. "Forgive my ignorance, but why is the Navy interested in zinc and bacteria?"

Quick returned his look. *He undoubtedly knows about my role at NRLI. And maybe even about ALCHEMY. So why the pretense?* "Like all American military branches, the Navy maintains a robust biological research program. My work centers on extremophiles, the bacteria that live in unusual or extreme conditions, such as in the scalding water found near undersea volcanic vents or in radioactive soups of nuclear waste."

She continued, "My current project targets bacteria that thrive in the presence of high concentrations of metals such as zinc, cadmium, or copper. These metal-loving organisms are essential for cleaning up toxic-waste sites like those sometimes found on decommissioned military bases." This was all true, she thought. *Which was why there's no need to add anything about the ALCHEMY project.*

Davies was then silent while the scientists recapped the

previous day's events, with the inspector frequently interrupting. After Quick described the Jeep's race down the mountain to the village medical clinic, Davies remained quiet for a moment.

Then he turned to Slater. "You said the assailants spoke a language unfamiliar to you?"

Before the Hawaiian could answer, Reyes cut in, "As I told your compatriots, Mr. Davies, I believe what Ms. Slater heard was one of the North African languages." He sighed. "On rare occasions, we are visited on La Palma by elements seeking to transit cocaine and heroin to Europe from Africa, which is little more than one hundred miles east of here. And we have recently received reports of such trafficking activities near La Garganta del Diablo. If Dr. Quick's expedition encroached on such endeavors, well, you can imagine. "

The inspector went on, "I believe that once Sr. Alcanzar regains consciousness, he will verify the language. Moreover, the remains recovered from the shaft"—Reyes's stomach churned as he recalled the corpse with the broken timber run through its abdomen and, worse, the pickax embedded in its neck—"are consistent with someone of North African extraction."

As he spoke, Reyes watched for any reaction from Quick to the mention of the man whom she—however justifiably—had killed. Her eyes gave none. He knew from his wife's Hollywood television dramas that American women were not to be trifled with. *But this scientist who so easily opened a man's throat with a pickax was something else.* His head's throbbing intensified.

Davies looked at Quick. "Just one more question for now: who cares enough about your work to kill for it?"

Reyes's head almost exploded.

And Sam Quick had her confirmation that Zach Davies knew exactly why she was visiting La Palma when he arrived at the Tazacorte police station.

TUESDAY, JULY 10
Island of La Palma

Quick looked around the table. "Shall we head to the hotel? It's been a hell of a couple days, and we've got another long one again tomorrow," she said more as a command than a question.

Hunt, Slater, and Davies nodded in agreement, and each hurriedly swallowed their final bites. The four Americans were seated in a simple, open-air seafood restaurant not far from the hotel. And they had just wolfed down their first meal of the day, after finally leaving the police station at nightfall.

Quick started to rise. But a glint across the crowded street running alongside the dining terrace caught her eye.

Then the waiter surged forward and leaned over the table to collect the tab, blocking her line of sight. When he pulled back, the reflection's source was gone.

Seeing Quick hesitate, Davies asked, "Something wrong?"

"Probably nothing." But Quick doubted the words as soon as she spoke them. *The camera had been pointed directly at them.*

Outside the restaurant, the Americans merged into the foot traffic drifting up the narrow street. They managed to slip rapidly through the crowds of tourists fingering trinkets at the storefront tables. Until they met a dense, barely moving wall of tanned and tattooed flesh blocking their way. The group—each member twenty-something, heavily inked and pierced, and wearing scant tribal-cloth beachwear—stretched across the lane, a dozen people deep.

The foursome threaded their way through the clique, and after they had left them well behind, Hunt said, "Not exactly your usual tour group back there."

"They're probably here warming up for this weekend's anti-globalization rally in Madrid, to protest the ICF," Davies said. Seeing Hunt and Slater's questioning looks, Davies went on, "The International Capital Forum is a summit where the world's major economies set trade policy for the coming years. Their choices affect everyone from"—he pointed across the lane—"that tapas stand owner to investment bankers in Hong Kong. And the ICF is the headline event for groups opposed to global capitalism—not the least of which because eight world leaders, including the president, will be in attendance."

"If the protest will be held in Madrid, why are they staying here on La Palma, a three-hour flight away?" Slater asked.

"Antiglobalization groups use places like La Palma as in-country staging venues to meet up, toke up, and hook up before their targeted events," Davies said. "A day or two before the ICF begins, they will converge on Madrid. And because they will already be in Spain, they will avoid crossing the border when the border patrol is on highest alert for incoming protestors, during the days just prior to the event."

"You seem to know all about this movement," Slater said loudly, as they passed another group of the tattooed youth, a few of who raised their beer bottles in toast to the Hawaiian, which elicited Slater's patented smile for putting off drunken frat boys at home.

"The State Department, along with the FBI and CIA, monitors myriad antiglobalization groups." Davies sighed. "And what I don't learn from embassy briefings, I hear from my little sister, who is"—his thumb pointed over his shoulder at the group behind them—"probably out there somewhere with those guys."

. . .

The Americans climbed the hotel steps. At the top, Quick turned and looked out over the street. She half-expected to see the camera-wielding man from outside the restaurant. But she found only red-faced vacationers strolling the plaza below.

Inside the hotel, at the second-floor landing, the foursome exchanged "good nights." Hunt and Slater split off down the corridor, while Quick and Davies resumed their climb, headed for their third-floor rooms.

On the second floor, Slater said, "So, what's Davies's story?"

"Good question. Sam seems wary of him," Hunt said.

"Yeah, I wonder. Anyway, he's interesting and kinda hot in a young-older-guy sort of way."

"Yeah, not bad, I guess," Hunt said, laughing, as they arrived at Slater's door. He stretched and started to turn for his room. "Well, good night."

"Eric?"

"Yeah?"

"I hate to ask this. But after all that's happened, I really don't feel like being alone. Would you be down for a sleepover? Totally nothing, you know—"

Hunt held up a hand. "No prob. I'll rinse off and be right over."

. . .

On the third floor, Davies put a hand on Quick's shoulder. "Look, I'm sorry about what happened to your guide."

She glanced at the hand and then straight into Davies's eyes. "Really? I'd have thought your only concern would be ensuring that we fragile scientists don't get sidetracked from the project. That is why you're here, isn't it—to keep an eye on us?"

Davies's eyes remained genial, but he withdrew his hand.

"And by the way, he's a friend, not just a guide," Quick added.

Davies nodded. "OK, sure, your friend. But whatever the relationship, we both know that the local authorities should handle the investigation. And that your team should safely finish your research and then return to NRLI."

"Thanks for the advice." Quick's room key sliced into its slot like a laser.

. . .

On the second floor, Hunt slipped into his room. The door closed.

Even at this hour, the air was hot and humid, and he wanted to get his sweaty body into the cool shower as soon as possible. He ignored the light switch and moved into the dark room, peeling off his shirt as he walked forward.

He felt his calf brush the bed.

He threw his shirt where he guessed the chair was.

He yawned and reached for his shorts.

That's when the pinpricks of light exploded across his field of vision.

. . .

In her dark room, Quick leaned against the door and took several deep breaths. Sending Davies was a typical patronizing move by her brass at NRLI. But what pissed her off was that she had let him get under her skin. And worst of all, she knew he was right. ALCHEMY mattered far more than any of this, even Manuelo getting shot.

After a final, long exhalation, she flipped the light switch.

First, she saw the scattered papers.

Then the overturned luggage.

Finally, her laptop case lying open and empty on the bed.

Quick spun, yanked the door, and rushed into the corridor.

"Zach," she shouted.

Down the hall, Davies stepped back from his half-open door. "Change your mind about that nightcap?"

"Dream on." Quick pushed past him into his room.

She hit the light switch. Jumbled papers and uprooted luggage also covered his bed and floor.

"What the hell?" Davies shouted, trailing Quick.

Quick grabbed Davies and dragged him toward the stairway. "Eric and Kalia."

-11-

TUESDAY, JULY 10
London

Hampstead Heath was a perilous place after dark, mainly populated by seekers of anonymous assignations, illicit drugs, or easy targets for violent acts. But Utley turned off Millfield Lane and strolled into the Heath as serenely as if he were taking a noontime promenade.

Under only the crescent moon's light, he smoothly navigated the curving pathway into the park. To his left, the single-sex swimming ponds glimmered like silvery amoebas. While all around him, the long shadows of the trees and the bushes lay unmoving.

After rounding a final bend, he stopped, took his position on a bench, and watched a path leading north. Several minutes later, a figure stepped from the trees bordering the walkway, into the dull sheen of the open range.

Watching the encroaching shadow, Utley felt no fear. He simply fingered the cool metal strapped to his ankle.

His hand remained locked on the grip of his Walther P99 until a light flashed three times from the shadow's direction. Then his fingers shifted to the penlight fastened alongside the pistol.

-12-

Quick and Davies rushed down the stairs and sprinted along the second-floor corridor. Quick pointed. "Try Eric." She kept running and then stopped at Slater's partially open door, as Davies began pounding on Hunt's door.

"Kalia?" Quick scanned the Hawaiian's room and then immediately returned to the hall. "She's gone."

Davies pounded Hunt's door again. "He's not answering either—"

"Sam!" The faint shout originated from down the hall, beyond a turn in the corridor.

Quick took off, yelling over her shoulder, "Get help at the desk!"

Guests peeking from their rooms, attracted by the noise, shrank back as the American woman hurled past. Quick traced the passage through a sharp right. Ahead, the hall ended at a large, open window.

Five more steps. She grabbed the sill and looked down. Below, a man was sliding down the fire-escape ladder using one hand, while his other one clamped her laptop and the expedition's sample case. Around his neck, a camera swung wildly from the chaotic descent.

The restaurant paparazzo.

The man dropped and landed beside a small orange car. A second man, at the driver's door, pointed up at Quick and jumped into the vehicle. Quick slipped out the window and leaped onto the fire escape.

The man dumped the stolen items and the camera through the car's open passenger window. Quick dropped from the ladder. The tires squealed, and the door handle ripped from the man's hand as the car sped off. The man spun and sprinted.

Quick looked after the car. Her heart somersaulted. Pressed against the back window was Slater's face.

She could never catch the car.

But she could capture a direct connection to it. Quick forced herself to turn away from Slater, channeling her rage into her arms and legs, as she began racing in the opposite direction.

Quick rounded out of the alley and saw the fleeing man push through a throng of people seventy feet ahead. She sprinted forward, tracking the man, as he veered down a side street toward the ocean.

She shoved between a pair of sunburned tourists, provoking a barrage of British-accented profanities, and then cut hard in front of a gaggle of teenage girls. The lead members halted, while the rear guard, noses to cellphones, smashed into their friends.

Quick jagged onto the side street. Here, the crowd thinned, and the shops gave way to residential apartment buildings and low-rise hotels. She ran as fast as she could, swerving around a couple kissing in a dark stretch. The gap closed.

Ahead, the man burst through a rectangle of yellowish light marking the lane's junction with the more brightly lit shore-side promenade.

Seconds later, Quick reached the beachfront walkway.

Thirty feet away, the man jumped down the stone steps leading to the main pier. As she hit the stairs, Quick heard the startled protests from a cranking diesel engine. She tore down the dock.

Her target was running out of pier. Then he made a blind leap.

When she reached the dock's end, all Quick could do was watch, as a speedboat carrying the man sent up a spray of wake and then disappeared into a constellation of bobbing lights scattered across the dark harbor.

. . .

"Ah, Dr. Quick, how very kind of you to join us this evening," said Inspector Reyes. He extended an arm toward Hunt's room, while his other hand continued rubbing his temple, which felt as if elephants were trampling it.

Quick pushed past Reyes and found a medic bent over Hunt, with Davies standing nearby.

"Is he OK? Did you see Kalia? She was taken in an orange compact car that shot from the alley onto the main square. We need to go after her now," she said, gulping air.

"I saw the car and Kalia from the hotel's front steps," Davies said. "Reyes and his officers are already searching for it. And they've alerted the air- and seaports, as well as the authorities on the neighboring islands. We'll find her."

A head rose from the bedcover. "Oh, hi Sam. What's up?"

Hunt blinked his eyes as if trying to focus. "I feel like I've been out drinking all night," he said. "And hello, who's this?"

The grad student attempted to rise up on his elbows, briefly fighting the pressure of the medic's hand against his chest, before surrendering and lying back, grinning at the Spanish man.

Her jaw muscle relaxed a hair, as Quick heard that Hunt's cognitive abilities remained roughly intact. But her brow wrinkled when a lightning bolt beside the medic's hand caught her eye. The tattoo, approximately two-inches long, was inked on Hunt's left pec.

Quick looked at Davies, who shrugged and said, "Eric's head took a good hit. The blow dazed him, but he never fully lost consciousness. The paramedics will transport him to the island clinic for an exam and overnight observation. They say a few pain relievers and a night's rest—"

"That still leaves one of my interns in grave danger," Quick cut in.

Knuckles rapped the room door. "Before we discuss Ms. Slater's whereabouts, may I first ask where you spent the previous fifteen minutes, Dr. Quick?"

"I did what your team has thus far failed to accomplish: I chased down the first lead in this investigation. Literally."

Quick looked hard at Reyes. "Inspector, do you know a large speedboat whose name begins *LAND—?*"

- 13 -

The two men leaned back on their heels. The straps securing the wooden crate snapped taut. The taller man released his binding, nodded at the adjacent crates, and said in Russian, "Let's check them all one more time."

The other man snorted. "Relax. We've already checked them twice. They're all fine. What do you think is in them? Delicate artwork? Eggs? *Nyet.* Too heavy. Probably unbreakable—"

"Excuse me," a voice said in heavily accented Russian.

The Russians turned around. Each man's hand slid behind his back onto the grip of the pistol wedged under his waistband.

Standing before them was a disheveled man wearing a fan T-shirt imprinted with the logo of the Azerbaijani national soccer team.

"You have a cigarette to spare?"

The Russians glanced at each other. Then the taller man nodded, and his hand parted with his gun and moved for his shirt pocket. The second Russian remained frozen, hand on pistol, while his associate gave a cigarette to the man.

As the man brought the cigarette to his lips, the shorter

Russian pointed at the other end of the cavernous cargo hold, where the other passengers sat. "Now get out of here."

The man nodded thanks to the taller Russian, then scowled at the shorter man and turned away.

When the man was out of earshot, the taller Russian sighed. "Now, let's check the straps one more time."

At the hold's far end, the man sat down and muttered, "Russian pigs and their precious cargo." Then he lit the cigarette and inhaled deeply.

Several minutes later, as the man crushed the smoldering cigarette butt on the metal floor, the Ilyushin's engines roared. At their end of the hold, the Russians hurriedly yanked a last set of straps and then took seats next to the crates.

The decrepit Il-76, a Soviet Cold War behemoth, started to move. The plane slowly gathered speed, until its worn tires finally released the crumbling pavement.

The plane shuddered and swayed, as it struggled to gain altitude. The dozen or so other passengers squeezed their eyes tightly shut, with their lips moving in an inaudible mix of prayers and curses.

But the stares of the Russians remained unwavering, locked on the crates, as the Il-76 dipped hard and then hung for a long moment, unsure whether to soar or sink.

Then the plane resumed its climb, lumbering northwest from Baku, toward the Caucasus Mountains and Europe beyond.

- 1 4 -

WEDNESDAY, JULY 11
Island of La Palma

A sheet of paper slid across Inspector Reyes's desktop. "This morning, we received this fax," Reyes said, looking from Quick to Hunt to Davies.

"'Americans, get out,'" Quick read aloud. "Pithy."

"Not such bad news," Reyes shrugged, desperately wanting to take more aspirin for his headache, despite the ulcer clawing at the lining of his stomach. "They've reached out. They want something. Perhaps we can hope to soon receive a ransom demand."

Reyes passed a second sheet to Quick. "As you see from this report, the slug recovered from Manuelo Alcanzar is nine millimeters. Moreover, its metallic composition is consistent with Russian manufacture." The inspector swallowed. "And in this part of the world, African hands hold Russian guns."

Seeing Quick's look, Reyes continued, "During the Cold War, to buy allegiance, the Soviets flooded Africa with their surplus weaponry and munitions. The bullet's provenance, along with Ms. Slater's report of the assailants speaking in, as I suggested, a North African dialect strongly supports my theory that African drug traffickers are to blame for the attack on your expedition and Ms. Slater's subsequent abduction."

"And the speedboat, Inspector?" Hunt asked. As the medic had predicted, the island clinic had released Hunt early this morning, no worse for wear after the prior night's attack, other than an egg-shaped bump behind one ear and his own dull headache.

"We are still searching for the vessel at sea. And my men are combing registration records looking for a craft whose name begins with the word "*LAND.*" Unfortunately, with only the partial name to go on, this process is taking longer than we would like."

Reyes sighed. "I, for one, shall be surprised if we find such a boat registered at all. Or if we do, I expect the vessel will be of either Moroccan or Western Saharan origin, the two African nations with the easiest sea access to La Palma."

Quick stared at the window behind Reyes, at a band of the tattooed-and-pierced youths from the previous night, who were passing outside, heading in the direction of the beach. "And what about Manuelo's condition, Inspector?"

"According to his doctor's report this morning, I am glad to say that Manuelo Alcanzar continues to improve, albeit he remains heavily sedated," Reyes replied, relieved to switch to a less contentious topic. "I plan to visit—"

"*¡Inspector! ¡Inspector!*"

The band of steel encircling Reyes's head tightened yet again, and he barely caught himself before he moaned aloud.

An officer ran in. "*¡Un barco se ha encontrado, quilla-para arriba flotante, cerca Fuencaliente de la Palma!*"

"A boat was found floating keel-up near Fuencaliente de la Palma," Davies translated. The Americans glanced at each other, as the officer added, "*¡El nombre del barco es LANDFALL!*"

Reyes and the man spoke in rapid-fire Spanish. Then inspector slumped back into his chair. His glasses landed on a stack of papers. And he rubbed his temples. "I'm afraid the boat offers no sign of survivors nor any information regarding Ms. Slater.

"Where the boat was found, Fuencaliente—literally in your language, the hot spring—is located on La Palma's southern tip. The currents there are very powerful and sweep directly into the open Atlantic, toward America. The Guardia Civil del Mar is towing the vessel to a beach near the village of Las Indias."

"Hot spring, did you say?" Quick asked. "Because I could really use a good soak." She looked at Hunt. "Care to join me?"

Reyes's brow wrinkled and then smoothed. "Of course, Dr. Quick, by all means go and look for yourself. And while you inspect the vessel, my team will search the registration records for the boat's owner."

Reyes snapped his fingers, and the officer scurried from the room. "But please be very careful. On that part of La Palma, the roads are quite narrow and tortuous. And sheep traveling to and from the shore frequently block them." He pulled some paper from the pile covering his desk and grabbed a pen.

"Sheep are ocean swimmers?" Hunt asked.

Reyes smiled. "No, Mr. Hunt. Rather both livestock and wild animals visit the water's edge to lick the sea salt from the shoreline rocks." He held out a hand-drawn map.

Quick grabbed it, already heading for the door, with Hunt and Davies right behind. They so rapidly crossed the station's main room that none of them noticed the officer who was tracking their movements with the precision of a laser guidance system.

Outside, Quick turned to Davies. "Reyes will take forever finding *LANDFALL's* owners—"

"So, you want our embassy assets to check out the boat," Davies cut in.

"And here I thought you were just another handsome face. That's exactly what I had in mind: you do that, while Eric and I visit the recovered craft." Quick threw her pack into the red Jeep.

"I'm happy to drive—," Hunt started to offer.

The cranking starter and grinding transmission answered. Hunt scrambled and jumped in, as the Jeep's rear tires spun, spraying gravel and inciting a verbatim replay of the British-accented curses that Quick had heard the prior night while chasing the fleeing thief. She waved at the twice-offended tourists.

Then Sam Quick spun the steering wheel and the shift lever into first gear. "I'll drive."

-15-

The wet aroma of freshly landed seaweed and spilled diesel crawled into their noses and lay down to stay. Beside Quick and Hunt, *LANDFALL* sat beached with its keel cutting into the black volcanic sand like a plow spreading fertile soil. Beyond the boat, a tan bluff walled off the beach. Terraced farms rose from atop the escarpment as if they were the slivered edges of a piece of green shale. Above the farms, the mountain sharply steepened into La Cumbre Vieja, the island's volcanic ridgeline.

The scientists climbed aboard the craft and started forward, their legs cocked to accommodate the deck's slope. They almost reached the wheel when a voice stopped them.

"Ah, you must be Dr. Quick."

Quick and Hunt turned to find a man gazing up at them. The speaker finished climbing the narrow stairs leading below and clambered onto the deck. He sported a closely shaven head, dark beard, and the green jumpsuit of La Guardia Civil del Mar. "Inspector Reyes alerted me to your imminent arrival. I'm Officer Alonso."

Quick introduced herself and Hunt.

"I suppose I could guess the Eric part," Alonso said, nodding at Hunt's T-shirt, which read, "iEric."

"Has *LANDFALL* revealed anything regarding Kalia Slater?" Quick asked.

"Nothing specific at this point about Ms. Slater," Alonso replied. "But what we are looking at is a botched ditch-and-sink job. But, as you see, they accomplished merely capsizing the boat rather than sinking it—"

"And who were 'they'?" Quick interrupted.

"Almost certainly drug runners."

Quick glanced at Hunt.

Alonso continued, "Whenever these elements believe a transport is compromised, they sink the boat or seaplane in deep water."

Quick pointed at the control panel. "This display is labeled 'UHF Penetrating Sonar.'"

"Yes, *LANDFALL* was undoubtedly once someone's personal watercraft, until it was stolen and put to nefarious use. Perhaps the boat's rightful owners enjoyed searching for buried treasure or sunken ships—"

A mobile clipped to Alonso's belt rang. The officer grabbed it. "¿Sí? Sí, Inspector Reyes . . ."

Quick whispered to Hunt, "UHF sonar is what my colleagues use to scan for undersea geologic formations, such as earthquake faults, hydrocarbon deposits, or mineral beds."

The phone clapped shut. "That was Inspector Reyes. Last week, a harbormaster on Tenerife reported *LANDFALL* stolen. As you might know, Tenerife is another of our Canary Islands, located approximately sixty miles to the east. The boat is registered to a firm based in Madrid. The harbormaster said the company representative wasn't particularly concerned by the craft's loss and said only that the insurance people would be in touch shortly."

Quick nodded. "Do you know anything more about the boat's owner?"

"Yes, the company is known here on the island for possessing many plantations and land tracts on La Palma's western half. In fact, coincidentally"—Alonso pointed at the summit of La Cumbre Vieja—"several years ago, they tried purchasing La Garganta del Diablo. But they were unable to surmount the bureaucratic red tape for securing the necessary environmental permits." Alonso smiled. "In Spain, we have an abundance of both bureaucrats and red tape . . . Dr. Quick? Dr. Quick?"

Hunt turned and followed Alonso's gaze, toward the dark hair disappearing below the boat's side, as Quick's voice called out, "Eric, I know a lovely paella restaurant on Calle de la Reina—"

A large wave slammed the shore. As the water's crash receded, Hunt and Alonso heard the end of Sam Quick's sentence: "In the heart of Madrid."

-16-

The trio split up. Gabriel headed alone toward a nearby brick building. Amanda and Jacob crossed the street, hurrying for a corner coffeehouse. Above, the sky was darkening. At the street's end, reflections of fast-moving clouds silently skipped across the Erie Canal like thrown stones.

Inside the coffee shop, Amanda and Jacob waited in line for the cashier to finish the previous order. Amanda watched the clerk's finger slowly roam over the register's touchscreen, occasionally pecking at various spots. The customer being serviced loudly sighed and tossed his money on the counter, while behind the cashier, a teenage boy wearing a manager's badge shook his head and reached to pull out one of his ear buds.

Amanda looked away, unable to watch further. The clerk was old enough to be her grandmother, she thought. *The old woman should be retired, watching TV with a cat curled in her lap instead of working for minimum wage, supervised by some twerp with terminal acne. She probably got laid off during one of the plant closings, and her pension, hosed in the corporate bankruptcy. And nobody gives a fuck.*

Her lip quivered. Well, soon, she fumed, they would care—soon the whole world would care. *That is if the whole thing wasn't some gigantic, fucked-up takedown.*

. . .

Inside the brick building, Gabriel approached a desk, as a woman rose behind it. Her peachy summer linen suite matched her smile. "So good to see you again."

Gabriel ignored her outstretched hand and slid into a chair facing the desk.

Her smile remained unflagging, as she withdrew her arm and reclaimed her seat. "I trust all is well with your family?"

"Of course."

She layered her hands in front of her, still smiling placidly. "So how may I be of assistance today?"

"I need to transfer some funds to Europe."

"Oh, Europe's lovely this time of year."

"It certainly is," he replied, glancing at a clock sitting on the woman's desk.

The woman smiled again and then slid a sheet across the desk. "Please just fill out this slip, indicating the transfer amount and the routing instructions."

. . .

From a window table in the coffeehouse, Amanda tore her gaze from the elderly clerk. She set down her cup and tapped at her laptop, which she figured cost more than what the cashier earned in a month.

On the screen, the little whirling ball stopped spinning and disappeared, leaving behind a euro sign trailed by a long string of digits. She smiled at Jacob and grabbed her coffee. Rising steam mingled as their containers bumped, and the first thunderclap exploded outside. "Got it."

- 17 -

The sharp jolt caused the passengers to clutch their seats. Two more hard bumps. Then the giant Il-76 finally glided into a patch of smooth air. The two Russians looked at each other. Then again at the wooden crates. Despite the flight's near-continuous turbulence, all the straps remained tight.

Outside the windows, treetops appeared level with the wings. Then a final hard smack, and the acrid smell of burning brakes invaded the cargo hold. The plane swung hard left and came to an abrupt stop. The engines shut down.

The Russians jumped out of their seats. The taller man pressed his face against a window. "The truck is here." He pointed at the first crate. "Start with that one, and I'll loosen this one. We need to get on the road within thirty minutes to make the deadline."

A grinding noise sounded. A nearby section of fuselage started to fall away, creating a ramp down to the tarmac. Outside, no other planes or an airport terminal lay in sight. Instead, just a collection of small, corrugated metal buildings lined the runway's far side.

The other passengers shuffled by the Russians, lugging suit-cases or cardboard cartons down the ramp, and then either climbed into waiting vehicles or congregated at the metal sheds.

Twenty minutes later, the Russians loaded the final crate onto the truck. The shorter man pulled open the cab's passenger door and started to climb in.

"Hey, don't forget—the instructions," the taller one said.

The shorter man snorted and stepped back down. "It's a waste, I tell you."

"No kidding. But they were clear. And for what they are pay-ing us, we leave them here."

The men walked over to a trash barrel. Two loud thunks, one after the other, sounded.

"Now, let's go," the taller man said, moving for the driver's side of the truck.

Moments later, a figure stepped away from a building and watched the truck speeding away on a service road paralleling the tarmac. The man flipped off the truck. "Rot in hell, Russian pigs and your precious cargo."

Then he walked to the trash barrel and peered inside. "Well, what do we have here?" he said. Then he reached in and pulled up a gun in each hand.

The man was still holding up the pistols, as a silver sedan pulled from alongside a building and turned onto the service road.

-18-

WEDNESDAY, JULY 11
Fuencaliente, Island of La Palma

His stomach pressed up against his heart. The Jeep whipped through the curve. The tires regained full contact with the pavement, and Hunt relaxed into his seat. Then Quick shifted the transmission into top gear and smashed down the accelerator.

Along the roadside, a rectilinear grid of salt ponds rushed past the Jeep, separating the pavement and the sea. Black volcanic rock outlined the pools, while a different shade of red, ranging from pink lemonade to fresh-spilled blood, tinted each pond. On the other side, the greens, purples, and blacks of a malvasia vineyard flashed by in a kaleidoscopic blur.

Hunt looked over at Quick. Her gaze was alternating between the road ahead and the rearview mirror. Her face betrayed no emotion other than a clear intent to return the Jeep as rapidly as humanly possible to Tazacorte. "Your nerves are metal, the way you stay so calm with Kalia missing."

The scientist glanced at Hunt. She wished she could explain how she expected contact from Slater's abductors asking for her stolen laptop's encryption keys. And how that request would lead to a series of events of escalating gravity that may or may not result in Slater's safe return. And how then she would worry. But explaining all of that would require explaining ALCHEMY as well. Instead, all she said was, "You'll understand soon."

She started to return her attention to the road, but her gaze caught on the rearview mirror. A spot was rapidly growing in the reflective glass. She depressed the clutch and jagged the shift lever from fifth to fourth gear. The gas pedal went to the floor, and the inrushing wind pushed both passengers deeper into their seats. But despite the Jeep's increasing speed, the reflection continued growing.

"Company," Quick said.

Hunt looked over his shoulder, just as an orange compact tore up behind them and stopped just short of the Jeep's rear bumper.

"Kalia's abductors," Quick said, watching the rearview mirror, the two faces grinning from the orange car's front seats. "But no Kalia," she added, scanning the rear seat.

"The fuckers," Hunt shouted. "Let's drive their asses off the road and beat the living shit out of them until they tell us where Kalia is."

"For some reason, I rather doubt they're here for a tête-à-tête," Quick replied, as the road flattened, and the centerline broke into dashes. "But we should at least be considerate and allow them to pass."

She let up on the gas pedal.

Quick, in the rearview mirror, and Hunt, over his shoulder, watched the gap between the two vehicles close and then stabilize, as the orange car precisely matched its speed to the Jeep's.

"So much for being friendly," Quick said, whipping the shift lever, popping the clutch, and flooring the gas. The tach needle flicked the red line. The engine screamed. The Jeep shot forward.

Quick relaxed back into her seat. Alongside the road, the salt farm narrowed to an end, with its rocky gridlines merging into a single, black stream of volcanic stone that narrowly separated the asphalt from the sea below.

Sam Quick looked at Eric Hunt. "Now, let's see if there's more to these boys than their pretty smiles."

. . .

The speedometer needle whisked past the 100-mph mark. The Jeep pounded ahead. The orange car held within inches of its rear bumper. Beside the road, white spray shot up and then collapsed on the rocks, while row after row of banana trees now roared by on the opposite side.

Over his shoulder, Hunt watched the occupants high-five. "They have their noses up our tail like dogs sniffing a new friend," he shouted over the wind noise.

Quick's eyes flashed to the rearview mirror. Then she hit the brakes, as the Jeep sliced into a tight, up-sloping turn. To maintain as much speed as possible, Quick swung wide into the opposite lane.

Coming out of the turn, the road began steeply climbing. To the left, the drop to the ocean grew sharply. Despite the upslope, the Jeep's speedometer needle resumed its clockwise sweep, passing the 110-mph mark.

"Does your phone have a signal yet?" Quick yelled.

Hunt checked his mobile again. "Negative. But there must be service in that village we passed—"

The Jeep juddered violently. Metal screeched. The 4x4 veered hard toward the drop-off to the ocean. The tires left the pavement; dust bellowed behind. Quick immediately countersteered into the skid. The Jeep swerved back into the lane. The engine shrieked as Quick jerked the shift lever down to second and slammed the accelerator. Behind them, the orange car held back, its front bumper flattened from the collision.

"Doing OK over there?" Quick shouted.

"If I knew getting my PhD would be this much fun, I'd have opted for dual degrees," Hunt yelled back.

"Oh, this is nothing—just wait for your oral exams," Quick hollered, checking the mirror again. "Hold tight."

Quick jagged the shift lever into third. The tachometer needle bobbed and then shot back for the red line. Keeping the gas pedal buried, Quick cranked the steering wheel. The tires howled, as they fought to maintain purchase through the curve.

The centerline leveled and broke into pieces. Banana trees blurred by. The Jeep's speedometer needle stabilized at the 120-mph mark.

Hunt watched the orange sedan break free of the last curve and then rapidly eat the gap to the 4x4. "Here they come again," he shouted.

"Brace!" Quick warned.

An instant before the orange car blasted into the Jeep, Quick swung into the oncoming lane, slammed the brake, and spun the wheel back hard right, hoping to sideswipe the other vehicle. But the car's driver stomped his brake pedal, slowing his lighter vehicle more rapidly. The Jeep, with a squeal of rubber, sliced into the right lane, missing its opponent.

Quick instantly jammed the gas. The 4x4 recovered, gained speed, and entered a long turn. Quick weaved the Jeep back and forth across the lanes as if she were stitching together sea and land. The sedan bobbed behind, unable to line up a hit. To the left, due to the road's ongoing climb, the shoulder now dropped ninety feet to the rocks and water below.

The Jeep rounded out of a curve. Quick tightened her grip on the steering wheel. Then she tried to shove the gas pedal through the floorboard.

"Are you sure about this?" Hunt shouted, staring at a herd of sheep swelling in the lane ahead, fed from the inland side by animals streaming through an open gate, heading for the shore and its salty rocks.

Quick answered by veering the Jeep hard to the left, slashing across the oncoming lane, where the sheep were now overflowing just ahead. The 4x4 hit the narrow gravel shoulder, the only bit of ground left before the dead plummet to the sea, the outer tires barely maintaining contact with land.

Then the tread grabbed stone, and the Jeep shot forward. On the passenger side, the lambs passed so close Hunt could have reached out and run his fingers through their matted coats if he'd wanted.

The Jeep broke past the flock. The sheep flooded the road in a panicked flight to the sea.

Quick slammed the brake and cranked the wheel. The Jeep whipped around 180 degrees, laying down a half-circle of smoking tread. The fleeing animals completely blocked the roadway. Quick and Hunt heard a squeal of rubber, the screaming rev of a downshifted engine, and the shrill blare of a car horn.

A cacophonous implosion of metal and glass preceded a huge splash. On the horizon, the final sliver of sun joined the orange car sinking beneath the Atlantic's cool surface. The only sounds remaining on the roadway were blats of warning and the fast click of fleeing hooves against asphalt.

Quick turned to Hunt. "See, I told you nothing to worry about—those guys couldn't even hurt a lamb."

. . .

The sounds of the squealing rubber and whining motors receded and then died.

The fork floated in front of Kalia Slater's lips, as she listened another moment, hoping to hear some sign that her rescue was imminent, or even just simple sounds of everyday life from the outside world. When none followed, she pushed the utensil into her mouth.

Chewing, she surveyed the small room for the thousandth time: the swept dirt floor, the four rough stone walls, the high window that, moments ago, switched from gentle red to blood-black, and the lumpy pallet where she had slept last night under a rough woolen blanket with one wrist handcuffed to its wooden frame.

Slater sighed, dropped the fork, and looked across the table. "After seven consecutive meals of rice, I've eaten enough carbs. Anything else on the menu?"

Only silence responded.

The grad student watched the man staring at her. He was sitting in same chair pressed up against the door, with one of his hands where it had remained constantly the entire time she had been there—locked on a T-shaped Micro Uzi lying across his lap.

He had said nothing during Slater's presence, only occasionally rising for food and water for one or both of them, or to relieve himself in a bucket in the corner. She had no idea if he understood a single word that she said.

But she would try again.

She had to.

"Let's start over. My name is Kalia. My friends and family are looking for me, and I would like to call them and let them know that I am OK," she said. "Can you help me do that—"

A knock sounded on the door.

The man jumped up, whirled around, and lowered the Uzi to his hip. Muffled words—in the language that Slater had heard at the mine and again when she was taken from her hotel room with the gun to her head—came through the door.

The guard lowered the gun and moved the chair. The door swung open. A second man, who could have been the gunman's brother, entered.

The men chatted loudly for a moment, all the time watching Slater. Then they circled the table. Her muscles tensed, and Slater looked away, toward the open doorway.

The silvery purples and greens of a vineyard lay closest to the building. Then an empty ribbon of blacktop. And beyond, the darkening sea. Kalia Slater's gaze rose to the crescent moon, which hung low with a bright planet or star glowing alongside it.

Then the black hood descended over her head, extinguishing all light.

- 19 -

WEDNESDAY, JULY 11
London

Utley lifted his wineglass. He swiveled his wrist and watched the spinning gold liquid climb the crystal bowl. After a moment, the wine settled. He took a deep drink. The chardonnay's oaken flavors mixed with the remnants of his last bite of pork belly, whose alternating layers of fat and meat had been as delicate as the pastry of a freshly baked croissant. Utley swallowed slowly, not wanting to free the mix of tastes from his month.

After several moments, he sighed and pushed back his chair. Normally, he would curse the tentacles of old age for pulling him from a meal to use the loo. But this excursion elicited none of those resentments. Rather, he felt quite ebullient.

As Utley neared the rest room, an approaching man nodded at him like a passing stranger might, seemingly preoccupied with his lapel buttonhole.

Without breaking stride, Utley nodded in return, acknowledging the signal, and then entered the men's room.

Utley walked directly to the second from last stall. Inside, he hung his jacket on the door hook and dropped his trousers and shorts to the floor. He slid onto the seat and immediately reached for the paper dispenser but then heard someone enter the restroom. He pulled back his hand and checked his watch.

After several minutes, he looked again at his timepiece. No need to appear rushed, he mused, finally reaching for the dispenser and unrolling some paper, which he discarded, unused, into the bowl. He reached again for the dispenser.

This time, his fingers slipped between the paper roll and the dispenser casing, moving upward until they stopped against a thin edge.

His shaking hand was causing more noise than he would otherwise want. But, he thought, should anyone hear these noises, he would only think him another old man fumbling to clean himself.

And, Utley smiled, *they would be righter than they could ever know.*

He pulled his hand from the dispenser and withdrew a sliver of metal and plastic. He slipped his mobile from his jacket and inserted the chip into a slot on the phone. Text scrolled across the mobile's display.

How delightful!

Utley removed the chip, bit down on it, and dumped the mangled piece into the bowl. The metal slowly somersaulted as it sank. Then with a roar, it shot away, destined for the River Thames.

-20-

Nin Zanin's polished red nails slid into the wavy salt-and-pepper hair, like scarlet snakes slipping down spring burrows toward unprotected, freshly borne prey.

"See, my darling, everything is unfolding as we knew it would, and the shipment is well on its way." Nin's hand was now fully submerged in her lover's mane, caressing his scalp.

"Shhhh—we must hear this." Sergei Sokolov pulled away and grabbed the remote control. On a flat-panel television affixed to the wall opposite his desk, the talking heads' whispers became shouts.

"In London," the newsreader continued, "against a backdrop of the ongoing plutonium investigation, the prime minister prepares to leave for the International Capital Forum, which he will attend this weekend in Madrid, along with other world leaders.

"The items high on the summit's agenda include the urgent need for additional loans from Chinese and Middle Eastern sovereign wealth funds to stabilize the European financial markets, and the role of Russia in ensuring a steady supply of critical hydrocarbon products to Western Europe.

"The prime minister has called the lack of energy security the gravest threat facing continental Europe and says that Britain is fortunate to enjoy diversified energy sources. In what is almost certainly the prime minister's final global summit—"

"Final without a doubt, wouldn't you say, darling?" Nin said.

"As always, Nin is right." Sokolov wrapped his arm around her waist and slid her onto his lap.

"Though, I do wonder about one thing," she said, as Sokolov reached for a lighter.

The flame shot up. "And what is that, my lovely Nin?"

"The loose ends on La Palma. They have eluded our men twice now. Perhaps we should arrange to dispose of them once and for all."

The cigarette danced with the fire, as Sokolov said, "No, the men were rash to take the American woman and chase the researchers. No need to attract more attention to the island at this point in the game. They are scientists, not soldiers. They must be scared now. They will run back to America hoping—no, praying, praying is what Americans do—for the girl's safe return."

Nin frowned but said, "As you think best, Sergei."

Sokolov inhaled long and deep, and then exhaled. Smoke formed his words, "We are so close, my love, so very close to achieving our goals. We must be very cautious."

Nin twisted her torso. Her lips brushed his neck. "Of course, Sergei, cautious, we will be."

Part II

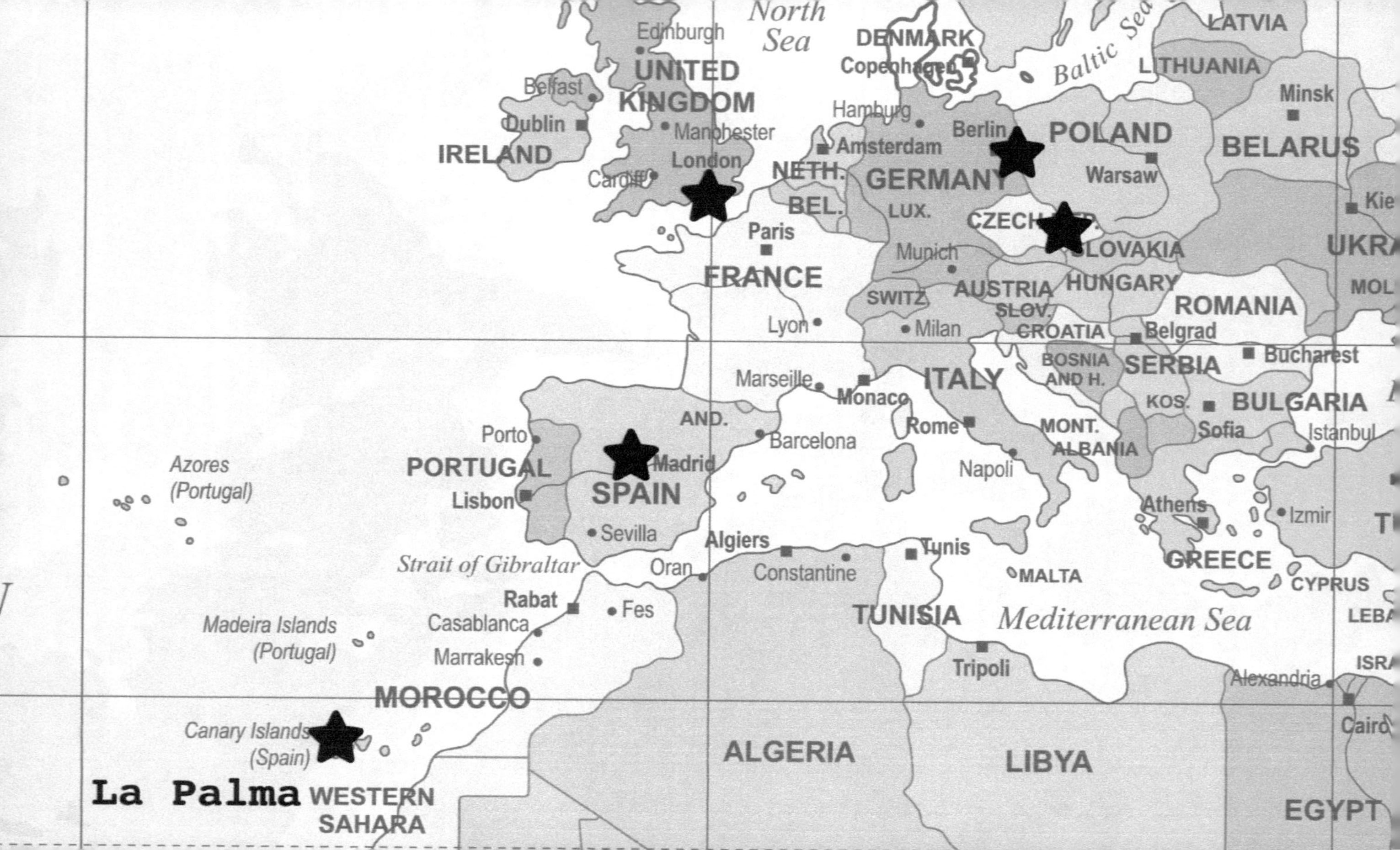

North Sea
Baltic Sea
DENMARK
Copenhagen
LATVIA
LITHUANIA
Minsk
Edinburgh
UNITED KINGDOM
Belfast
IRELAND
Dublin
Manchester
London
Cardiff
Hamburg
Berlin
POLAND
Warsaw
BELARUS
Kie
UKR
Amsterdam
NETH.
BEL.
GERMANY
CZECH
SLOVAKIA
LUX.
FRANCE
Paris
Munich
AUSTRIA
HUNGARY
SWITZ.
SLOV.
ROMANIA
MOL
Lyon
Milan
CROATIA
Belgrad
Bucharest
ITALY
BOSNIA AND H.
SERBIA
BULGARIA
Sofia
Istanbul
Azores (Portugal)
Porto
PORTUGAL
Lisbon
Madrid
SPAIN
Sevilla
AND.
Barcelona
Marseille
Monaco
Rome
Napoli
MONT.
KOS.
ALBANIA
Athens
GREECE
MALTA
CYPRUS
LEB
Strait of Gibraltar
Algiers
Oran
Tunis
Mediterranean Sea
Madeira Islands (Portugal)
Rabat
Fes
Constantine
TUNISIA
Tripoli
Alexandria
Cair
Casablanca
Marrakesh
MOROCCO
ALGERIA
LIBYA
EGYPT
Canary Islands (Spain)
La Palma
WESTERN SAHARA

-21-

The Russian driver was furious. "The road signs were unhelpful," he granted. "But other factors also played a role." He looked at his shorter companion and then pointed at an empty vodka bottle rolling around the passenger foot well.

"Regardless," the other Russian retorted, "we can't afford even a moment's more delay if we hope to arrive at the instructed hour." Then he suggested the driver shut up and focus on the road.

The driver grunted. He looped the truck onto the next exit ramp and then charged back onto the expressway, now heading in the opposite direction. Still immersed in the argument, neither man noticed a silver Peugeot sedan complete an identical maneuver in their wake.

The truck exited at the proper junction, made several rapid turns, and eventually veered onto an industrial cul-de-sac. At the dead end, it pulled into a parking lot and stopped beside a bay door of a large, windowless warehouse.

The Russians checked their watches and instantly forgot their anger. The on-time bonus alone would pay for American-style braces for the driver's son and a seaside vacation for the passenger's parents.

The warehouse door rose. Several men stepped out.

After a brief exchange, the Russians and the welcoming party began hauling wooden crates, one by one, from the truck into the warehouse.

As they placed the fourth and final crate in the building, the Russian driver raised a brow at his partner and tilted his head at the descending bay door.

"Perhaps they wish to keep the cooled air within the warehouse," the other man whispered, as the metal sill clattered against the concrete floor.

"They can dance a waltz for all I care, just so long as they pay us first, so we can get to the whorehouse in Barcelona," the driver whispered back.

Outside, several parking lots away from the warehouse, inside the silver Peugeot sedan, the car's two occupants watched as the bay door closed. A cellphone rang. They exchanged a look.

Inside the warehouse, the sharp crack of nails pulling from wood echoed throughout the space. The warehouse men pulled off the crate's top. The lead agent reached inside. A few feet away, the Russian truck drivers shifted to better see.

The agent's arm rose, and a glinting reflection caused the Russians to blink. Then the agent altered the angle of his arm, and the reflection died, revealing what he held: a large suitcase clad in brushed metal.

The Russians glanced at each other again. They were both thinking the same thing: *whatever that case held, whether money or drugs or God knows what, it was none of their business.*

The warehouse agent set the suitcase carefully—gingerly even, the Russian driver thought—on the floor. The process was repeated for each of the remaining crates, until four brushed-metal suitcases sat aligned in a neat row.

The Russians shifted nervously while the warehouse men stood for several moments just looking at the cases. Then the lead agent turned to the truckers and nodded.

The warehouse men led the Russians to a nearby office.

The truckers entered.

Cold clarity rushed them, as a hollow cylinder pressed into each Russian's back: they now knew exactly why the instructions had ordered that they abandon their pistols on the airbase in Jince.

Their hearts beat wildly. Clogged arteries futilely shunted blood from their cirrhotic livers and ulcerated stomachs to their flabby arms and legs. Lungs, hobbled by decades of cheap tobacco tar, desperately sucked up oxygen in preparation to either fight or flee.

But neither Russian had a chance to move.

Lead slugs tore through their shirts, past the sweaty skin, into the thick layers of fat and muscle. The bullets shredded the truckers' thrashing hearts and then completed the reverse journey before finally exiting their chests.

The Russians slumped. The warehouse hands grabbed the collapsing truckers and, using the falling bodies' momentum, thrust them forward.

The driver's body landed slack on the cold cement. The passenger's body hit the floor still violently spasming.

Muzzles pressed the Russians' heads. Control shots—the

punctuation marks to no alphabet other than assassinations in the victims' hometown of Moscow—rang out.

As the echoes died in the warehouse, outside, in the silver Peugeot sedan, the driver lowered his cellphone and looked at his companion. "He's landed."

-22-

THURSDAY, JULY 12
Madrid

Late-morning Madrid was ferocious. Even with the embassy's triple-layer, blast-resistant glass, waves of heat radiated from the inner pane. But Quick ignored the thermal assault. Staring out, all she could see was Kalia's face pressed against the rear window of the abductor's car.

Finally, she had heard enough. Quick turned from the window. "So, Inspector, what you're telling us is we still have not received a ransom note for Kalia?"

Reyes's voice answered slowly from the speaker of Davies's desk phone, "Unfortunately, Dr. Quick, that is exactly the case. We have, however, finished recovery of the orange car that found its way into our lovely Atlantic. It was a rental stolen two weeks ago. Both occupants were male. Neither man carried identification. The driver was mangled beyond recognition, while the passenger was more or less intact." A pause was followed by the sound of swallowing. "And based on this man's facial features, we believe that he was not local."

"Let me guess, you think he was North African," Quick said.

"Yes, Dr. Quick, the dead passenger appeared to be of North

African extraction, possibly Moroccan." A sigh came from the speaker. "I'm afraid all roads continue leading to the involvement of an African drug-smuggling ring in Manuelo Alcanzar's shooting and Kalia Slater's disappearance."

"Inspector, anything new on *LANDFALL?*" Eric Hunt asked, sounding very much as if he meant every word printed across his T-shirt, which read, "No, you can't be my friend," ended by a yellow smiley-face emoticon.

"The adjuster from a London-based insurance company is due to arrive today to inspect the vessel. Doubtlessly, *LANDFALL* will be deemed a total loss. My officers are still trying to contact the boat's owners—"

"We plan to visit their offices this afternoon," Davies cut in.

Another sigh from the speakerphone. "I suppose speaking with the company's representatives cannot hurt."

A man entered and handed a folder to Davies, and Quick said, "Thank you, Inspector. Please immediately contact us if any new leads arise." Her finger stabbed the phone, cutting off Reyes's reply. "OK, what do we have?"

Davies leaned back in his chair and thumbed through the printouts. "The boat is owned by a private partnership founded in 2001. Spanish tax records list 'oil and natural-gas exploration' as their primary commercial activity." Davies frowned. "The company's only shareholders are a handful of private Russian corporations, all of which are wholly owned by one Sergei Sokolov, aka, 'The Falcon,' as the name translates to." Davies slid a photo from the file and handed it to Hunt.

"A face like raked ashes." The grad student passed the sheet to Quick.

Davies continued reading, "Sokolov is Russian born, birth year unknown but estimated circa 1950. During the communist era, he was a small-time criminal who ran brothels located in various major cities in the Soviet republics, mainly stocked by teenagers and young adults of both sexes from Eastern Europe and Central Asia—usually unwilling inventory at that."

His brow rose. "But the recent decades have favored the Falcon: he is now one of Russia's richest men, one of the mega-wealthy, post-Soviet industrial oligarchs. When the Soviet Union imploded during the '80s, Sokolov seized control of various state-owned industries by either bribing or blackmailing the Politburo officials who frequented his brothels and were unwittingly filmed in compromising positions."

Davies turned the page. "Sokolov, using state loans, then extended his empire to include coal mines, chemical plants, and manufacturing facilities: first across the former Soviet Union and then the West. Purportedly, Sokolov is now worth in excess of 50 billion-with-a-'b' dollars. And the Madrid firm is likely a shell corporation used to shield profits from the Russian and other tax authorities.

"If this guy's already a multibillionaire, then he is therefore unlikely to be involved in Kalia's kidnapping. I'm afraid Reyes might be right about us wasting our time on this lead." Davies swiveled his chair toward the window, where Quick had returned. "What do you think, Sam?"

Looking out at the sluggish traffic, Quick silently computed the odds of a boat owned by an oil-and-gas exploration company and commissioned in the theft of an ALCHEMY laptop being due to random chance. *I'm all-in on this one.*

Sam Quick turned from the window. "I think it's high time we visit their offices."

. . .

The airliner glided. To the north, dry mountains squat against the horizon. To the east, the summer sun was racing for its zenith. To the west and south, the city rolled and stretched without end. Then the jet's tires smacked the concrete, and the reverse thrusters sucked the scorching morning air, roaring in victorious arrival.

Inside the plane, the passengers stretched and yawned, ran fingers through hair unsettled by the night flight, and gathered their tablets and noise-canceling headphones. In first class, a trio of young people stuffed wafer-thin, titanium-clad computers into sleek carrying cases.

To the other passengers, the threesome looked as if they had landed for a fashion shoot or perhaps to open an art exhibit. The two men were clad in blue blazers, with white cotton shirts open at the collar, and form-fitting jeans. A hint of blond stubble shadowed the taller man's face, while dark shag carpeted the jowls of the shorter, heavyset man.

Anyone looking at them might suppose them young men of means with wilder streaks, hinted at by the now empty holes lining their ears. Certainly, no one would ever guess the existence of the tattooed mushroom cloud and exploding American flag hidden beneath the blond man's expensive clothes.

The group's third member, the woman, wore nearly the same outfit, albeit with no jacket, and the white shirt gathered at the buttons overlying her chest, its line distorted by the ample flesh beneath. Her face was free of cover, and her dreadlocks were bundled into a regal headdress, bound with a golden silk scarf.

After exiting the plane, at the immigration counter, each member of the trio presented their American passports. Each time, the border-control officer glanced at the photo, looked up, and—seeing the expensive uniform of those who travel in the front of planes and the back of cars—immediately slammed down his stamp.

On the freeway, as their taxi merged into traffic, Amanda gazed out her window, still lost in the fog of transoceanic flight, staring but seeing little. She tried to make her mind work. But, as the cab crept toward Madrid, Amanda could not for the life of her remember how it had all gotten this far.

. . .

Nin Zanin sniffed the gritty mixture of exhaust and dust, smiled as if the air were sufficiently unhealthy for her tastes, and then climbed into the car's rear compartment. Her red heels stabbed the tiny Persian carpet serving as a floor mat. The heavy door glided shut and latched with a gentle click.

The driver hurried around to his door. He glanced at the small business jet parked nearby, at the ten-feet-long metallic cylinders affixed beneath each wing, one beside each engine. He shrugged and climbed inside.

Nin leaned back and closed her eyes. She was tired after the stopover in Prague and the two-hour weather delay this morning. Hearing the driver slide behind the steering wheel, she barked directions without raising her head and then stabbed a button on the armrest. A smoked polycarbonate divider silently rose, sealing her off from the front compartment.

As the car began to move, she grabbed the newspaper lying on the other seat. Her lips moved, as she read the headline.

"London plutonium mystery!" she snorted and pushed away the paper.

A mobile slipped from her purse. After a moment, she spoke, "I've landed . . . Yes, the shipment arrived safely at the warehouse . . . I should arrive at the office within the hour." She smiled. "Yes, darling, looking forward to seeing you, too."

Nin set down the phone and glanced at the window. The car was threading through surface-street traffic. She checked the console display. The temperature reading was impressive even for Madrid in July. She looked again at the Spaniards walking outside, chatting and laughing as if the day were as cool as Moscow in May. *If this infernal heat does not drive them indoors, then we must turn up the flame.*

-23-

Hunt whistled softly, while Quick and Davies moved in and quietly surveyed the office's unmanned reception area. Heavy furniture and massive oil paintings liberally adorned the space, and a large, colorful carpet comprised of geometric tribal patterns covered the floor.

Davies nudged Quick. The scientist looked where he was pointing, at the largest oil painting. Of a wolf crouched with its jaws latched onto the pale throat of a young maiden, with a falcon perched nearby, its eyes glinting, awaiting its turn at the fresh kill. Davies whispered, "The Falcon welcomes you to his lair."

A side door opened, and a woman marched out. Seeing the visitors, she paused. Then she recovered and asked in good English, without smiling, "May I help you?"

"Yes, I think you can," Quick said, taking in the woman's softly lush facial features and shiny black hair, and the short skirt, blazer, and heels, all in the same bright red. Her gaze flicked to the legs. *And given those calves, she definitely takes the stairs.*

Quick smiled at the woman. "I'm Sam Quick, and these are my associates, Eric Hunt and Zach Davies. We're investigating a boat that capsized off La Palma, in the Canary Islands—"

"Of course"—the woman relaxed—"the silly boat. You must be with the insurance company. I'm Solta Zanin, the managing director."

"Yes, that's exactly right—we're with the insurance company," Quick said, as Hunt and Davies nodded in agreement.

Solta shrugged. "The island police informed us of the loss. Undoubtedly, the accident was the result of some joyriding children who found more of a thrill than they bargained for." Her brow rose. "But Ms. Quick, why are Americans—you are American, no?"

Quick nodded.

"Why are Americans working for a British insurance company on a claim against a boat that capsized in Spanish waters?"

"That's globalization for you. No borders remain, we simply go where they pay us most."

Solta sighed extravagantly. "Now even the Americans must leave their homeland to find good-paying work." She shrugged again. "So, what can I tell you about *LANDFALL?*"

"Perhaps you could first explain why your firm keeps a speedboat in the Canary Islands?" Hunt asked.

"Simple, we use *LANDFALL* for entertaining visiting executives and government officials who might be helpful to us."

"What sort of help does your company need?" Davies asked.

Solta's lip curled. "I'm afraid that is proprietary information."

"Was the boat ever used for oil or gas exploration?" Hunt asked.

"Certainly not. *LANDFALL* was in no way equipped for that."

A lie. But let it pass. Quick instead asked, "Is Mr. Sokolov aware of the vessel's loss?" She watched the woman's eyes widen and then swiftly narrow.

"Mr. Sokolov? This, I cannot say. I informed Moscow and assume that they, in turn, told Mr. Sokolov."

"And has Mr. Sokolov used the craft recently?" Hunt asked.

"I'm afraid that I fail to see this question's relevance. Nor, in any case, am I at liberty to discuss Mr. Sokolov's schedule."

Solta looked at her watch. "Speaking of schedules, I expect a *scheduled* visitor at any moment. Now, may I answer any further questions before I must return to my work?"

"Just one more. Who named *LANDFALL*?" Quick asked.

Solta's lips gathered again. Several seconds passed. Then she said, "Why, Mr. Sokolov, of course. He names all the company's vessels, large and small."

Her arm rose toward the entry door. "If additional questions arise, please call before you visit, and I shall happily arrange a mutually convenient appointment."

Moments later, Solta Zanin picked up a handset. When the Americans unloaded from the elevator at the lobby, the ringing of a mobile phone greeted them. As they crossed the checker-board tile, each couldn't but help stare at the gorgeous woman entering from the street, whose bright red nails clasped a mobile to her ear, and whose eyes briefly widened and flitted their way.

As soon as they were outside the building, Quick turned to the men. "Did you see what I saw? Solta Zanin and that woman were identical other than a large beauty mark high on the new arrival's cheek—twins."

-24-

Six city blocks away, only Utley noticed. But the couple standing a few paintings from him spent more time assessing the Prado's collection of visitors than they did surveying the surrounding masterworks of art. Probably not American, he figured, Canadian possibly, but definitely an advanced recon team.

He slowed and pretended to examine a Velázquez that he had always thought overrated, while he watched the couple re-sweep the room. Several minutes later, he saw the pair nod at each other and then step into an adjacent gallery.

Utley followed the couple into the next chamber and then stopped before a five-century-old wood panel. *Now, this was a painting.* Out of the corner of his eye, he caught the couple join hands and then leisurely head toward the main stairway. *My, aren't they putting on quite the show.* But, he thought, at least they're moving on before my visitor arrives.

His gaze returned to the medieval panel, and the sounds of the surrounding low conversation faded from his consciousness.

"Cave Cave Deus Videt," he murmured aloud. Yes, he thought, beware indeed. From the painting's center, a monocular

eye—with the accession of the Christ figure reflected in the pupil, and the phrase "Beware, Beware, God is Watching" inscribed in Latin on the iris—stared out at him.

Utley mouthed the words circling the eye: "*Accidia, Gula, Avaritia, Invidia, Ira, Superbia.*" He paused before saying the final one: "*Luxuria.*"

His gaze moved to the painting's tiny scene of torture and ruin representing hell. *Before long, this is where I'll call home. And if I have any say in the matter, Sergei Sokolov will welcome me warmly.*

"So old chap, which one was your downfall?" a voice said from over Utley's shoulder.

Utley gaze didn't leave the Bosch. "You don't reach my age without having landed at least once on each of these sins. Of course, I've spent more time on some than on others."

"Quite so." The voice continued in a volume and tone suggesting a discussion of artistic merits, "I assume you've noticed that company is in the house?"

"Yes, no doubt tidying up in advance of the ICF reception that's scheduled here for Sunday night," Utley said.

"Yes, which is also why I'm here in Madrid in person: I'm on the PM's detail."

"And the shipment?"

"It remains housed at an industrial warehouse located in some godforsaken city north of here called Zaragoza. Our assets are in place, watching and waiting.

"Excellent. Any progress on the London incident?" Utley asked.

"Suspicions are high that London will suffer a follow-up to

the 7/7 bombings of 2005, with a dirty bomb this time. Plutonium spread about London and whatnot. You could read the relief on the PM's face when we left British airspace. Though the order that he gave his wife to remain behind in London—too much uncertainty about security in Madrid, he told her—might also have factored into his levity."

Utley chuckled.

"I assume the Zaragoza shipment is heading this way?" the man said. "Anything too hot to handle?"

"Who can say?" Utley responded evenly. Not telling his long-time ally about the totality of the danger was now just another betrayal bobbing in the wake of Utley's life. But, staring back into the painting's all-seeing eye, Utley vowed that this infidelity—unlike those past—would bring no harm to its victim. "Anything else?"

"No."

"If—"

"Of course."

Utley was alone again before the painting. He pulled his hand from his pocket, and his trembling fingers approached the oil, stopping an inch from the wooden panel. Then he jumped, and the gallery sounds grew loud in his ears.

As he hurried away, his cheeks glowed bright red, and his fingertip burned in shame from its tremor-induced contact with the scene of hell.

-25-

The evening was hot. People chatting and drinking filled the chairs scattered about the plaza. A fountain sprayed arcing lines of water into the fading sky. Jugglers tossed wooden pins and twirled large hoops around their undulating, gold-painted torsos.

In a quieter corner of the square, away from the fountain, Quick raised her espresso cup. "Here's to being one step closer to finding Kalia." Then she downed the dark liquid.

Davies's brow wrinkled. "Maybe I missed something."

"Haven't you realized that Sam Quick is always two steps ahead?" Hunt turned to Quick. "So what exactly did we learn today beyond those twins having pricey decorating tastes?"

"Let's start with Solta Zanin," Quick said, "and her lie about *LANDFALL* being equipped for exploration. Contrary to what Officer Alonso assumed when Eric and I visited *LANDFALL*, the craft's sonar was most certainly not used to hunt for sunken vessels. No, the *LANDFALL's* gear looked much deeper into the earth. And to me, a simple ranch girl from New Mexico, that sounds like exploration. The question is what were they looking for around La Palma."

She pulled out her cellphone. "And I know just the person to answer that query."

After several rings, a voice crackled from the speaker, "Sam? Honey, what the hell is going on over there?"

"Molly, listen, I have you on speakerphone." Quick introduced Hunt and Davies and then briefly relayed the previous days' events, ending with a description of the boat's sonar and the visit to the Madrid offices of the craft's owner.

"Sam, any reason—"

"Not at this time, Molly," Quick cut in, still unready to discuss ALCHEMY in front of either Hunt or Davies. "But we need to know what those folks were searching for around La Palma with *LANDFALL*'s sonar? Oil? Natural gas?"

"More likely, minerals or metals of some kind. Let's start with the macro picture"—Matson's voice gathered as the geologist warmed to the topic—"La Palma, like its sister islands, started life as an undersea volcano that eventually grew high enough to break the ocean's surface.

"Volcanic lava, or magma as it's called when still within the earth, is laced with metals such as zinc, silver, and gold. Hence La Palma's rich zinc deposits and La Garganta del Diablo mine, which supplied the metal to Europe . . . that is until the eruption of 1949 and the Big Slip."

"Big Slip?" asked a deep voice, causing Matson to wonder about Davies's appearance.

"That's right, the Big Slip was the showstopper of the '49 eruption, when a seven-mile-long fault line ripped open along the island's ridgeline, and kicked off a colossal landslide—"

"All this was due to seismic activity?" Hunt asked.

"The eruption's associated earthquakes were only part of the equation," Matson explained. "More important was the composition of the island's rock: Much of La Palma's stone is very porous. And this rock soaks up the abundant winter rains, turning the mountain into a wet sponge. And in June 1949, the sponge was wringing wet."

"Uh-oh," Hunt said.

"Uh-oh indeed," Matson replied. "In the buildup to the eruption, two-thousand-degree magma rose up from the magma chamber lying under the island into the mountain. The rising magma heated the trapped rainwater. And most liquids, water being one, expand when heated. Thermal hydraulic expansion on a massive scale cleaved that mountain just about right in half." Matson paused. "Then the actual eruption hit."

"And?" Hunt and Davies asked simultaneously.

"The mother of all landslides ensued. La Palma's western half—half the whole damn island—broke free and began collapsing into the ocean," Matson answered. "In the shoreside villages, the docks sunk under the waves. Water rushed in. Buildings collapsed. People ran for their lives."

"And then?" Hunt and Davies prodded.

"Then it just stopped. The rocks locked in place." Matson sighed. "And we should be real thankful it did: because if that mountain had completely collapsed, then the landslide would have displaced so much ocean water that the resultant tsunami would have obliterated nearly the entire Atlantic coastline."

The geologist chuckled. "Of course, that was just a temporary reprieve: someday—fifty or five hundred or five thousand years from now—the volcano will blow her nose hard enough to finally knock that picturesque hunk of island into the Atlantic, and then it's bye-bye birdie for us here Florida and all along the eastern seaboard."

"Molly, the sonar—," Quick cut in.

"Righto, getting back to what they used that boat's sonar to search for, my money is on gold or diamonds. Due both to the direct deposition of ejected volcanic material and to landslide debris, the island's surrounding seabed is volcanic in origin and therefore likely contains significant mineral and metal deposits."

Quick picked up the phone. "Thanks for the info. I hate to run, Molly, but I need to get these men out on the town."

"Anytime, sweetie. You take care. Ciao."

Quick disconnected the call and looked at the men. "So, we can say *LANDFALL* served as something more than the company toy. And to Eric's point about the expensive decorating taste: the pieces filling their reception area were the real deal: the Dutch oils, an exquisite tribal rug, and the nineteenth-century furniture lifted straight from the Hermitage. An easy couple mil' adorned that room."

"We figured that Sergei Sokolov used the firm to funnel money away from the Russian tax authorities—the furnishings are likely just another place to quietly park his assets," Davies said.

"The furnishings themselves don't interest me," Quick explained. "No, what the high-value décor tells us is that a very sophisticated security system likely protects those offices."

She looked at Hunt. "Any ideas how we might handle that issue?"

The grad student simply grinned, without looking up from his smartphone, which he was already furiously typing on. While beside him, Davies's brow wrinkled anew.

"Great, I thought you just might." Then Quick added, "Drink up, gentlemen—the next round of caffeine is on me."

-26-

THURSDAY, JULY 12
Calatayud, Spain

Angry red streaks sliced across the darkness ahead as overtaking cars cut back into the lane ahead.

"Can't we go any faster?" Amanda said, as she ground her dreadlocks into the headrest and reached for the joint. Outside, a road sign seemed to crawl by the BMW, while on the center console, the digital clock seemed as if it had been frozen at 9:15 for the past twenty minutes.

Like her companions, since arriving this morning from New York, Amanda had shed the expensive look designed to smooth their entry past border control. Now the metal piercings again lined her ears, and she wore a T-shirt and jeans.

From the driver's seat, Gabriel laid a hand on her thigh. "What's the rush? You want the police to stop us for speeding and then expel us from the country for carrying pot, all on the eve of the twenty-first century's defining event?"

He looked in the rearview mirror at Jacob, who lay sprawled along the rear bench, pressed against a door. "Just sit back and enjoy the ride, kids—we're right on schedule."

Amanda sighed and passed the joint over her shoulder to

Jacob. Then she peeled Gabriel's hand off her leg, shoved it away, and rubbed her hands before the dash vents as if trying to wash them clean in the outrushing air.

"I tell you: I still think this is a setup," she started. "We wire the money and then, bam, some pervy counterterrorism agents throw black hoods over our heads and then ship us to Romania for torture and interrogation in a secret prison."

These were the doubts that Amanda dared articulate. But what she really wondered was whether her family would even recognize her after all was said and done. *And my so-called boyfriend is really starting to piss—*

"Just maybe she's got a point. Because, yeah, why'd some Russians want to help us, anyway?" Jacob said. "What's in it for them?"

"Now you're starting to sound like her. We've been over this, like, a hundred times. It's rather simple: what's in it for them, like we've said, is a hell of a lot of my family's money." Gabriel laughed. "The pot is making you two paranoid."

He held up his hand and snapped his fingers. Jacob handed him the joint, as another passing horn droned. Gabriel inhaled deeply, pulling the soothing smoke into his lungs.

Finally, he said, "Yes, my friends, soon the world will understand how false and empty our leaders and their materialistic greed really are."

Then another car cut off the BMW. And the red slash of its taillights pointed to a sign reading, "Zaragoza 80 km."

-27-

FRIDAY, JULY 13
Madrid

They waited. At three a.m., the narrow street angling off the Puerta del Sol was just as hot and dusty and, until an hour ago, as crowded as at midday. Now the steady crush of pedestrians had thinned to irregularly spaced clumps.

Quick surveyed the street, which was finally empty for a block in either direction. "OK, everyone remembers the plan?"

Davies swore softly, while Hunt nodded.

"All right, let's move then."

They crossed the street to the midrise. At the building entrance, Quick opened a large purse bought from a street vendor for this occasion and started pawing through it as if looking for her keys. As she did this, Hunt discreetly held his smartphone alongside a keycard reader affixed beside the entryway.

Churning numbers filled the phone's screen, and Quick and Davies shared a brief glance, both impressed by Hunt's delivery. Before she had finished outlining the plan in the plaza, Hunt had downloaded a decryption hack for unlocking doors secured by swipe-card readers. Exactly like the card reader that he had earlier seen when visiting the building. The hack would not work for military-grade security systems, but for the customary installations found at commercial or governmental buildings, his phone was now a master key.

After twenty seconds, a green light flashed on the card reader, and a buzzer sounded. Hunt pulled open the door and looked from Quick to Davies. "After you."

Inside the lobby, they crossed the entry hall, ignoring the noisy elevator as planned, and instead filed onto the staircase spiraling up around the lift.

Halfway up the first flight, Hunt whispered, "I hope the Spanish authorities accept cards for bail because I'm fresh out of euros." His voice deepened and roughened, "American Express, don't break in without it."

"That's why we let the embassy guy tag along—his diplomatic immunity is our get-out-of-jail-free card," Quick said.

"Hilarious." Davies momentarily locked eyes with Quick.

They continued climbing and finally stepped off at the fourth-floor landing. At the office door, Quick knelt. She slipped a small portfolio from the purse and removed a long, slender tool that looked like it was used to clean teeth in dental offices. A second instrument joined it, and the tools slid into the keyhole.

"So, this is how scientists unlock life's mysteries," Davies said, watching the hall.

"Tools for collecting samples," Quick replied, as the rods jagged and tacked as if a knitter were weaving his hundredth afghan. "In high school, I ran a little business in the student parking lot opening vehicles in which keys were locked."

A clicking sound came from within the door, and the metal rods withdrew.

"Not for the money. But mainly to hear blockheaded jocks stammer while asking for a girl's help, particularly with errors involving the rolling extensions of their peripubescent manhoods." She flashed Davies a smile. "If you ever happen to lock your keys in your car, Zach, I'd be most glad to assist."

"I bet," Davies grunted.

The instruments returned to their case, and Quick said, "Eric, you're up."

"Check."

Quick opened the door. A beep greeted them. Then another. And another. With the interval between each beep shorter than the last.

The Americans slipped inside. Scanning the reception area, Hunt caught the wolf and falcon staring directly at him from the massive oil painting, the predators seemingly weighing his potential as their next meal.

"Eric," Davies whispered, "the alarm."

The grad student crossed to the opposite wall, where red lights flashed on a display, in unison with the beeping. He held his smartphone alongside the panel and tapped a button. A series of six whirring numbers appeared on the phone's interface. From the left, the digits began stopping one by one, like a digital slot-machine's readout.

As each number locked, Hunt punched the alarm pad's corresponding button. The first three numbers resolved almost immediately. But the last three digits were still spinning away, as the flashing red light and beeping pulsed ever closer together.

"Time's running out, Eric," Davies said, while Quick studied one of the paintings.

The fourth number locked, and the fifth and sixth digits remained in play. The beeps nearly merged into the continuous squawk of a flat-lining cardiac patient. Then the fifth number nailed, and Hunt hit the button on the alarm panel. His index finger continued roaming over the keypad, ready to stab the sixth digit when it came up on his phone.

"Eric, hurry—," Davies started as the last beep gave way to a continuous tone. The grad student punched a button, and a steady green light flashed on.

"Hey, your phone." Davies pointed at the smartphone and the still-spinning sixth digit.

Hunt shrugged. "Sometimes you gotta go with your gut."

Quick's flashlight beam pegged the inner-office door. "Zach, you're on lookout duty. Eric, bring your phone and your . . . um, gut."

Hunt followed Quick, while Davies moved for the reception desk, muttering, "Great. I'll just keep the wolf and the falcon company."

Inside the office, pale light spilled from a huge window overlooking Madrid. Quick went behind the desk and started pulling drawers.

Hunt gave a low whistle. "The inner sanctum makes the reception area look like a thrift store." Hunt pointed at a flag stretched across most of one wall. "And what's with the mutant bird?"

Quick glanced up. The panel's background was butterscotch colored. And a black, double-headed eagle filled its center, with each head topped by a crown. "Well, vexillology was never my strong suit," the scientist paused, "but I'd say that's the Russian royal standard."

She nodded at the desktop computer. "I'm more interested in what's on this baby."

Hunt squinted at the bizarre bird one more time, as he circled the desk, pulling a cord from his pocket. He tethered his phone to the computer and then grabbed the desktop keyboard. A few moments later, he shook his head. "The files are encrypted"—another barrage of keystrokes—"I can copy them. But opening them will require some help."

Hunt's gaze rose from the monitor and followed Quick to the wall opposite the flag, to a large portrait. In the painting, a man was seated with a woman standing behind him, her hand on his shoulder. The figures were dressed in regal vestments and adorned with glittering jewels. Both wore crowns. And they were situated in front of the Russian royal flag.

"The Falcon," Hunt said.

Quick pointed at the other figure, at the beauty mark high on its right cheek. "And the woman from the lobby earlier today."

. . .

The cold metal and whalebone slid along her inner thigh, and the downy hair on her forearms stood at attention. The Beretta Bobcat—with its owner's name, "Nin," obliquely scrimshawed in cursive script across the gun's whalebone grip—entered the leather holster strapped high on her leg, under her short, red skirt.

Nin smoothed the fabric and smiled at her sister, who was performing the same maneuver with a Bobcat identical except for the name "Solta" carved on its grip.

Then Nin barked some orders at the driver, who was holding

open the rear door of the big sedan. Nin and Solta climbed into the car, while the driver's eyes snapped to the muscular thighs and calves now jackknifing below the tiny skirts as they slid in the vehicle's rear compartment.

Seconds later, the engine's twelve cylinders roared. In unison, the sisters tilted imperceptibly to the side, as the car whipped around a corner.

"You should not worry so much." Solta patted her sister's leg. "In less than a week, everything will be over."

Nin pursed her lips and said nothing.

Several minutes later, the sedan glided into an alley and rolled to a stop. The driver jumped out and opened the rear door. The twins exited. Solta fished a cellphone from her pocket. She spoke for a moment, then ended the call. "That was the technician in Moscow. The intruders just signed off the office computer."

"Good," Nin said. "If we hurry, driver and I will catch them on the fourth floor, and the cleanup team can haul them down the service elevator. And in case Dr. Quick runs, Solta, you watch the front entrance."

Solta nodded and headed down the alley.

Nin swiped her ID card against the reader for the building's service entrance. The door buzzed.

"Well, don't just stand there drooling," Nin growled at the driver. "Get moving."

. . .

"Are you almost finished?" Quick and Hunt heard Davies call from the outer office.

Hunt nodded at Quick and untethered his phone from the

computer. The two scientists retreated, and Quick waved at the fantasy portrait of Sokolov and his tsarina. "See you soon."

"What did you find?" Davies asked, as the pair emerged.

"We won't know until we decrypt the files." Quick nodded at the alarm panel. "Eric, the honors, please."

The grad student punched in the deciphered code. The beeping and flashing returned. The trio hurried from the office.

They neared the stairs, when the sounds of rapid footsteps came the hallway's far end. A couple came into view, walking rapidly toward them.

"Company, a man and woman." Quick pointed at the stairs. "Go. I'm right behind."

She watched for a moment longer. The approaching figures started running toward her. She jumped onto the stairs, a half flight behind Hunt and Davies. The staircase echoed with their hammering feet. Quick caught up to the men as they rounded down onto the second floor, as the sound of shoes hitting the staircase crashed above.

Quick edged past Davies. "I suggest picking up the pace."

Two flights up, with the driver at her heels, Nin whipped down the stairs. Her hand glided along the railing, while the other dove up her skirt, its red nails finding Beretta's grip.

Outside, from across the street, Solta watched the building. She had heard no shots yet. Then the entrance door flew open. And the Americans, led by Quick, burst out and started running up the street. She pulled her Bobcat and immediately aimed for middle runner's torso, stroking the trigger, as she lined up the shot. *Put down the boy, and the other Americans will surely stop to help him—.*

Shrill laughter broke her concentration. Solta glanced sideways and narrowed her eyes at an approaching cluster of scantily dressed young women in animated conversation. The Bobcat plunged under her skirt, just as Nin and the driver surged from the building. Solta pointed at the fleeing threesome and began running after them, with Nin and the driver on her heels.

Ahead, Quick, Hunt, and Davies ran down the middle of the street, cutting around the strolling Madrileños who had replaced the street's automotive traffic, and who ignored the trio as if runners were common during Madrid's predawn hours.

Quick checked over her shoulder and saw the two women and their male companion crash through a slow-moving clump of pedestrians, eliciting drunken shouts.

"Now three in pursuit. And those aren't cellphones they're holding," Quick yelled, pointing at a side street.

The passage was hardly more than an alley. Halfway down the block, the first low pounding of a disco beat reached them. The street cut hard right, revealing a small square. The thumping beat sharply intensified.

The Americans rapidly scanned the little plaza. People smoking and chatting packed the stone pavement. Rope stands and steroidal guards marked the source of the music. And Sam Quick, Eric Hunt, and Zach Davies immediately realized why the beat reverberated so loudly here—buildings enclosed the square on all sides, except for the narrow passage that would soon deliver their hunters.

-28-

Quick scanned the crowd for police presence. Finding none, she grabbed Hunt and Davies and charged the men past the night-club's doorman before the giant Spaniard could raise himself from his stool. Inside, the music was deafening. The Americans ran the only way forward, down a flight of steps and then along a red-lit hall lined by glossy black walls. At the corridor's end, they spilled through a neon-framed archway.

A vast, writhing subterranean cave lay before them. Darting amoebas of colored light washed over sweaty, jostling dancers, many shirtless and almost all well-muscled. The air was heavy with cigarette smoke and aerosolized perspiration, with the glinting particulates pulsating at the music's 110 beats per minute.

"I feel a bit out of place," Quick shouted, seeing no signs of other female life.

"What now?" Davies yelled over the noise.

"There must be a second exit," she shouted back.

Hunt pointed at an unmarked doorway located on the opposite wall. "Let's try that way."

They cut through the crowd. As they burst through the

doorway, the odor of ammonia and a phalanx of muscular backs fronting a wall of urinals met them.

"Dead end," Hunt yelled.

"Where now?" Davies shouted.

Quick one-eighty-ed to the dance floor, followed by the men. They searched the black walls for an exit but saw none. Quick pointed toward the street entrance: their pursuers stood on the top step, with heads jerking side to side like fast-moving security cameras.

Quick did not see the guns, but she knew they had undoubtedly also arrived. One of the women pointed in various directions. The new arrivals split up, with the man stalking directly toward the Americans.

Still finding no other exit, Quick shouted, "Back into the restroom."

Inside, Quick led the men past the urinals to an inner room with four, tightly closed stalls lining each long wall. Quick began pushing on the closed panels, with Hunt and Davies joining in. Each door held fast. Until finally one tried by Davies swung inward twenty degrees, and Spanish shouting erupted from within.

A young, sweaty face appeared in the space created by the door's movement. "*¡¿Que hace usted?!*"

Davies rapidly asked the man in Spanish to vacate the stall.

The man inspected each of the three Americans, his gaze lingering on Hunt. Finally, he said in heavily accented English, "Just hold on, now I am done anyhow." The door closed. The Americans looked at each other, and at the restroom entrance where at least one of the armed pursuers would arrive at any moment. Then the door reopened, and the man stepped out, carrying a beer bottle and shaking his head.

Quick shoved Hunt and Davies into the empty stall. She pointed at the toilet. "Eric, you and I crouch on the seat. Zach, you sit, so anyone looking under the stall door will see only your legs."

"And what if that doesn't deter them?" Davies shouted over the music, which the restroom's tiled walls amplified like an echo chamber.

"Then we go to plan B." Quick jumped onto the toilet and crouched into one corner, while Hunt did the same in the opposite one.

"Which is?" Davies asked, as he sat on the toilet.

"Let me get back to you on that," Quick said, scanning the tiny enclosure and finding no weapon more lethal than a half-used roll of toilet paper.

On the dance floor, Solta Zanin moved toward the DJ booth. The driver headed for the men's room. And Nin circled the central bar, her Bobcat unobtrusively palmed, as she slipped between the dancing patrons like a cougar through swaying grass.

The driver entered the restroom's outer chamber. Not finding the Americans, he marched into the adjacent toilet area. He eyed the closed stall doors, spit on the floor, and swore.

His fist slammed against the first door, popping the lock. From inside the stall, angry shouts answered. Then the occupant, seeing the gun pointed at his face, threw up his hands and rushed out.

The driver scowled, moved to the next door, and applied his fist again. He moved from door to door this way, in each case provoking furious outbursts that soon morphed into panicked flight.

At the last door, he gave the panel an extra hard blow, slamming it into the person inside. But the door bounced back, opening no more than an inch.

Inside the stall, Quick, Hunt, and Davies braced themselves for the next onslaught. They now faced no choice other than fighting: any cries for help would go unheard over the pounding music.

The driver turned sidewise with his shoulder out and prepared to rush forward.

Then the bottle smashed into his head. The green glass shattered. Beer ran down the man's neck. Bits of glass ricocheted off the tile wall.

The driver slumped to the floor, and his gun clattered free on the tile. The Americans scrambled out, climbing over the fallen man.

Holding the bottle's broken-off neck in one hand, and grinning at them, was the Spanish man who had vacated the stall. "Lucky for you, I take a long time washing my hands and see this not-so-friendly guy come looking for you. No wonder you want my stall so bad."

Quick grabbed the gun off the floor. "Thank you for your help. Unfortunately, he is the least of our troubles. Do you know a back way out of this club?"

The man turned and pointed at the restroom doorway. "*Sí, por supuesto,* follow me." He looked back. "By the way, my name is Jorge—Jorge Delgado."

The Americans ran after Delgado, out into the main dance area, with the start of a seventies disco song greeting their arrival.

Delgado pointed at a black curtain hanging along a far wall.

"Over there. Behind the curtain and then up the stairs."

They started slipping through the crowd. Hunt grabbed Quick's arm and pointed. Twenty feet away, Nin was emerging from behind two tall German tourists. Her eyes immediately locked on the Americans. Her arm went up and pointed their way. Thirty feet to her right, bobbing among the dancers, Solta's head jerked in their direction. The sisters nodded at each other and began moving.

Hunt shouted, "They're both heading our way, and Solta is blocking our route to the exit."

Quick clicked the gun's safety off. But looking around, she figured hundreds of dancers filled the room. *Any gunfight would surely hit bystanders.*

"Jorge, are you sure about this exit?" Quick shouted.

"*Sí,* most definitely. I use the fire exit when I want to avoid my exes."

"Good," Quick said, "because that's exactly what we need—a fire exit." Then she raised the gun, aimed high, and pulled the trigger.

The sprinkler head exploded. Water sprayed down onto the dancing crowd below. People shouted and began running. The human tide picked up the Zanin sisters and swept them along as if they were swimmers caught in an inexorable rip current. While Quick and the men ran behind the black curtain and up the stairs, as the disco beat played on.

☢

-29-

FRIDAY, JULY 13
Zaragoza, Spain

They crushed against the wall like dried weeds rammed into stone. Amanda leaned back and shook her head from side to side, sweeping her dreadlocks over the wall in frustration and sighing loudly. "How much longer are we stuck in this sewer? I'm cold and hungry, and I have to pee." Her nostrils contorted. "And what the hell is that awful smell?"

"Will you just keep your mouth shut? It'll take as long as it takes," Gabriel said, from his seat beside her. "No one can help that the bank f'd up the wire transfer."

"We were supposed to be out of here, like, eight hours ago." Amanda's voice lowered to a whisper, "I tell you, they get the money, and then they off us right here and now."

Jacob leaned forward on Amanda's other side. "Dude, I'm beginning to wonder if she's right."

Gabriel looked at his companions. "Both of you—"

The door crashed open, and the trio jumped. Two men entered, both similar in appearance: dark-haired, unshaven, and wearing military fatigues. And their Micro Uzis were pointed directly at the seated threesome.

For several moments, the only sounds were the soft whoosh of cold air spewing from the ventilation grates and the accelerating pounding of three young hearts drowning in adrenaline.

One of the new arrivals nodded. "Our bank on Guernsey finally received your funds." The muzzles swept down to the floor. "Although I had worried that your check would bounce, some of our men were most hopeful: they were relishing the prospect of some target practice."

The men laughed. Then the speaker looked at Gabriel. "Perhaps you are ready to receive your purchase?"

The gunmen turned and walked from the room. The Americans looked at each other and then jumped up. Gabriel and Jacob hurried after the gunmen, followed by Amanda, who moved more slowly.

In the main warehouse, the gunmen led the trio toward the rented BMW, which was parked beside the bay door.

A large suitcase sat alongside the vehicle. The case was clad in a silvery, brushed metal and was a rolling bag, with wheels attached to one corner, and a folding handle affixed opposite. At an airport baggage carousel, it would be perfectly at home with the other high-end luggage.

Gabriel ran forward and knelt beside the suitcase. His cheek melded with the brushed metal, and his hands caressed the case's rounded edges. After a moment, he looked up. The metal shell reflected the overhead light, casting his upturned face a deaden, bluish hue.

He said only two words: "Thank you."

Amanda watched all this unfold as if in a dream. She had almost wanted it to be a setup. *But it was real. Too real.*

"Mind if I open it and take a look?" Gabriel asked.

The lead gunman shrugged and grinned. "Just don't touch anything inside."

Gabriel gently turned the suitcase on its side. The snap of the latches echoed in the warehouse. Gabriel slowly lifted the lid. Then he sat back on his heels, silent.

Jacob whistled, while Amanda leaned forward and looked over Gabriel's shoulder. To one side of the open suitcase lay a small control panel with a 3X3 matrix of unmarked buttons and a blank digital readout. Beside it, surrounded by foam padding, rest a large black cylinder. Amanda squinted, trying to read the writing on the canister. She gave up after making out that the text was Russian.

Then she grabbed the Gabriel's shoulder. "What the hell is that?" She pointed at a yellow-and-black trefoil symbol affixed below the print. "Is that thing radioactive? What the fucking hell? That wasn't the plan. You said a conventional bomb. We were just gonna shake things up. Send the swine a little warning. Right, Gabe?"

Gabriel remained transfixed, staring down into the suitcase.

"Gabe, fucking answer me," Amanda shouted, grabbing Gabriel's T-shirt, pulling and twisting the fabric. "What the fuck is that thing?"

Gabriel's gaze finally broke. He stood up and faced her, grabbing her arms and placing them at her sides. "Nothing is ever going to change if we think small, Amanda. The world can't go on the way it is. Someone's got to put a stop to the shit. It's all up to us. We're in control now."

Amanda looked at Jacob. "What is he talking about?"

Jacob merely looked at the floor. She turned back to Gabriel. "Is this some sort of dirty bomb or what?"

"Think big, Amanda. Ultimate big."

Her dreadlocks whipped back and forth. "Are you telling me this suitcase is some kind of full-on nuclear bomb? Gabe, is that what you're telling me? Is it?"

Gabriel smiled. "Bingo, Amanda."

"Are you crazy? Do you know how many people will be killed? Do you, Gabe?" Getting no response, she turned to Jacob, who was still looking away. "What about you? This wasn't the plan. We were supposed to just scare them!" She shook her head. "My fucking brother lives in Madrid. No, you can't do this. I won't let you."

Gabriel frowned. "I'm sorry to hear you say that, Amanda. I really am."

Five minutes later, the warehouse's bay door clattered closed. The BMW crawled across the parking lot and then slowly entered the cul-de-sac. Several lots away, in the silver Peugeot sedan, the driver returned the binoculars to his eyes. "The blond man is behind the wheel as before. The heavyset kid is sitting in front, lighting a joint."

He handed the binoculars to his companion. "But where is the woman with the dreadlocks?"

-30-

"What do you mean they didn't find anything worthy of further investigation, Inspector?"

Hunt jumped up and leaned over the desk. The words, "Only the Stupid are Happy," printed across his shirtfront nearly brushed the speakerphone. "Didn't they see the crazy Russian flag with the double-headed eagle? Or the portrait of Sergei Sokolov and his concubine tricked out like a tsar and tsarina?"

"Mr. Hunt, I am afraid those items point to nothing more nefarious than poor taste. I assure you my Madrid colleagues, although perhaps not as efficient as my Tazacorte team, thoroughly searched the premises. And they found nothing relating to Ms. Slater's disappearance." The speakerphone gurgled with the sounds of liquid being gulped.

"What about Solta Zanin?" Davies asked.

"We can find no addresses or financial associations for a woman of such name in Madrid. And we ran an Interpol check and found, as you say, zilch."

Behind Davies, Hunt started typing on a laptop, where he had been futilely working since dawn on decrypting the files he'd copied.

"Inspector, last night, we were chased at gunpoint by Solta Zanin, her twin sister, and their associate—none of whom were of African descent, torpedoing your Moroccan drug-smuggling theory," Davies replied, his tone now straining the outer bounds of diplomatic suitability.

"But Mr. Davies, we have absolutely no evidence of any connection between these people and Kalia Slater. In fact, they may well have chased you precisely because you broke into their office, a crime, I don't need to remind you. In any case, the Madrid police found no man unconscious in any dance-club restroom nor any women in red running around with guns. Until they are located and questioned, I'm afraid we must assume they were simply pursuing those who had invaded their offices."

Sam Quick turned from the window, where she had stood silently so far during the call, watching Madrid stumble on through another day's impossible heat. "Thank you, Inspector. If any new information turns up, you'll let us know as soon as possible, won't you?"

A sigh came from the speakerphone. "Of course, Dr. Quick, if any leads develop in regard to Ms. Slater, you'll be the first to know."

Quick nodded, and Davies killed the connection.

No need, Quick thought, to discuss the unspoken on the call: *Still no ransom demand. Time was running out for Kalia.*

Hunt watched a long look pass between Quick and Davies. He cleared his throat. "You might want to check this out."

"You cracked the files?" Quick asked, as she and Davies hurried behind Hunt. On the laptop, overlapping dialog boxes tiled the screen. Lines of numbers and text filled each little window.

"Not exactly," Hunt said.

"What are we looking at?" Quick asked.

"The Sokolov computer networks are heavily protected. But the company directory is publicly accessible via their main website. So, I wrote a script—a simple computer program—that attempts to log on to the network using the employee names as the IDs."

"But what about the password?" Davies asked.

"That was the easy part. My script didn't even make it halfway through the directory before I found a Sokolov employee using the universal password."

"Which is?" Davies asked.

Hunt grinned. "'Password.' We are now logged into Sokolov's main network under the account of a midlevel financial analyst who has access to the company's administrative servers—financials, inventories, facilities, etc."

"So, we're going to audit Sokolov?" Davies asked.

"*Nyet.* I'm guessing where Eric is going is"—Quick leaned forward—"travel charges." Her finger tapped the screen, on the words *Madrid/Falcon*, which were printed beside yesterday's date. Her finger slid along the line entry to a string of numbers and then to an amount in rubles.

Hunt's finger pinned a matching numeric string listed in another dialog box, beside a line item starting *Prague/Falcon*. "Someone used the same corporate account yesterday at a small airport outside Madrid for something called the *Falcon,* and the night before in Prague, again for the *Falcon.*"

Hunt pointed at a third dialog box. "And according to this

asset list, the *Falcon* is a Sokolov corporate jet, an Embraer Legacy 600."

Davies whistled. "That's a nice ride. In one of those babies, you can hop from New York to Geneva without stopping, flying at nearly the speed of sound."

"And"—Hunt tapped a fourth dialog box—"according to Sokolov property records, in Prague, the only facility owned by the company is at this address. And"—Hunt fingered a fifth window—"the same day, a company credit card paid for a restaurant meal one block from that address, a credit card assigned to one," he pointed at the last bit of text: "Nin Zanin."

Sam Quick clamped the men's shoulders. "The same Nin Zanin who must be the twin sister to Solta Zanin, and the faux-noble subject of that vainglorious portrait in the company office. Nice work, Eric." She reached for the phone. "It's time to call Florida."

-31-

She wished she could vomit. The acrid stench of her stomach juices would be a welcomed change from the putrid odor that had filled her nose since fucking Gabriel and Jacob had stowed the suitcase in the BMW's trunk and tore from the warehouse as fast as they could. Leaving her with the gunmen. Who had hooded, bound, and locked her in a room.

Then the first noise sounded in what seemed like hours: the clunk of a turning lock, followed by the whoosh of an opening door, and finally the snap of a tight electrical switch changing positions. Light pricked the fabric covering her face.

Amanda sat up. Blood reentered the bony points where the concrete had borne her weight, picking at her like icy spikes. Heavy shoes slapped the floor. Hands pulled on her upper arms, roughly hauling her up into a standing position.

She stood as best she could on the single pole of her bound legs, while unknown fingers dugs into her underarms' soft flesh. Near her feet, a snap sounded; the ring of pressure around her ankles was gone. The hood flew upward, caught for a moment on her dreadlocks, and then broke free of her head.

She blinked several times and then looked from side to side, first at the men gripping her arms, then around the room.

Contrary to her assumption, this room was not the office where she had waited with Gabriel and Jacob for the suitcase's delivery. Her gaze locked. If she had recently taken any food or liquid, her earlier wish to purge would have been fulfilled. Instead just the sounds of her dry heaves mingled with wet laughter from the men at her sides.

After a moment, she recovered enough to open her eyes again. The two corpses were piled against a far wall. But the glistening lake of blood and other bodily liquids stopped only a few feet shy of where she had lain.

They pushed her forward. She was certain her body would join the heap. But they instead steered her through the doorway, into the main warehouse, and she nearly fainted with relief as she gulped clear air.

They pointed at a cargo truck with its rear door open, parked near the rolling bay door.

Her body tensed rock-tight. "No! That's not the fucking deal. My friends are coming back to pick me up after it's done. Right here at this warehouse. I'm not going anywhere. Forget it." She tried collapsing down onto the concrete floor.

The men looked at each other and laughed. Then the lead man smiled at her. "Come back to get you? Now why would they do that? So, you can rat them out? Do you really believe your boyfriend, Gabriel, asked that we hold onto you? No, he asked that we dispose of you. No one is ever coming to get you." Then their hands dug in under her arms, squeezing deeper into the soft flesh.

"No! That's not true. Let me go!" She twisted and curled with all her might. "Let me go!"

The men just keep laughing, dragging her writhing body across the concrete. At the truck, rough arms slid under her thighs and tossed her up onto the cargo bed.

"You can't fucking do this! You motherfuckers. Let me go!" Amanda yelled.

The men jumped up after her. Their arms looped under hers and dragged her along the metal bed as if she were a sack of potatoes. They shoved her against something hard.

"Listen, listen! My family has money and connections to the U.S. government. Let me go, and I'll get you anything you want."

She looked around wildly. She was leaning against a wooden crate, which sat alongside two identical packing containers. The cargo space was otherwise empty.

"They can get you anything, any amount of money. They can make your rich."

She watched the men move toward the door as if they were preparing to jump down. But instead, they pulled it shut, killing all light.

"My family will come looking for me. They will never stop until they find me," she cried out into the darkness. But as she spoke the words, she sickeningly realized her statement would soon be the furthest thing from the truth.

She heard their boots clumping against the metal floor, as they returned toward her.

"Please just let me go." Tears flowed from her eyes, her bound hands useless to wipe them away.

She felt and smelled the men sit down, sandwiching her

between their sweaty bodies. The truck's engine started with a diesel roar. Gusts of hot, fetid breath bathed her neck. Then the truck jerked and started to move.

FRIDAY, JULY 13
Key Biscayne, Florida

The yellow ball whizzed within a half inch of the racket's edge. Its trajectory unaltered, the ball smashed just inside the baseline. The young man spun and watched it bounce up, over the line, en route to the high fence enclosing the court.

He turned back to the net, his teeth sparkling against a deep tan and a frame of longish, black hair. "Nice shot, Dr. Matson."

Matson tipped her racket. "Thank you, Jake." Despite her prowess on the court, the sexagenarian knew that her opponent, a ranked college player, should have returned that shot. *All morning, the boy had been as slow as a man admitting a mistake.* Matson wondered if he had been up late the previous night. *And if so, with whom?*

"Excuse me, Miss Molly?"

Matson looked toward the gate, where Dolores, her housekeeper, stood holding a cordless handset in one hand and a sweating pitcher of lemonade in the other.

"Dr. Quick is on the line. She says it's urgent."

Matson jogged to a courtside table, grabbed the phone, and slid into a chair. "Sam?" Then she sat listening, watching her opponent, as he plopped into the adjacent chair, pulled a chilled towel from the cooler, and began wiping the sweat from his face and neck.

Matson vigorously nodded at the lemonade cascading from the pitcher into a glass and mouthed a "thank you" to Dolores. Then she said, "Sam, hold on a sec, sweetie."

Matson turned to the young man. "Jake, why don't you run up to the house and have a swim while Dolores pulls lunch together? I think you'll find some old trunks in the cabana." She shrugged. "And if not, don't worry—we're real casual around here."

Matson watched him simultaneously trot away and pull off his shirt. *Well, whoever had kept him up late was certainly one lucky gal*—her brow wrinkled—*or fella. You just never knew these days.* She sighed and punched a button on the handset.

Matson laid the phone on the table. "Sam, I figured our foreign friends would have called for the decryption codes to your laptop in exchange for your intern by now."

"Me, too, Molly," was the only reply from the speakerphone, but it told her plenty about how worried Quick was.

"And what about the computer files you swiped?" Matson asked. "Do they point to this Sokolov and his girls allying with our foreign friends?"

"That's why we've called, Molly," Quick said. "The files' encryption algorithms are military grade, untouchable by Eric, our resident computer hound, or even by the embassy spooks. But I'm hoping that if we put the NRLI mainframe to work—"

"That they'll open like clams in a paella pan over a hot fire? Fine, get 'em over here."

"Our people will send the files right away, Dr. Matson," said Davies, and the geologist again tried picturing what he might look like.

"I'll put my emeritus status to good use and get the boys at the Institute working on them straight away. OK, kiddos," Matson continued, "I've gotta run: I've a guest to whom I must explain that he'll be lunching alone." His glistening lats flashed in her mind. "Which is a real shame, as I do hate being a bad host. Bye, Sam. Ciao, fellas."

Matson tossed the phone onto a chair cushion, stood, and started a fast trot toward the pool. The white-haired scientist knew perfectly well that no swimsuit would ever be found in her poolside cabana.

-33-

FRIDAY, JULY 13
Madrid

Utley frowned. His fork clinked against his plate. He hated interruptions during a meal, especially during a repast as sublime as the late-afternoon snack lying before him: a wedge of tortilla with its creamy center of egg and potato, a hunk of hard bread, and a glass of cold Spanish beer.

Utley watched the visitor finish the exchange with the cashier and then walk toward his table. A small soda bottle landed beside his plate.

Utley raised a brow. "Well?"

"We tracked the BMW and the two men to an apartment block in Madrid. They apparently left the dreadlocked woman at the warehouse—we aren't sure why, perhaps as collateral."

"And?"

"The car is parked in the apartment-building garage. Our men have visual contact with the vehicle at all times—and the package remains stowed in its trunk."

"And the American men?" Utley asked.

"Both the blond and the heavyset man have stayed in the apartment building since they returned from the warehouse.

Though the blond periodically comes down to the garage and stares into the car trunk. Inbound, however, they have received several deliveries of food and two visits from a Spanish youth—a low-level drug dealer."

"And the other suitcases?"

"A truck left the warehouse several hours after the American men departed. We followed it to a small airstrip outside Zaragoza. We observed the three crates and the woman being transferred to a Legacy 600. Fifteen minutes later, it taxied and took off."

"I assume we are tracking the plane?"

"We were."

Utley frowned and raised a brow.

"Our resources tracked it as it flew due south over the Mediterranean and into African airspace. Ten minutes over Algeria, the plane disappeared from the screen." The man shrugged. "A disabled positioning transponder and bribes to Algerian flight controllers to ensure that the signal loss went unnoticed."

Utley inhaled sharply. "Fully fueled, a plane like that has an operating range of several thousand miles. If they continue south, they could fly as far as equatorial Africa." He sighed. "Is that all?"

The visitor nodded.

"Keep me informed."

The man tipped his head and walked away wordlessly. Before he had passed through the exit, Utley sank his fork into the tortilla. As he savored a large bite, Utley thought of the other bombs, now lost to the silent undertow of the global arms trade.

What untold destruction would they someday bring? But he reminded himself of the lesson learned at the Academy so long ago: his goal was successfully completing the mission, not saving the world. He swallowed the mixture of egg and potato with an extra-large chaser of beer.

Then Utley smiled at the little Spanish boy who, sitting at a nearby table, was imitating the tremor of his hand.

- 3 4 -

SATURDAY, JULY 14
Island of La Palma

The metal band encircling Inspector Reyes's head was no larger than a wedding ring. He was sure his eyes would explode from their sockets at any second. And this, he knew, would only be a prelude to the brain matter that would soon to erupt from his head's every orifice, like grayish lava simultaneously spewing from all the volcanoes dotting La Palma.

Reyes pulled at the bottle with all his might. The cap abruptly conceded, and dusty aspirin tablets scattered across his desktop. Shaking fingers pinched up two pills. Then he shrugged and grabbed two more tablets, making it an even foursome. His molars ground the buttons to a fine powder. Cold espresso was added, creating a caustic mud, which oozed down his esophagus like drain opener down a clogged pipe.

The inspector looked around his office, at the piles of reports and authorizations that summarized his thirty years on the Tazacorte municipal police force. He felt the wet fingers of the early morning air stirred by the overhead fan. From the open window, he smelled the Atlantic's pregnant musk and heard the sounds of morning: the shouts and laughter of delivery men, the sleepy conversations of tourists debating between a day at the beach or up the mountain, and the gentle clink of flatware from the open-air cafes lining the narrow village streets.

Through the doorway to the station main, he watched the cocky men who served beneath him and who now sat in silence at their desks.

He sighed and lifted his telephone's clunky handset.

"Hello, Dr. Quick? . . . No, the speakerphone is unnecessary—I think it's best that we talk alone."

. . .

After Madrid, Prague was a jungle. The travelers stepped from the humid afternoon air into a cab. For the first time since the jet had left the tarmac of Madrid's Barajas Airport, Sam Quick spoke, and her voice was clear, and her directions, precise. The driver's brow rose, and the taxi sprinted from curb.

During the drive, neither Quick nor Hunt nor Davies noticed grand Prague Castle, regally situated across the Vltava River from the motorway. Nor did they see, after the cab began maneuvering the surface streets, the history of Western art unfurl outside the sedan's windows, the city's rich mosaic of buildings from every artistic epoch: medieval fortifications, baroque spires, renaissance churches, art nouveau facades, and modernist glass towers.

The cab finally stopped before a drab cement edifice that stood out amid the city's architecture like a poor child in a school class otherwise populated by brightly dressed students. Pallid bricks clad the façade, while vertical columns of narrow windows rose to the roofline.

Entering the building was like stepping back into the

communist era. Every stark line, hard surface, and low-watt bulb droned in bureaucratic monotone of enforced scarcity and repressed expression. The smell was the building's liveliest element: a sickly-sweet presence that immediately assailed the nose.

The Americans stopped at the lobby desk, and Quick handed the receptionist a slip. The women studied it and then lifted a rotary telephone handset. She spoke in Czech for several moments. Then the receiver returned to its cradle, and she jotted a diagram on the back of Quick's paper. The slip just barely returned to the scientist's fingers in time to make the journey deeper into the building.

The receptionist stared after the threesome, slowly shaking her head. Who were these people? she wondered. Hollywood stars researching roles for a new television forensic drama? Perhaps the handsome man with the salt-and-pepper hair would play a coroner. The blond boy, a police rookie. And the beautiful but too thin woman, the smart cop. Before she could flesh out the plot, all that remained of the Americans in the gray hall was the echo of their footsteps.

. . .

The Americans stepped into an office where only the ceiling was free of books. Bursting shelves lined the walls, and teetering stacks sprouted from the floor like wind-bent saplings.

"Ah, you must be Dr. Quick," said a man in perfect English, as he rose and circled the desk. He wore a spotless lab coat. A horseshoe of light brown hair circled his otherwise bald head. He reached out a hand.

"Hello, I'm Dr. Linzer, chief of pathology." His head dipped toward a second man, who had the flattened face of a grouper fish and was rising from a chair. "And this is Captain Svoboda of the Czech State Security Police."

Linzer continued, "I am honored to meet you, Dr. Quick—I just wish the circumstances were different. I have encountered your papers in numerous scientific journals. And I find your work with extremophilic bacteria most exciting. In my spare time, I fancy myself a bit of a microbiologist—"

Quick held up a hand. "Please, Dr. Linzer, what can you tell us about what the police found?"

Linzer pointed at the chairs fronting his desk. "Please."

After everyone was seated, Linzer started, "At 4:15 this morning, municipal police officers on foot patrol responded to screams coming from a path along the Vltava in central Prague. The officers arrived to find a couple—a Danish tourist and a local man—who had taken advantage of last night's hot weather and had strolled along the Vltava in search of a secluded spot for an outdoor rendezvous. However, while undressing beneath a bridge, the couple realized they were not alone but rather were in the company of the body of a young adult female."

Linzer paused and looked to Quick. "I'm not sure how much detail about the body you wish to hear—"

"All of it."

The pathologist glanced at Svoboda and then nodded. "Very well. The corpse was nude and lying in a fetal position alongside the river. The hands and feet were missing." Linzer cleared his throat. "As was the head."

He reached into a pile on his desk. "The police found this beside the corpse: Ms. Slater's passport." He handed the booklet to Quick, who, without a glance, passed it to Davies.

Davies thumbed through it. "It appears real."

Linzer continued, "We know the decapitation was performed at another location based on the absence of collateral blood splatter. The body's core temperature and the degree of rigor mortis set the time of death at between seven and eight hours before the amorous couple stumbled on it.

"The corpse's height and weight, extrapolating for tissue loss, match those of Ms. Slater as listed in the Interpol alert regarding her disappearance. Of course, until we receive DNA samples from Ms. Slater's family, we cannot definitively identify the victim."

He looked at Quick. "If you know of any identifying features or marks that Ms. Slater bore, this information would be most helpful."

"I need to see the body," Quick replied.

"Dr. Quick," Linzer said, "I must object to that course of action. We have photographs, which, in themselves, are upsetting enough—"

Svoboda shook his head and interrupted in a halting English, "This body is no sight for a woman!"

Quick shot him the look that she usually reserved for the handful of dinosaurs at NRLI who treated women as if they were fit for little more than filling coffee cups. "I'll do my best to neither faint nor launch into a fit of hysterics, Captain. But if this body really is that of Kalia Slater, then I need to see firsthand what they did to her."

Quick stood. "Now."

Linzer sighed and slowly rose from his chair. "All right, Dr.

Quick. But I must caution that if you've never seen—"

"You two wait here," Quick said, cutting him off, looking at Hunt and Davies. Both men nodded at Quick's back, which was already halfway to the door.

SATURDAY, JULY 14
Madrid

Before the Spaniard could take a single step, President James surged across the stage, clasped his host's hand, and vigorously shook it, all the while looking straight into the Spanish leader's eyes.

During his ascent to ever-increasing heights of political office, Jasper James had long ago honed this technique for projecting power and decisiveness. At public debates or shared speaking forums, James always swiftly moved to greet his opponent before the challenger could take even one step forward. He was not an overly aggressive man by nature. But this tactic often cemented his dominance in the viewers' minds before one word was spoken, and it always unsettled his opponents.

The Spanish leader nodded at the president. Then the hands parted, and the two leaders turned and walked to their respective podia. The Spanish leader spoke first, giving his welcome and a string of sound-bite-worthy introductory remarks. While President James stood, turned in the direction of his host, appearing to closely watch and listen.

But James barely heard a word. His mind was elsewhere, on

the tough discussions that would take place during the coming days of the International Capital Forum, particularly with the Russian president about energy supplies for Western Europe. *And that rotten business with the theft of plutonium from the British research lab.* If what his CIA director said was true, then enough plutonium had been stolen to create a dirty bomb capable of rendering London—or New York City—uninhabitable for the next forty thousand years.

The applause broke his thought, and his mouth reflexively started moving, delivering his speech in the careful, gravelly Western tones that reassured his male supporters and that attracted his female voters, or so the polls said. The president spoke without hesitation, without even a glance at the prepared text on the teleprompter.

Ten minutes later, after a brief round of questions from the journalists, President James followed the Spanish leader off the dais. The men joined the other world leaders, who were gathered alongside a stone railing overlooking the reception hall of Madrid's Palacio Real.

President James smiled and shook hands with each leader in turn. With the German president, he bent forward and kissed her right cheek. Despite her makeup, he discerned a slight reddening of her face. Good, he thought. *Because we sure as hell need her rock solid on the Russians.* The President continued along, finally reaching the last person in the lineup.

James stared directly into the unblinking Russian eyes and firmly pumped the man's unyielding hand with an intensity lacking in his greetings heretofore. The other leaders, still smiling widely, eyed the encounter with a mixture of envy and thanks.

Each head of state present was acutely aware that the Americans remained the only counterweight to the Russian bear growling on Europe's eastern flank. And although they all silently wished for the power wielded by Jasper James, they were equally glad for their freedom from having to lead the world's only superpower.

. . .

Watching the proceedings unfold on the television screen, Gabriel inhaled deeply and then, after a twenty-second pause, released a grayish cloud, which swirled and somersaulted before him.

He shook his head. "Nothing but walking corpses. Expansion of global trade and new economic opportunities and new world order. A bunch of blah, blah, bullshit. And what do any of them know about real life and the troubles that working men and women face? Not one thing, that's what." Ash fell to the sofa cushion. "Well, they're about to learn a friggin' thing or two about the hardships of the common man."

Beside him, Jacob slowly nodded, gazing at the screen with half-open eyes.

Then the shot cut from the politicians to a crowd swaying behind metal barricades on a sidewalk opposite the Palacio Real. Signs bore pictograms of globes overlaid by red slashes. Sticks beat drums. And hundreds of tanned, tattooed youth, with fists raised, chanted behind the barriers.

Jacob exhaled, and the smoke joined the cloud hanging over the sofa. "Dude, I don't think we'll ever see her again."

"I told you to stop sweating it. I worked it all out with them. Why would they renege?" Gabriel answered. "She is simply insurance that we don't turn the Red over to the authorities." He pointed toward the television. "Besides, if she doesn't return, she'll be a hero for the cause, like the rest of our brothers and sisters—"

A ringing cellphone interrupted. Gabriel grabbed it and, after checking the caller ID, stabbed a button. "Hey . . . Yeah, another bag A-double-SAP." He raised a brow at his friend and pointed a thumb toward the ceiling.

"Hell yeah . . . definitely, bring us a chick."

-36-

The room was a glittering ice field studded with green hillocks. Everywhere, shiny metal instruments reflected the light from the overhead work lamps, while dull-green sheets draped irregular mounds on three of the chamber's six exam tables. Amid all this, a young, uniformed police officer sat hunched on a stool positioned adjacent to one of the shrouded bodies.

"I must ask, one more time—"

Quick held up her hand.

Linzer sighed and signaled the patrolman, who jumped up and practically ran to the exit. Beside Linzer, Captain Svoboda watched the retreating officer, shook his head, and then took a position alongside the table opposite Quick.

Quick nodded. The green sheet peeled back. The scientist's face remained smooth. After several moments' consideration, she started examining the exposed corpse: first the jagged strands of white and red tissues marking the body's neckline, then the severed wrists and ankles, and then the bronze flesh.

As Quick walked the table end to end, Linzer closely watched her. If this horrific sight, which had beckoned the stomach contents of seasoned police detectives—and from the looks of Svoboda, threatened to do so again—affected Sam Quick, he could see no sign of it. *Not only a beautiful woman and respected scientist, but she's also as hard as Czech granite.*

Quick stepped back and took in the entire body. *The skin coloration was roughly the same golden brown as Kalia's. And Linzer's right, both the height and weight were approximately correct.* From the moment of receiving Inspector Reyes's call, she had suspected the sad truth.

But Quick had to be sure.

She turned to Linzer. "I need to see the back of her left shoulder."

Linzer nodded and grabbed a pair of industrial-weight gloves from a tray. The rubber snapped around his forearms. He reached over the corpse and curled his fingers beneath the left shoulder and torso. He pulled, and the headless corpse lifted its shoulder as if turning to offer a bed companion a day's final kiss.

Svoboda averted his gaze. But from the corner of his eye, he watched Quick bend and peer into the space that had opened between the metal table and the dead flesh.

Quick needed to see the jumping dolphin, the small tattoo that she had admired earlier in the week, on the beach in Tazacorte when the team had rinsed off after the long day of setting up equipment at La Garganta del Diablo.

Staring at the corpse's shoulder, Sam Quick realized she was right.

A mix of emotions rushed her: sadness for the young woman who had suffered such deadly insult; rage toward the brutal people who had committed this terrible crime; and most of all, the thrill of knowing that only one reason could cause someone to attempt such horrific deception. *Kalia Slater must still be alive.*

. . .

2200 miles away, Kalia Slater had no idea whether it was day or night. She felt as if she had slept for twenty-four hours. *But I might have only had an hour of hard sleep.* She sighed. *In either case, nothing here would give any hint.*

Slater lifted her head and inspected the small chamber again. Although lacking temporal orientation, she had an excellent idea of her general location: *the red walls, the hulking timbers, and the warm, dead air.* Slater knew she was in the Devil's Throat. Handcuffed to a metal cot in a small, suffocating room.

She recalled Manuelo explaining how La Garganta del Diablo extended for miles, on myriad levels, like the underground farm of giant-sized ants. No one really knew, he had said, how far or how deep the shafts traveled, because whole sections of the mine had already been long abandoned by the time of the 1949 eruption and the mine's closure. *I could be anywhere in the mountain.*

She shook her head. *I must keep trying.* A smile broke across her face as if she were greeting a longtime friend. "Hi, my name is Kalia. And my mother, father, and family are very worried about me. Can you help me call them? Do you have a little girl? What's her name?"

The man simply stared at her, from his chair ten feet away.

"My name is Kalia," she repeated. "What is yours?"

The man sighed, shut his eyes, and lowered his head.

After several more attempts at conversation, Slater dropped

her head back down to the cot's rough canvas. She had tried engaging him and all the other guards who rotated through the chamber, each bid earning the same result: silence.

She shook her arms in frustration, clattering her handcuffs against the cot's aluminum frame. The man's chin shot from his chest. His lips curled into a leer, revealing two incomplete rows of brown-webbed teeth. Slater continued fighting the binds, watching the guard's grip tighten on the Micro Uzi lying on his lap.

"You can shove your gun straight—"

A barrage of guttural language cut off Slater and wiped away the gunman's grin. A second man marched into the chamber. After a brief exchange with the seated guard, which was incomprehensible to Slater, the new arrival pointed toward the entryway. The seated man said something else, in a harsher tone. Then he stood, shoved the pistol-sized Uzi at the new arrival, and stomped from the room.

The new man settled onto the chair, with the gun on his lap. He stared at Slater through the glassy eyes of a spider surveying prey struggling against its web.

And Kalia Slater, like any captured creature, began plotting her escape.

- 3 7 -

Utley pulled open the door to his room. The waiting valet said, "Good evening, sir."

Utley nodded in reply, and the young Spaniard moved for the two pieces of luggage waiting by the door.

When they reached the lobby, the valet held back, as Utley first settled his bill, then handed an envelope with the usual tip to the concierge, and finally, for just a moment, stared up into the lobby's majestic dome.

The old man wished that daylight still lived. The dome's colored panes were like a beautiful woman, he thought, always best under the sun's warm gaze. He nodded goodbye to it for what, he was nearly certain, would be the last time.

He sighed and slipped his trembling hand into a pocket. The valet's smile breeched its widest, as Utley pressed a hundred-euro note passed into the man's palm.

At the hotel entrance, the doorman opened the silver Peugeot's front passenger door. Utley climbed in, while the valet deposited his bags in the trunk. The car door thumped shut.

Wordlessly, the driver slid the transmission into gear, and the sedan pulled away from the hotel and then turned onto the Paseo del Prado. Utley craned his head to watch, mesmerized, the museum glide by, its up-lit stones glowing like unpolished gold.

After several blocks, Utley spoke for the first time since entering the vehicle, "Status, please."

"The two men are still holed up in the apartment, presently entertaining a woman whom we assume is a prostitute," the driver replied, glancing at his passenger.

"Just one?" Utley chuckled, as he absently smoothed the front of his linen shirt. "How very economical of them to share. Any visitors other than the woman?"

"Only the Spanish youth—the presumed drug courier—who previously visited them."

"And the package?"

"The suitcase remains in the BMW's trunk, in the building's garage, with our men watching at all times as ordered." The driver glanced at Utley again. "However, we may have a problem."

"Oh? Pray tell."

Utley sat silently as the driver explained.

When the driver finished, Utley merely nodded and turned toward his window.

"Should we take action?" the driver asked.

"No. It sounds like this problem may sort itself out. Let's monitor the situation," Utley replied, still staring out the window. Then he fell into silence, and the only sounds in the car were the soft rush of chilled air and the muffled bleats of impatient autos.

The driver glanced between the road ahead and the hands fighting atop Utley's lap. The suitcase's contents were never mentioned. But he could guess. He hoped the old man was up to the task.

As he watched Utley's left hand lose its battle to calm the trembling right, a million taillights flashed red, and he slammed the brakes just in time.

-38-

Quick jumped out the shower and crossed the Italian tiles, dripping water as she ran. She grabbed the buzzing cellphone lying on the vanity.

"Yes?"

"Sweetie, are you all right?"

"Molly." Quick pushed the speakerphone button, set down the mobile, and snatched a towel from a nearby stack. She raised her voice and began drying herself. "I just spent the afternoon admiring an example of Czech craftsmanship that won't ever make the tour books. Any luck with the computer files?"

"I don't know exactly what these folks have to hide. But it must be something mucho major. My boys"—Quick pictured the young computer techs at NRLI who were always ready to perform a favor in exchange for either a smile from Quick or a promise from Matson to abstain, if only temporarily, from patting their rears—"needed every last one of their terabytes to break the encoding. And even then, they apparently had to hijack a couple hundred thousand Canadian home computers to help with the processing, or some such no-no that gets them all hot and bothered."

Matson went on, "The way I pushed those silly energy drinks to keep them moving at full speed, I felt like a crack dealer—"

"The files, Molly, the files . . ."

"Right, well, the thing is, Sam, I can't for the life of me understand why this data was so heavily encrypted. Unless those folks plan to drill for oil beneath downtown Madrid, these files are as worthless as ice skates in Miami. They contain nothing more than subterranean infrastructure maps of the Spanish capital: underground utility passages, subway routes, and sewer tunnels, some dating back to the Roman era."

"Nothing regarding La Palma or any seabed exploration around the island? The boat? Or Kalia Slater?"

"Not a thing, I'm afraid, hon. It was all just a tour of underground Madrid." Matson tried to adopt a hopeful tone, "Anything further information there?"

"Davies should be on a call right now with the embassy, to see if the intel assets have captured any chatter regarding the abduction of an American. And against my better judgment, I've sent Eric to check out a Sokolov facility here in Prague. He suggested going solo, and given it's a brothel, I could hardly argue, much less get pass the door."

Matson chuckled. "Perhaps the young man wants to pursue some personal investigations during his visit to the red-light district."

A soft chime sounded from the other room. "Molly, I gotta run. Keep me posted if you find anything else."

"Ciao, sweetie."

Quick dumped the towel and grabbed a robe hanging on the

door. Crossing the main room, Quick slipped it on and gathered it at the waist. She put an eye to the peephole and found Davies standing outside. She stepped back, checking that the V formed by the robe revealed no more than she wanted.

Then Quick grabbed the doorknob.

. . .

"I hope I haven't caught you at an inconvenient time."

The speaker wore a short, red skirt and a matching blouse. The beauty mark high on her right cheek complemented her silken dark hair. And her Beretta Bobcat drilled into the slot between Davies's seventh and eighth ribs.

Quick held open the door. "Think nothing of it, Ms. Zanin . . . Ms. Nin Zanin, is it not?"

"You've done your homework—"

"They don't call her Sam Quick for nothing," Davies interjected in a wry tone.

The woman smiled. "Surely they do not. And yes, Dr. Quick, my name is Nin Zanin. But just 'Nin' will suffice."

Keeping her gun jammed into Davies's side, Nin nodded over her shoulder, at a man stationed directly behind her. "I believe you have already met my colleague."

"Indeed." Quick looked at the man. "I hope your head is feeling better after your night out in Madrid."

The man just stared her, as Quick nodded at Nin's gun. "That's a handsome Beretta. The scrimshaw—that's a whalebone grip, is it not?—is indeed a classy touch." She glanced at the man, who was also holding a weapon. "Albeit not as powerful as your colleague's polymer-framed CZ 100, your Bobcat is certainly luckier: you have seven shots to his thirteen, if I recall correctly."

Nin's brow rose. "Impressive, Dr. Quick. I'd love to chat more about our firearms and their capacities for killing"—she looked past Quick—"but would you mind terribly inviting us in first?"

Quick stepped aside. "By all means, please do." She looked into Nin's eyes. "But shouldn't we wait for Mr. Sokolov, or will he join us as the evening is in progress?"

"Unfortunately, Sergei cannot be with us tonight—affairs require his attention in Moscow." Nin's teeth flashed. "You are probably also wondering where the spritely Mr. Hunt is."

Quick shrugged.

"Mr. Hunt is a naughty boy, I am afraid," Nin went on. "We found his room empty. But then Mr. Hunt looks like a young man who easily makes new friends." The teeth flashed again. "Not to worry, we'll meet up with Mr. Hunt later—I am certain of it."

The Bobcat turned its attention to Quick. "Now, really, Dr. Quick, I must insist, after you."

Quick turned and walked into the room, with Davies and Nin at her back, followed by the man. The door clicked shut behind them. The Bobcat pointed at the sofa. Quick and Davies took seats, side by side, on the couch.

"What a lovely suite, Dr. Quick," Nin said, inspecting the large room. "But rather extravagant on a scientist's salary, is it not?" She shook her head. "Oh, that's right, our research said that you come from a wealthy cattle family—which also explains your knowledge of firearms—from someplace dreadful like Texas."

"New Mexico, actually." Quick's eyes sparked. "Now, where the hell is Kalia Slater?"

"Of course, New Mexico, an enchanting land, I think they say." Nin sighed. "As for Ms. Slater, by now you know the one place where she is not—the Prague Morgue. Counterfeiting a passport is such a trifling matter in this age of . . . what is it called? . . . high-resolution printing? You should see what we do with hundred-dollar bills and fifty-euro notes."

"Aren't the railcars full of rubles garnered through corruption and blackmail enough for you and the Falcon? Need you also stoop to currency counterfeiting as well?" Davies asked.

"Ah, Mr. Davies, how naïve you are. After a point, Sergei and I care little for money. However, destabilizing our enemies' currencies is much more interesting." Nin walked to the window, while the man positioned himself opposite the sofa, with his CZ 100 ranging back and forth between the American foreheads.

The brocade drapes parted. Prague Castle filled the window.

"You chose wisely, Dr. Quick. The uninformed always ask for a room on the hotel's front side, while I always prefer the side suites facing the Castle. As you may know, the Castle is a monument to Prague's endurance—some parts are more than one thousand years old."

Nin turned from the window. "Are either of you perhaps familiar with the Defenestrations of Prague?"

"You refer to the medieval uprisings when political officials were thrown to their deaths from high windows," Davies said.

"Bravo, Mr. Davies. Yes, The First Defenestration of Prague occurred in 1419, when a Hussite priest led his congregation to Town Hall to petition for the release of some prisoners. But when they failed securing their associates' liberation, being simpler times, the crowd threw the recalcitrant council members from a high window onto some upturned spears handily waiting below.

"The Second Defenestration of Prague came in 1618." A red nail tapped the window glass. "Right there at Prague Castle. A group of Protestants was upset about some land deals, so they decided to throw two imperial governors and their scribe, all of who happened to be Catholic, from a window high on the Castle's Bohemian Chancellery."

"And today's Wall Street bankers think they have it bad."

"Well put, Dr. Quick."

Nin turned a brass knob and pushed open the window. A yeasty breath billowed the drapes, and sounds of traffic rose from the boulevard below.

"Interestingly," Nin said, "during the latter defenestration, the trio of grandees survived the fall—thanks to a fortuitously placed pile of manure—and the Catholics claimed angels had cushioned their landing."

Holding the window with one hand, Nin leaned out and looked downward. After a moment, she turned back to the room.

"Unfortunately for you, I have just confirmed that, six stories below at the foot of this hotel, no cherubs pose as excrement."

Nin's arm shot toward the open window. "Now, which of you would care to go first?"

- 39 -

The woman frowned. She looked from the T-shirt that read, "Cyber: Not Even Virtually a Good Time," to the overhead red bulb. Her head shook and a finger stabbed a button on the handheld reel. The retracting leash jerked the poodle away from Eric Hunt's leg. And the woman hastened her step, dragging away the little dog with its manicured nails scraping against the pavement in protest.

Hunt shrugged and pressed a button beside the door. After a moment, a red LED light blinked above a plastic half-sphere affixed at head height in the doorframe. He smiled at the orb, as its lens rotated and focused on his face. After a few seconds, the door buzzed. He grabbed the handle and pulled.

Stepping inside, Hunt was hit by a fast one-two: the bass beat of hard music was immediately followed by an overpowering mix of long-trapped cigarette smoke, cheap perfume, and alcohol-infused perspiration.

His eyes fought to compensate for the near absence of light inside the entryway. Before he could back out, fingers encircled his wrist and firmly pulled him in.

"Good evening," a voice purred in good English, as the fingers dug deeper and pulled harder. The door clicked shut behind him. Hunt's eyes were still adjusting, as someone grabbed his other wrist and pressed a sweaty glass into his hand.

"Welcome to our fair city of Prague. From where are you visiting? America, no?"

"Uh . . . yes, from the U.S."

"Excellent. Lots of American college boys visit us. We like American college boys very much, don't we, girls?"

A chorus of lackluster, heavily accented "yesssses" responded from, Hunt could now finally make out, a semi-circular banquette wedged into one corner of the room. Hunt saw women of various ages, shapes, and sizes lining the bench, all dressed and posed as if they were models in a lingerie catalog.

Hunt looked around the chamber. An array of monitors, all playing different erotic videos, filled one wall. Opposite the banquette, two burly men who looked more like prison guards than bartenders staffed a small bar. But the grad student saw no sign of what he really wanted—a computer.

He looked closely for the first time at the woman gripping his wrist and nearly jumped. *The same black hair, round face, and almond-shaped eyes as the Zanin sisters. And she was wearing that same tight, red outfit. Some relative?*

The nails dug insistently into Hunt's wrist. "Drink up—it'll help you relax, college boy."

Hunt feigned a shy smile, shrugged, and sipped from the glass. His eyes widened. The oily fluid smelled like rubbing alcohol.

The woman smiled at him. "Now, you brought cash money

with you? Euros or dollars are fine: sixty euros or eighty dollars."

Hunt nodded and reached for his pocket, while the woman's hand remained locked on his wrist, even as he fished for the bills.

As the American twenties emerged, the woman nodded. "Very good. Now, you choose your hostess for the evening, and she will show you upstairs."

She pointed at the bench, at an emaciated young woman with eyes undergirded by heavy black circles and a head framed by curly blond hair. "Svetlana likes American college boys very much. Or"—she pointed at a large-bosomed woman with a red silk garment straining around her middle—"perhaps you prefer someone motherlier, such as Helga?"

Hunt inspected the lineup for a moment. Then he pointed at a nondescript, brown-haired woman who looked like she might normally teach grade school. "She looks nice."

"Helena, a very good selection." The woman held out her hand. Hunt's bills landed in her palm. Her fingers snapped, and Helena stood up, looked Hunt up and down, and shrugged.

The woman grabbed the glass from Hunt's hand. "Two rules: One, be dressed and downstairs in one hour. And two, if Helena calls for help, my friends crush college boy's legs."

The bartenders waved at him.

"Now go have fun, American college boy."

A rectangular box—with two antennae sticking out, affixed to the ceiling in a corner—caught Hunt's eye.

Eric Hunt turned and grinned at the woman. "Oh, I think I will, ma'am."

SATURDAY, JULY 14
Prague

Quick watched the thug's eyes mow the V-shaped patch of tanned skin exposed by her robe. And Sam Quick recalled a fact that she frequently exploited in her Florida lab: *A strand of DNA is only as strong as its weakest hydrogen bond.*

"I see we have no takers," Nin said, still holding her arm toward the open window. "Perhaps a bullet in Mr. Davies's kneecap would facilitate a decision?"

Quick rubbed her leg against Davies. He glanced at Quick and then followed her line of sight, as it subtly triangulated between the gunman, the coffee table, and his own face.

Then Quick stood. "As the hostess, I guess I should go first."

Davies shrugged at Nin. "You heard the lady."

"So much for chivalry. But not to worry, Mr. Davies," Nin purred, "your turn will come soon enough." She crossed the room and joined her gunman. "My helper will escort Dr. Quick to the window and, being a proper gentleman, he will help the her out. Then will come Mr. Davies's turn. Although this may provide little solace, but for reasons that you will never have a chance to understand, tonight's events will undoubtedly earn the definitive title of The Third Defenestration of Prague—your places in the history of not only this fine city, but of the world are assured."

Nin aimed her Bobcat at Davies's head and nodded at her man, who tucked the CZ 100 into his belt and looked to Quick.

The scientist bowed her head as if she were accepting an invitation to dance. She and the man moved to the window and stopped. Quick glanced out at Prague Castle.

Then she turned and faced the man, looking into his eyes. "I'm ready when you are."

Nin's brow furrowed, while the man reached for Quick.

Continuing to stare into his eyes, Quick relaxed her grip on the robe's front. The thick cloth sagged like a sail losing wind. With the man laser-tracking its collapse and the spreading exposure of Quick's nude torso.

Nin shouted, "You fool!"

Quick rammed her knee into the man's groin. The ashtray from the coffee table smashed into Nin's arm, with Davies following right behind it.

The man jackknifed.

Quick grabbed his belt as if grasping a hay bale on her family's ranch. Using all her might, she threw him at the open window, grabbing the CZ 100 from his belt.

She whipped around and aimed.

The lamp exploded. The darkness silhouetted Quick diving away from the window, as another shot exploded from the dark. Shattering glass punctuated the thuds of diving bodies and overturning furniture.

Another explosion.

Quick blasted two shots.

Someone screamed in the room next door. Light from the hallway spilled into the room.

Blood, like water, flows downhill. Outside, the man's ran off the sidewalk, into the gutter, pooling behind a parked car's worn tire. Screams and shouts in Czech, English, and German climbed from the street.

In Quick's room, Davies's blood soaked into the powder-blue carpet, turning the rich wool a sickly purple. Quick clamped his brachial artery shut with one hand. The other locked the CZ 100 on the open doorway to the corridor.

She eyed the gun and the doorway, desperately wanting to chase after Nin Zanin. But Quick kept the pressure steady on Davies's arm.

- 4 1 -

"You are very sexy man."

"Uh, thanks." Hunt smiled at the young woman and then surveyed the second-floor room where Helena had led him. The space was smaller than an American walk-in closet. A narrow single bed was shoved against one wall, leaving just enough open floor space for a person to walk alongside it.

Sketchier, Hunt thought, was the sick noise and smell. Up here, the monotonous music was both twice as loud and punctuated by occasional moans, and the terrible mélange of odors, doubled in strength.

The young woman sighed. "Please sit down."

Hunt eyed the worn sheets covering the thin mattress. "Uh, thanks, but I think I'll stand."

Helena looked at Hunt for a moment and then nodded. "Ah, yes, I understand." Her negligee dropped to the floor, and she plopped on the bed and reached for Hunt's jeans. "So, you like—"

"Whoa"—Hunt gently intercepted her hand—"that won't be necessary."

Her brow furrowed. "You don't like me?"

"No, it's not that"—he held up his hands and smiled at the naked woman—"you're . . . very hot, I'm sure . . . " Hunt shook his head. "No, what I need, Helena, is a small favor."

The woman looked at the door and then again at Hunt. "Don't try anything funny, college boy, or you know what will happen to you."

The grad student reached for his pocket. "This is your lucky day."

The woman's jaw set. "I warn you—"

Hunt slipped out a thick wad of twenties and offered it to Helena. "All you need to do is relax for the next hour. Take a nap, if you want."

"But—"

Hunt's finger went to his lips again. Helena looked back and forth between Hunt and the money. She shrugged, grabbed the twenties, and snatched up her teddy. Then, hugging the cash and the silk against her chest, she scooted to the bed's far end. "So, what do you want?"

Hunt pulled out his smartphone and held it up. "I just need—"

"No pictures or I scream!"

"No, no—no pictures. I just need to check out something on the Internet."

She groaned and lulled her head against the wall. "This place is making me so old and ugly—I can't even win against the web anymore."

"Not at all, Helena." Hunt started tapping the phone. "I'm just into some strange things. And right now, I really need to concentrate on penetrating this root directory using a little technique that I developed of iterating with a nifty asynchronous, multivariate Gaussian algorithm."

As the phone beeped, Hunt grinned at the woman. "That, Helena, is my idea of foreplay."

. . .

The coupe roared down the ramp. The steering wheel cranked hard to the right, inciting shrieks from the high-performance tires. The sleek hood nearly rammed the concrete wall.

The driver's door flew open. The smell of singed rubber and burning brake pads mingled with French perfume. Muscular calves followed a pair of red shoes out of the car. Firm thighs led to a short, red skirt. And the faint outline of a Beretta Bobcat surfaced, as the skirt's fabric was pulled taut by the driver's emergence.

The car door slammed shut.

Nin stalked across the garage and ripped open the door. The stairway echoed with tiny staccato explosions. At the ground-floor level, Nin charged through a jagging series of corridors until she reached a curtain, which she whipped aside.

"Ah, there you are, dear cousin . . . ," the woman said, her voice faltering as she absorbed Nin's disheveled hair and blouse. She snapped her fingers. The women sitting on the bench scurried for the staircase, and the bartenders locked their gazes on the glassware that they were polishing.

"The hotel visit did not proceed as planned: The American scientist defenestrated my driver. Luckily for him, because I would otherwise have castrated him with my bare teeth for his infernal weakness."

The woman shook her head. "The Americans are still—"

"Yes," Nin growled, "still breathing. I wounded one, the diplomat. Quick, the scientist, I don't know. Sergei will not be pleased. And then the student, the blond boy with the eyebrow jewelry, was not even at the hotel, probably instead out prancing about Vinohrady—"

"Eyebrow jewelry? University-age with a blond, military haircut and a silver ring above his eye?"

Nin nodded. "How—"

"He's upstairs with one of our girls. Right this instant!"

Nin sucked in her breath. "They somehow connected this property to Sergei." Her head whipped around, and she pointed at the Wi-Fi access point attached to the ceiling. "The computer network—rip out the wires. Now!"

The men scrambled from behind the bar and ran toward the back. Nin's hand slipped under her skirt and returned with the Bobcat. She looked at her cousin. "Show us the room."

. . .

The silver eyebrow ring tilted on its axis, upset by the wrinkling of Hunt's brow. A message was flashing on his smartphone: "Access Lost." His fingers rained on the interface. Then the concentric arcs indicating Wi-Fi signal strength disappeared.

Hunt looked at the young woman lying curled on the bed, intently watching him and the phone. The silk negligee was balled forgotten in the corner, and the wad of twenties lay loose on the dingy sheet.

"And I thought my Internet service back home was unreliable," he said, as the phone dove into his pocket. "Helena, is there a back way out of here?"

The woman glanced at the money and then smiled at Hunt. "Sure, college boy. Out in hall, go right, metal door at end, and then down the stairs. At bottom is garage. The big door will open automatically—unless they see you on the security camera."

Hunt leaned down and kissed the young woman's cheek. "Thank you. Now, for your own good, I suggest you hide that money and then, on my signal, scream your head off."

Hunt yanked open the door and looked out. To the left, an older man blocked most of the corridor, with a tiny woman clad in a black leather bustier prodding him toward the staircase. To the right, the hallway lay empty, lined by little doors, each one sealed shut. Thirty feet away, a full-sized metal door marked the corridor's end.

Then the fast, hard thuds of someone running up the stairs sounded beyond the heavy man. Hunt looked back at Helena— who remained naked on the mattress, but with no cash in sight— and gave a thumbs up.

"Good luck, college boy." The young woman waved. Then her guttural shrieks filled the hallway.

Hunt cut to the right at a full sprint. From behind him, mixed with Helena's screams, Hunt heard other female voices shouting.

The little doors began crashing open. Young women warily peered around the doorjambs. Beyond them were more narrow beds, most topped by large piles of lily-white male flesh fumbling for discarded garments.

Hunt looked over his shoulder. The heavyset man slammed face-first into the wall, with a familiar figure in red wedging her way past him, led by a gun.

Hunt kept running. He passed a room where the male occupant had joined the woman at the door; Hunt grabbed the naked man and jerked him into the hall, leaving him shouting Italian profanities from the floor.

He reached the hallway's end and the metal door. To his right, in an open restroom, a plainly clothed woman knelt beside a toilet bowl with a sponge in her hand, staring up at him. He slammed past the exit door and found the stairs leading downward. Then he turned back and dashed into the restroom.

He grabbed the bucket of sudsy water. "Do you mind if I borrow this?"

He ran back out and looked back down the hall. Nin and the other woman were trying to get past the naked Italian, who was shouting and wildly gesticulating.

Hunt threw open the metal door. Just behind him, the women broke past the Italian. At the top of the stairs, Hunt dumped the bucket. The water cascaded down the concrete steps.

Hunt grabbed the metal railing and jumped over it, landing halfway down the next flight, below the wet treads. He pounded the steps three at a time, using the railing to whip around corners.

Down two flights, he heard the door above crash open. A second series of thudding steps joined his. Then a scream, shouting, a series of thuds. The grad student smiled and ran faster.

At the bottom, he shoved open a door. The garage still smelled of exhaust and burnt rubber. Sprinting, he traced a pair of black streaks up a ramp.

Ahead, through the grated garage door, he saw cars passing on the street. He reached the top of the ramp. At shin-level, on either side of the door, little red electronic eyes glowered.

Hunt kicked the beam.

Nothing happened.

Below in the garage, the door from the staircase slammed open.

Hunt frantically waved his lower leg back and forth. "Come on, come on!"

Still nothing.

He looked around. At the ceiling, near the rolling-door mechanism, the security camera glared at him.

He kicked the beam one more time. Nothing.

Then the door shuddered and started creeping up. Footsteps rang from the garage below. Hunt dropped and shimmed under the metal sill.

Nin ran up the ramp. The Bobcat whipped around the corner and searched the street. But the gun found nothing other than nighttime traffic.

In the office, the two bartenders high-fived each other. Before them lay the wires ripped from the computer network—including for the monitor for the garage security-camera feed.

SUNDAY, JULY 15
Prague

Quick stared at Prague Castle. She wondered which window had disgorged the victims of the Second Defenestration of Prague. Davies's voice eventually replaced the receding scream of the man whom she had thrown to his death from her hotel window just an hour earlier.

She turned and locked eyes with Davies.

"Yes, I promise . . . And if I hear from Amanda, I will definitely call you right away," Davies said. Then he put down the phone and shook his head. "Mothers worry too much."

Quick crossed to his bed. "I'd say having a son shot would give even the most iron-hearted mater pause," she said, laying a hand on Davies's forearm, below the fresh bandage.

Davies glanced at the hand and then at Quick. "Actually, I think she is more concerned about my sister who fancies herself the antiglobalization activist." He pointed at a muted television hanging on the wall, and the flashing images of Madrid and chanting protestors.

He laid his hand over Quick's. "By the way, thanks for staying with me back in the hotel room; I've never had a beautiful scientist tend my wound with one hand and wield a gun with the other, to hold off the bad guys."

Quick rolled her eyes.

"I'm just sorry if I stopped you from going after Nin. I guess you've figured out I really am just an embassy attaché and not some CIA undercover agent."

"I don't know. You were a decent shot with that ashtray, kinda stealthy even."

Davies grinned. "Yeah, not bad for a diplomat, huh?"

"Perhaps you should try out for the Yankees," said an unsmiling Captain Svoboda from the doorway. He motioned with his hand, and Hunt followed him into the room.

"What did you find at the Sokolov property?" Quick asked, pulling her hand free of Davies's arm.

"Well, let's just say our friend Nin Zanin gets around." Hunt relayed the events at the brothel, ending with his sprint away from the building. "I didn't have much time on the Sokolov computer network. But when I saw that Nin Zanin was also visiting Prague, I made additional inquiries."

He held up his smartphone. "And fortunately for us"—he shrugged at Svoboda—"the Czech government's networks are not nearly as well protected as Sokolov's. A flight plan was filed for Nin's jet from Ruzyne to—"

"Madrid," Quick interrupted.

"How—," Hunt started.

"Nin Zanin went to awful lot of trouble to get us to Prague— and out of Madrid." Quick pointed at the mute TV and an image of protesters outside the Palacio Real. "My father advised: 'Don't hit a growling dog with a stick, because he'll bite as you fend him off. No, what you do,' he said, 'is throw the stick, which the dog will chase, giving you time to grab a shotgun.' And like any dog, we followed the stick right to Prague."

"I fail to understand that expression," Svoboda said.

"What Sam is saying is that she"—Hunt glanced at Davies's bandaged arm and the IV tubing snaking up to a plastic bag hanging adjacent to the bed—"and I are returning to Madrid."

"What?" the captain exclaimed, as Quick waved at Davies, passing through the doorway, with Hunt following close behind.

Davies's call of "Be careful" jumbled with the captain's shrill, "I must protest . . ."

. . .

"Ruzyne please," Quick said, and the cab shot away from the curb. She pulled out her phone and held it between her and Hunt.

A sleepy "Hello?" issued from the speaker.

"It's Sam and Eric calling, I hope we haven't wakened you."

They heard mumbled confirmations from both Molly Matson and a voice fainter yet discernibly deeper and younger than Matson's.

Quick raised a brow at Hunt. "My apologies to you . . . both. Listen, Molly, I dropped something out the window of my hotel suite in Prague, and the folks at the front desk raised a ruckus. Eric and I are now on our way back to Madrid. We need another favor. The computer files, the maps of Madrid's subterranean infrastructure, did they chart any particular area of Madrid?"

Quick and Hunt heard Matson say, "I have to talk business. Go have a rinse." After a pause, Matson's full voice returned to the speaker, "Sam, the files contained hundreds of maps—of varying detail and scale. I would need to run a full analysis to say for sure. Why?"

"Molly, we need a spatial correlation of the locational frequencies of those maps against the meeting sites of the International Capital Forum in Madrid where world leaders will be present—"

"Whoa, Sam, honey, what's the connection between the ICF meetings, these maps, and Kalia Slater?"

"I'm not entirely sure myself. But Sokolov and his twins, and the tattooed antiglobalization crowd, some of who were on La Palma when Kalia was abducted, may be connected. And tonight, one of the twins paid us a personal visit in Prague, and now she's rushing back to Madrid in her private jet. Kalia's abduction might not be about ALCHEMY after all. Rather, Kalia Slater might be a pawn in some sort of geopolitical blackmail having to do with the ICF."

"Oh criminy, why can't kids just burn their bras anymore?" Matson replied.

"Molly, if you could run some models using the computer files, I'd be forever grateful."

"No problem. My techies are probably just sitting around in their skivvies playing video games at this hour anyway. And all I had on my agenda for tomorrow morning were a few lessons for my tennis pro—"

"Don't you mean *from* your tennis pro?" Hunt asked.

"Eric, I may be nearing the age for Medicare eligibility, but I assure you that Molly Matson always means exactly what she says. Ciao, kiddos."

Quick slipped the phone into her pocket and looked at Hunt. "Molly has a certain . . . oh, never mind. You'll probably see for yourself someday."

They continued in silence, watching the Vltava's dark waters race by at 80 mph. As Prague Castle receded from view, Quick said to herself: *Hold on, Kalia: we're coming.*

. . .

The driver set down his phone. "They survived. Somehow."

Utley continued staring out the front passenger window of the silver Peugeot. "Did they now? Well, my, aren't they resilient."

"Nin Zanin is flying back to Madrid. They will follow." The driver glanced at the rearview mirror, at the third man, who was sitting in back seat, shrugging. He turned back to Utley. "They're getting closer. They may cause you a problem. Should I have our people divert them?"

"*Au contraire*, they're beginning to prove quite useful. By all means, let's stay out of their way."

His gaze traveled up the building's dark façade. His trembling finger stilled as he pressed it against the glass, pinning the building's one window burning with light, nine stories up.

"The boys will move soon. When they do, we shall know what to do."

-43-

SUNDAY, JULY 15
Island of La Palma

Her body sank deeper under the water. Kalia Slater tasted the sea's salt, felt the water's warmth, and saw the shifting, shimmering schools of brightly colored fish. But as she sank deeper still, the receding sunlight turned from white to blue to green through a thickening filter of plankton and algae. Thousands of tons of water pressed down on her. And Slater began to struggle.

The fading point of sunlight turned into an orange sea snake shooting down, directly at her. She tried to turn over and swim away, but she could not. The blazing serpent neared. She screamed. Water filled her mouth. She realized the snake was actually a cascade of glowing-hot lava sinking into the ocean.

For a second, the budding volcanologist in Slater took over, and she wondered how lava could continue glowing orange at such depths. The lava neared her face. But instead of the burn of fire, Slater felt the sting of cold.

She whipped her head back and forth. Water flew from her face and hair. She tried to sit up. But the restraints kept her pinned down. Opening her eyes, she could only wonder which nightmare was worse—boiling alive in an underwater lava flow or waking to find an unwashed man standing over her with an empty plastic cup clamped in one hand, and a semiautomatic machine gun in the other.

The grad student wished her mouth were not so parched from the combination of irregular access to water and the Devil's Throat unrelenting heat, because she really wanted to spit in the bastard's face. Instead, all she could do was imagine her captor taking her place beneath the lava-fall of her nightmare.

The man crumpled the cup and threw it onto a trash pile growing in the room's far corner. His Micro Uzi landed on the wood planks stretched between a pair of upright barrels. His browned teeth flashed at her. And Slater felt the tiny warning hairs on the back of her neck rise.

He leaned over her pinned body. She grimaced, as his fetid breath and sweaty chest brushed against her. But Slater did not flinch. She had been through this routine enough by now.

The man backed away, returning the handcuff key to the chain around his neck. Slater, her hands now free, sat up and carefully made a show of rubbing the red marks ringing her wrists. Her captor retook his seat, while she eyed the gun tabled five feet from her.

Although she was certain that she could grab the weapon before the guard could, Slater did not know whether she could simply pull the trigger and blast away the man's face. Or whether she instead needed to first find and switch off a safety mechanism. If the latter, then the guard would overpower her before she could figure it out. *No, better that she stick with her plan and wait for an opportunity offering a greater chance of success.*

A second guard's almost immediate arrival confirmed her

hunch. This man spoke rapidly and loudly to the seated guard, who scowled and snatched the gun from the table. The new arrival shook his head and handed Slater a bowl of unadorned white rice and a cup filled with water.

Sitting on the cot, Slater used her fingers to shovel the rice to her mouth. After she finished eating, one of the guards pointed toward the covered bucket at the room's far end. Slater stared straight back at them, as the men watched while she used the bucket to relieve herself.

As the Hawaiian returned to the cot, a commotion outside the chamber's entrance caused her and the men's heads to turn. The sounds of footfalls and shuffling followed.

A third man, also holding a gun, stomped into the room. Behind him followed someone or something—with rope loosely binding its feet, filthy shorts and a shirt covering its body, and an oddly misshapen, black blob resting where its head should have been. A fourth man trailed, his gun stuck into the hostage's back.

The tattoos circling both ankles ruled out both Quick and Hunt. So, who was this? Slater watched the men force the figure toward her cot, with the captive moving with the short steps that the bindings demanded.

The men shoved the body down beside Slater, and a squeal erupted beneath the black hood. A guard pulled out a new set of handcuffs and locked the new arrival to the cot.

The men turned their attention to Slater. The handcuffs clicked closed behind her back. Slater balled her fists and pulled them against the metal rings with as much force as she dared, as she had been doing each time the cuffs were applied to her. The men stepped back and admired their bound prey: Slater and her new companion sitting side by side.

The men spoke rapidly, elbowed each other, and laughed. A guard stepped toward the cot. With a snapping sound, the spandex hood broke free from the new arrival. The head shook, and dreadlocks lashed against the rock wall. Big, dark eyes blinked and opened. They looked first at the guards and then at Slater.

Then she said, "Hi. I'm Amanda."

Part III

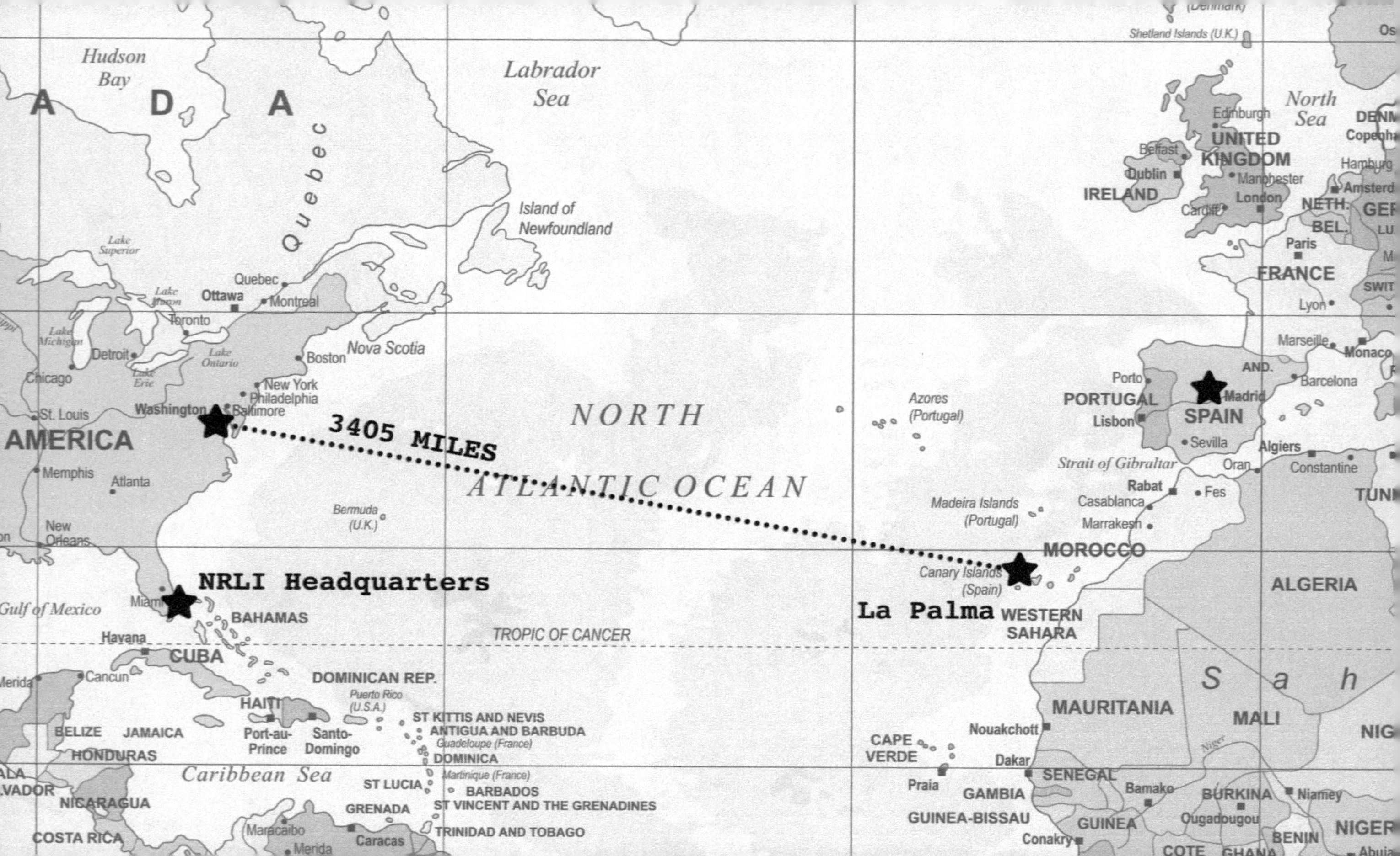

Hudson Bay
Labrador Sea
Shetland Islands (U.K.)
(Denmark)
North Sea
DENM.
Copenh.
Hamburg
Amsterd.
NETH.
BEL.
GER.
LU.
UNITED KINGDOM
Edinburgh
Belfast
IRELAND
Dublin
Manchester
London
Cardiff
Paris
FRANCE
SWIT.
Lyon
Marseille
Monaco
AND.
Barcelona
ADA
Quebec
Lake Superior
Lake Michigan
Lake Huron
Lake Erie
Lake Ontario
Chicago
Detroit
St. Louis
Memphis
Atlanta
Toronto
Ottawa
Montreal
Quebec
Boston
Nova Scotia
New York
Philadelphia
Washington
Baltimore
Island of Newfoundland
AMERICA
New Orleans
NORTH
ATLANTIC OCEAN
3405 MILES
Bermuda (U.K.)
Azores (Portugal)
PORTUGAL
Lisbon
Porto
SPAIN
Madrid
Sevilla
Algiers
Oran
Constantine
Strait of Gibraltar
Rabat
Casablanca
Marrakesh
Fes
TUN.
Madeira Islands (Portugal)
MOROCCO
Canary Islands (Spain)
La Palma
WESTERN SAHARA
ALGERIA
NRLI Headquarters
Miami
BAHAMAS
Havana
CUBA
Cancun
Merida
TROPIC OF CANCER
Sahara
MAURITANIA
MALI
NIG.
DOMINICAN REP.
HAITI
Port-au-Prince
Santo-Domingo
Puerto Rico (U.S.A.)
ST KITTIS AND NEVIS
ANTIGUA AND BARBUDA
Guadeloupe (France)
DOMINICA
Martinique (France)
BARBADOS
ST LUCIA
ST VINCENT AND THE GRENADINES
GRENADA
TRINIDAD AND TOBAGO
BELIZE
JAMAICA
HONDURAS
Caribbean Sea
NICARAGUA
COSTA RICA
VADOR
ALA
Maracaibo
Merida
Caracas
Gulf of Mexico
CAPE VERDE
Praia
Nouakchott
Dakar
SENEGAL
GAMBIA
GUINEA-BISSAU
GUINEA
Conakry
Bamako
Niger
BURKINA
Ouagadougou
Niamey
BENIN
NIGER
COTE
GHANA
Abuja

$$\circledast$$

-44-

SUNDAY, JULY 15
Madrid

The extended hundred-euro note metastasized into a finger-thick pile. A loud pop of air exploded from the gum in her mouth, marking the disappearance of the money into a shoulder bag.

"*Muchas gracias, señores,*" the woman said, as she smoothed her neon pink skirt and grabbed the doorknob. The woman—who might have been a fashion model if not for a thin, ropey line of scar tissue running from her upper lip to her left nostril—was eager to leave. The windfall, she figured, would allow taking off the rest of the month to spend time with her angel. *As soon as I get home, the cellphone goes into the drawer. And tomorrow, I take my little girl to El Prado to see the colorful pictures that my Maria loves so much.*

Fifteen minutes after the woman's departure, a phone chirped. Gabriel scrolled through the text message and then grinned at Jacob. "We're on."

After rapidly dressing, each man grabbed a plastic jug. The men ran from room to room, dumping clear liquid from the jugs onto the piles of dirty clothes and take-out containers that littered the room. Much of the fluid vaporized before hitting the intended targets, filling the room with a thick chemical haze that mingled with the pot smoke.

The men slipped into the building hallway and pulled the door almost closed behind them. Gabriel struck a match against the stucco wall. The stick cartwheeled through the space left by the cracked door. The men ran for the stairs.

The blast wave slammed the Peugeot and the line of parked vehicles. The cars shook as if hit by an earthquake. Alarms shrilled. Hot splinters of glass and aluminum danced on the Peugeot's hood and roof.

Utley and his companions craned their necks, looking upward through the windshield and sunroof, and found orange flames chasing a curl of black smoke from the ninth-story window.

Utley slid his phone from his pocket. Despite his finger's tremor, a long line of digits sprouted on the display without the mobile's backspace key ever feeling pressure. The phone beeped and then returned to his pocket.

He looked around the passenger compartment. "The time has arrived for parting's sweet sorrow. I have initiated the transfers. Provided you meet the remainder of your contractual obligations, including divulging none of this week's events, you will receive your first payments fourteen days hence."

Utley pointed at the Metro station. "I suggest that you leave Madrid with all dispatch. Goodbye, gentlemen."

. . .

The 737-300 glided just north of Madrid. The orange flash on a midrise building held her eye for only a second. Then Sam Quick turned from the window, slid the vibrating phone from her pocket, and checked the display.

"Molly," she said to Eric Hunt, who sat beside her in a row midway back in the crowded plane. She raised the phone between her and Hunt. "What have you found?"

"Sweetie, you sure know how to give the boys a workout. First, we had to determine which locations appeared most frequently on the encrypted maps. Then the boys correlated these locations to the sites of those International Capital Forum meetings where world leaders would be present."

"And?" Quick asked, as a gentle bump shook the plane, and the PA announced a welcome to Madrid.

"We found only one match: a network of former coal-cart tunnels beneath the location of a champagne reception slated for this evening at the Prado."

"Great work, Molly," Quick said. "Please further characterize the location."

"The coal tunnels were part of a subterranean network formerly used to deliver fuel to municipal buildings during the late nineteenth and early twentieth centuries. After coal burning was phased out, the tunnels were converted to utility shafts. They now carry steam pipes, high-voltage lines, communication cables, and water and gas mains. And the site of interest is a tunnel that runs directly beneath the museum."

"How do we access the tunnel network?" Hunt asked.

"The easiest entry point lies in the Atocha subway station, near the Prado."

"Can you send a map to Eric's mobile?" Quick asked.

"I just need the number, and it's done."

"And can you track Eric's phone?"

"My wunderkind here is nodding in the affirmative"—Matson's voice weakened for a moment before returning to full strength—"but he says only when you're above ground. The cellular signals won't penetrate far enough underground to reach the coal tunnels."

"Understood," Quick said, followed by Hunt relaying his phone number.

"Got it," Matson said. "Now, you two be careful."

"We'll try our best, Molly." Quick pressed the disconnect button and looked at Hunt. "I hope you have change—we're taking the subway."

. . .

Utley watched the stream of escaping residents thin into clumps. By now, flames and black smoke spewed from several windows located on the apartment tower's ninth and tenth floors. Onlookers clogged the sidewalk alongside the Peugeot. Red lights and siren wails bounced off the buildings lining the narrow street.

The flow of fleeing people petered, as firefighters, trailing streamers of canvas hose, ran inside. Utley's attention remained locked on the garage entrance. A firefighter appeared. He was pulling along two straggling young men, hauling them and their metal suitcase away from the building.

The firefighter deposited the men at the curb with a shake of his head. Utley, not bothering to remove the ignition key, climbed from the Peugeot and then slipped into the crowd.

The heavyset man wheeled the bag right past Utley, while the second man—the tall blond—walked alongside with his hand resting on the metal suitcase as if calming an anxious pet.

Utley watched the men and the suitcase jag across the street, as they carefully lifted the bag over the turgid fire hoses and shards of window glass, and weaved among the firefighters and police officers.

Utley started moving when the suitcase was three car-lengths away. He walked slowly, periodically turning his attention to flaming building, as any onlooker would. With each step, his Walther P99 rubbed against his calf.

The blond man grabbed the suitcase's handle and boosted the suitcase onto the curb. Utley smiled as the brushed metal began sinking from view—down into the Madrid Metro.

-45-

Rice again. But Kalia Slater did not care. Desperation is an emotion that does not share its soil, and Amanda's arrival had withered her fears at the root. Plus, she thought—feeling the burn of chafed skin on her wrists—her plan was working.

Slater looked into the big eyes hovering above the rice bowl opposite. She smiled, cupped her fingers, and scooped a load of rice from her own bowl to her mouth. Because of the enforced silence, Slater could not explain why to Amanda, but she needed the other woman to eat every one of the little pellets of energy. Her head nodded slightly but firmly in the direction of the other woman's dish.

Amanda's gaze shifted from Slater, toward the guard, who was seated a few feet away with his Micro Uzi. The last thing she felt like doing was eating. *Somehow, I must let my brother know what is happening.* She turned back to Slater, who was still subtly nodding at her. After another moment of hesitation, Amanda dipped her hand into her bowl.

Good girl, Slater thought.

Chewing the flavorless rice, Amanda watched Slater and

realized this woman who barely knew her—with the comforting nudges on the cot and, here at the table, the encouragements to eat—had showed more care for her than had any of her so-called friends, the ones who had looked straight ahead as they had driven from that warehouse, leaving her behind as if she were a bag of trash.

But what would Kalia think if she knew how or why I was brought to this hellish mine or whatever it was. Somehow, I need to let my brother know what is happening.

Her thoughts broke, as another man entered the chamber. The red laser of this new arrival's gun sight pointed to the cot. Amanda looked at Slater, who nodded. The women rose and moved toward the bed.

After they were seated, the guard set his gun on the table and stepped to the cot. Grinning, he bent forward, wrapping his arms around Amanda, who averted her face and shrunk herself as much as possible. An overpowering smell of garlic and onions confirmed that his diet included more than plain rice. Behind her, a series of short clicks sounded as her handcuffs locked.

The man shifted his attention to Slater, giving her an especially long leer as he crouched to hug her. But Slater did not pull away as Amanda had. Instead, she maintained as much bodily contact with the man as possible, smiling at him and inflating her chest.

All the better to keep him distracted. As she balled her hands against the closing cuffs.

The guard pulled back from Slater, grinning wider than ever. The two men said something, fixing their eyes on the women and laughing. Droplets of saliva felt like splattered hot grease on Slater and Amanda's faces.

The guard took his seat, still staring at the woman. The other man gathered the dishes and left the chamber. Slater rubbed elbows with Amanda, who looked first at her cot-mate's face. And then, following the Hawaiian's eye signals, behind Slater. At the hands quietly working against the metal cuffs.

SUNDAY, JULY 15
Moscow

The red bits sprayed from Sokolov's mouth like sparks from a fireplace fueled by green wood. The mother-of-pearl scoop dove anew into the fish eggs. Then the paddle returned to his face and dumped another load of caviar into his mouth.

The eggs dissolved on his tongue, as Sokolov stared at the wall-mounted screen hanging opposite his desk. The pixilated image of two young men—one tall and blond, the other dark-haired and heavyset—wheeling a metallic suitcase filled the enormous display.

The men stopped at a nondescript door. Sokolov leaned forward.

The heavyset one started pressing buttons on a keypad affixed to the wall beside the door. The pause between keys grew longer with each new depression of a button, and the typist looked ever more frequently at a slip of paper.

Sokolov jumped up and crossed to the monitor.

The blond man snatched the paper from the other man and then continued the keying. Finally, he jerked open the door. The men and the suitcase slipped past. The door closed behind them.

Then the screen filled with people hurriedly walking in front of the door, to and from the turnstiles and shops at the edges of the camera shot, just as it had been before the men's arrival.

Sokolov snorted. For another minute, he watched the scenes of everyday life in a subway station continue to unfold. *Too bad this couldn't be shown live.*

He pictured the monitors in the command center of the Spanish antiterrorism taskforce. The displays normally fed by a data stream from this subway-station camera. But that, at this very moment, thanks to his technicians, instead showed a loop of video filmed months ago, footage of nothing but the mundane passage of transiting Madrileños and tourists. Only on his display and in his own command center did the intercepted, real-time video play.

Of course, Sokolov mused, reruns of the actual footage, of the metal suitcase disappearing through the subway-station doorway, carried by the two American activists would be the most re-played video of all time.

Undoubtedly, at this very instant, his technicians in Moscow were burning the real video onto the hard drives at the Spanish antiterrorism center, which was a safe thirty miles from central Madrid.

"A video that will be seen by more people than," he said aloud, as he scooped more caviar, "even those of the assassination of President Kennedy or 9/11."

The fish eggs poured into his mouth, as he walked over to the wall map. The X drawn by Nin Zanin in caviar juice remained covering Washington D.C. Sokolov dipped his finger into the liquid left on the roe scoop. Then it slashed down the U.S. eastern seaboard. The black line sliced off a twenty-mile-wide strip of shoreline running from Florida to Maine.

-47-

SUNDAY, JULY 15
Madrid

The doors parted. Hunt was first off the train, followed closely by Quick. The grad student glanced at his smartphone, then cut into the thick crowd, and jumped on an up-bound escalator, weaving between the standing riders, climbing the grooved steps two at a time.

At the top, Hunt stopped in the middle of Atocha Station's main level. A buzzing hive of newsstands, map-wielding tourists, and fast-walking locals surrounded him and Quick.

Quick pointed at Hunt's smartphone. "Which way now?"

The grad student scrolled his screen and looked around the space. His gaze landed on a nearby concession fronted by racks of tabloids and shelves filled with candies and bottles of water

"There." Hunt pointed at a metal door set in the wall adjacent to the store.

They moved for it. Quick nodded at the keypad affixed to the wall. "This is one is all yours."

Hunt tapped at his phone. "Just need to send this . . . " He pressed a few more keys. "OK. Ready."

Quick turned and faced into the station. Behind her, Hunt

held his phone alongside the keypad. Churning numbers filled the screen.

Quick watched the escalator deposit two uniformed police officers less than twenty feet away. She prepared to grab Hunt. Then she saw a pair of tight-topped American college students unfurl a map near the officers.

The young women heard a jaunty "*Buenos días, señoritas*, are you lost?" as Quick and Hunt slipped inside.

The door clicked shut. The station's noise and frenetic energy died. The scientists found themselves in a narrow hallway that appeared to double as a stockroom for the concession stand: stacked cardboard boxes of magazines, books, and toiletries lined one wall, while humming meter boxes and thick electric conduits girded the other.

Using the phone, Hunt led them forward. The boxes gave way to dented trashcans. After another thirty feet, the overhead lights grew less frequent. Everything vibrated as a train passed through a tunnel beneath them. In the darkest patches, their shoes squished jellyfish of used rubbers and anthills of discarded cigarette butts.

After traveling another hundred feet, Hunt stopped. A pitch-dark staircase descended directly ahead. Beside it, a metal gate lay retracted against the wall.

Quick pointed at a cut-open padlock lying on the ground. "Apparently, we aren't the only ones with a penchant for breaking and entering."

Hunt checked his phone again. "We're dead on Molly's route. These steps lead down into the utility tunnels."

His arm swept outward, and his phone display lit the upper

steps, while the lower stairs remained a black pool beyond the screen's illumination.

"Ladies first," Hunt said to the back of the figure already diving into the dark water.

. . .

4400 miles away, tanned fingers dug into the shoulder. "Hell's bells, where did they go?"

"Dr. Quick and her companion's cellphone are too far below street level to get a GPS read, ma'am—they're in the tunnels now." The officer nodded at a computer screen, which showed a close-scale 3D rendering of Madrid's museum district. "They need to resurface before we can retriangulate their position."

"And Sam can't get a signal to call out?"

"Yes, that's correct, ma'am."

"I don't like this one bit."

The geologist bent forward, reached around the officer, and grabbed a handset anchored to the control panel. She pulled the receiver to her ear and, with her free hand, ruffled the man's crew cut.

"Be a sweetie and dial the base operator for Molly—I need to make a transatlantic call. And while you're at it, stop calling me 'ma'am' or I'll put you right over my knee."

Her eyes twinkled at the red-faced officer. "Unless of course, that's the way you want to play it."

-48-

"Go away. You'll get us fired," he whispered in Spanish to the other waiter.

Then Jorge Delgado turned forty-five degrees, flashed his bright teeth, and leaned forward. The woman standing before him, in a dress that made her look like a toffee wrapped in cellophane, collected the precious token between her thumb and finger.

Delgado winked at her and said in a stage whisper, "Take another: they're small."

The woman's heavily plumped lips spread into a smile. She plucked another piece from Delgado's tray, shoved it in her mouth, and then dashed away in a life-or-death pursuit of the crab puffs that were drifting by on another server's silver platter.

The Prado's main gallery was a blur of mid-level diplomats, their spouses, and the catering staff. The diplomats and their spouses were filling with food and wine before the arrival of the heads of state, cabinet secretaries, and section ministers, at which time their sole mission would become preening for their and their partners' bosses.

Captive witnesses to this frenzy were the immortalized members of the Spanish court whose portraits lined the walls, with each aristocrat or royal mutely staring down on the melee. Along the gallery's midline, a parade of large bronze statuary depicted scenes of horsemanship and battle victories long past. And at the hall's far end lay the exclusion zone protected by velvet ropes and suited men in sunglasses stationed at each bollard, where the presidents, prime ministers, and chancellors would soon gather safe from the hoi polloi.

Delgado turned back and stood shoulder-to-shoulder with his colleague, who had ignored his command to move away. He shook his head. "These people are so ravenous, you'd think they'd just escaped from a refugee camp."

The other waiter snorted. "Yes, but just wait. Because the only people more famished than bureaucrats are journalists. Once the reporters are admitted, they would trample Velázquez himself"—he nodded at a large oil hanging on a nearby wall—"if he stood between them and a spear of limp asparagus wrapped in dry *jamón serrano*."

He lifted his tray of crostini slathered with fava-bean puree. "Speaking of hunger, I wonder if perhaps *Monsieur l'Ambassadeur* would care for a bite?"

Delgado followed his colleague's gaze to a man in a crisp, slim-cut suit. "Possibly, but unfortunately for you, probably not yours."

"Perhaps, but I'll take my chances." The other waiter nudged Delgado. "We can't all be so lucky as you, Jorge, to have a muscle-boy American scientist chasing us with text messages after we rescue them in the nightclub restroom from crazy psycho killers in red skirts. Tell me, Jorge, how long since the last text from your American?"

Delgado shot his colleague a look. "He's not *my* American—Eric and I have just exchanged a few messages, that's all."

"Oh, calling him Eric now are we—"

The men jumped as phlegm, an inch behind their adjacent ears, rattled. They turned to find the brushy brows of their stout Castilian supervisor reared in standoff.

"*Señores*—and I use the term most loosely—you are here to serve food to the guests, not to cruise the guests." Her chipped incisor glinted. "Besides, the American secret service agents"—her head tilted at a blue-suited duo with thin wires spiraling down from their ears, standing near an exit—"those are the real targets."

She grabbed the tray of crostini from the other waiter. "More men than either of you boys can handle. Get another platter from the kitchen and then go ply your Frenchman with shrimps."

Delgado and his empty-handed workmate watched the Castilian approach the agents. As she spoke, the American faces turned a shade that perfectly matched the red strips of the flag pins affixed to their lapels.

. . .

One story directly below the blushing agents, in a locker located in a basement-level staff room, Jorge Delgado's cellphone blinked. Bright-red letters burned on its display: "CRAZY TERRORIST STUFF GOING DOWN. GET OUT OF MADRID NOW. NO JOKE. ERIC."

. . .

Another story directly below Delgado's glowing cellphone, two snaps sounded. The noise reverberated throughout the subbasement, echoing off the three massive coal-fired boilers that had once heated the museum and a frozen landslide of concrete and bricks occluding a staircase.

The top shell of a metallic suitcase rose. The lid stopped at the point of a yellow arrow, which, along with a string of geographic coordinates, was spray-painted on the center boiler's rusted iron.

The men glanced at each other. Then they looked down at the black cylinder that filled half of the case, at the silvery Russian inscription, the trefoil symbol, and the circuitry glowing in the flashlight beam.

Fingertips caressed the cylinder, as Gabriel whispered, "Time to light the fuse on this Red."

Jacob handed him a sheet of paper. For the hundredth time, Gabriel stared at the slip. Then he laid it on the dusty floor and lifted the plastic cover of a small box inside the suitcase, revealing a three-by-three matrix of unmarked keys.

Gabriel read the instruction's first line again.

Then again.

And finally, after several more seconds, his finger depressed the array's central button.

The finger retreated.

The button rose up.

Neither man breathed.

Gabriel read the second demand three times before his finger went back to the keypad.

On the fourteenth directive, Gabriel forced himself to stop the repetitious reading after a tenth scan of the line. He looked at his friend, who slowly nodded.

His finger pressed a series of four buttons.

A loud beep sounded.

The men scattered.

Except for two wildly beating hearts, silence fell in the sub-basement. After several long moments, the men released each other, crawled forward, and peered down into the case.

They checked their respective watches and then looked anew at the red stick figures flashing on a glossy black strip inside the suitcase: *50:55 . . . 50:54 . . . 50:53 . . .*

They jumped and ran. First down a narrow ramp opposite the boilers. Then past the heavy metal door that they had earlier found half ajar, its welded edges cut.

Now in the tunnel, Gabriel in the lead, they sprinted. The passage was six feet wide and not much taller at the centerline of its rounded roof, offering just enough space to accommodate its originally intended occupants: a stooped man, a straining dray horse, and a wooden cart piled with coal.

Without slowing, Gabriel looked over his shoulder, grinning at Jacob. "Right now, we're the two most powerful people on the fucking planet."

Then the bullet smashed into his ear. The projectile shattered his cranium, dragging along the metal ringing his ear's outer edge. He slammed against the brick wall. The lead slug and tangle of jewelry lost its momentum at the midline of his brainstem.

He slid down the wall and buckled to his knees. He collapsed forward, crashing facedown on the ground. His shirt rode up, exposing the exploding American flag inked on his back. Coal dust blackened the white of his upturned eye.

For a second, light shone on the body. Then the flashlight clattered to the tunnel floor. Jacob tried to turn around, but he felt like he was fighting through molten lead. His legs seemed to be going in every which direction, bent at unnatural angles. Great, wild slapping steps sounded as he started running.

A controlled, staccato clip of heels on brick overlaid the sounds of his scrambling retreat.

Utley stopped at Gabriel's body. He planted himself with his shoes spaced an exact shoulder's width apart, drew himself to his full height, and pushed out his arms into a prow-shaped formation. His lower hand clenched his flashlight, while the upper one gripped his Walther P99. His beam jittered over the diameter of the tunnel.

The gun locked on target. Now with flowing grace, it followed Jacob as he crashed from side to side, running as fast as his short legs would carry him.

Utley squeezed once.

Between the momentum of his barely controlled forward motion and the force of the bullet striking his back, Jacob tumbled forwarded. He landed face-first and skidded along the dirty bricks, until he stopped sliding after five feet.

The tunnel was silent. Powder smoke and stirred-up coal dust swirled in Utley's beam.

Utley squeezed again. The bullet slammed into the delicate V formed by the man's splayed legs. Jacob's lifeless body merely jiggled like a block of gelatin flicked by a bored child's finger

"I guess this makes me the most powerful person on the fucking planet." Utley sighed and jammed his again-shaking hand and the Walther into his pocket.

. . .

The old man walked swiftly, stepping over the second body. After traveling another dozen yards, he landed his flashlight beam on the neat lettering of a half-open door: "El Prado." He slipped inside, went up the ramp, and scanned the room. He headed for the middle of the three boilers.

Utley looked down into the suitcase, as the display flashed 41:17.

Plenty of time provided the disarming sequence is unchanged. "And if it has changed," he said aloud, as his finger trembled above the cylinder of packed plutonium, "then none of it will have mattered anyway."

He flicked open the keypad cover, and his finger shook so violently that it brushed several buttons. Finally, it landed on the center button, and the suitcase beeped in acquiescence.

His eyes were on the keys, but Utley saw himself walking into the Oval Office. He was alone except for the president, who was rising from behind the desk. His hand was clasped. The president thanked him and pressed the medal into his hands. The usual murmurs were made about wishing how this ceremony could have been a public presentation. And Utley's finger danced across the keypad like a tender ballerina on the stage of the Royal Opera House.

- 49 -

"Daddy, this is a most unexpected surprise!"

Utley's finger hovered a quarter inch above the key.

"But a delightful one in any case—it's been so long."

Utley looked at the blinking red numbers: 38:32.

He turned. The tiny blood vessels webbing his brain bulged like old garden hoses. The dark-haired beauties standing side-by-side between him and the ramp were nearly thirty years older. And they now held matching Beretta Bobcats. But to Utley, they were same teenage girls holding tumblers of laced scotch all those years ago, on the night leading to the horrible pictures.

"Well, what fine women you've become," Utley said.

Nin Zanin stepped forward, her Bobcat locked on Utley. "Thank you, Daddy . . . you do still like to be called 'Daddy,' do you not? You certainly did that night in Prague."

She shrugged at Utley's silence. "First, Solta and I must thank you for saving us the trouble of dispatching those spoiled little boys who thought they could change the world by buying a bomb, as simply as if they were purchasing a bag of their smelly drug to get high. We certainly couldn't have them running around with what they knew."

Her teeth flashed. "Next we must say how much we admire your patience. In your position, a lesser man would have retaliated years ago against those who had wrought his downfall.

"Ah, but of course"—Nin glanced at her sister—"you want more than revenge: you want your good name back." She nodded. "And what better way to accomplish this goal than by averting the assassination—by the means of something as dramatic as a nuclear bomb, no less—of your pathetic president. Bravo, Daddy, a truly inspired plan."

"Alas," Solta Zanin said, "you will fail on both counts. The only shame is that you'll miss the real show tomorrow with our other little friends"—her Bobcat nodded at the suitcase—"on the island."

Utley grimaced. *The other bombs were in play.* He realized how foolish he had been thinking that the assassination of the world's most powerful leaders would satisfy his old enemy. *They have grander plans.*

"Now, now, sister, let's not bore Daddy." Nin glanced at the suitcase timer. "We really must hurry to the airstrip. Sometimes Madrid's dreadful heat is simply too much to bear. And I feel just such a spell coming on—in little more than half an hour."

Utley's hand shot for his pocket and the Walther.

But the Bobcats reached it first. Two bullets permanently ended his hand's tremor.

Utley held up his arm, looking at the bleeding pulp lying at his wrist's end and then at the sisters.

He sighed. "Brava, my dears, brava."

"I'm afraid the only word left to say is 'adieu,' Daddy," Nin said.

Two bullets, one from each Beretta, tore into his chest. He collapsed backward, landing on his back in the dust.

The sisters shoved their Bobcats under their skirts. Nin bent down and pressed a series of keystrokes on the pad. A long beep sounded. And the displayed continued its countdown, flashing 31:50.

Nin offered an arm to her sister. "Shall we? We haven't long to escape the blast range."

"But the control shot?" Solta asked.

Nin glanced at Utley's body and its burbling red springs. "The old man is dead."

Solta shrugged. The two women blew kisses at Utley. After a few seconds, "Goodbye, Daddy" drifted up from the coal tunnel. Then all was silent.

-50-

"Talk about a piercing session gone bad," Hunt whispered, as he pointed at the fist-sized crater where the ear should have been.

Quick nodded at the arm. "Look familiar? These tattoos are the same pattern as the ink on the antiglobalization crowd on La Palma."

Hunt nodded. "An old coal tunnel is an awfully strange place to hold a protest."

"Sure is." Quick said, grabbing the flashlight lying beside the body. "Let's keep moving."

After traveling another forty feet in the tunnel, Hunt whispered, "And here's number two."

"Someone's been awful busy." Quick barely slowed to step over the heavyset man's leg.

From the boiler room, Utley heard the approaching footfalls and cried out. But only a frothy, red effluence dribbled from his mouth and ran down over his collar. His eyelids fluttered in resignation. His one functioning hand skittered over the dusty floor, while he stared straight up, seeing the Bosch painting with its seven deadly sins and its images of heaven and hell.

In the tunnel, Quick pointed at the words printed on a partially open door: "El Prado." The flashlight went dark. Quick slipped past the door with Hunt following. Above them, a faint red light flashed.

They crept up the ramp. The blinking light revealed the center boiler. Hearing only a soft, regular beeping, and a louder, chaotic gurgling somewhere closer to them, Quick snapped on the flashlight.

"Number three," Hunt whispered.

They moved in and crouched, one on either side of Utley. Red teeth grinned up at them. The eyes, heavily bloodshot due to the vessels bursting from the pressure spike during the bullets' incursion, seemed to stare at the ceiling in wonder.

"Except this one doesn't share the others' affinity for tattoo parlors," Hunt said.

Quick's gaze traveled over the wounds. "Though I'm afraid in a minute, he'll have something else in common with them." She laid a hand on Utley's shoulder, and his eyes broke from the ceiling and locked onto Quick's.

He struggled to clear his airway. Then he managed to say, "Dr. Quick . . . "

"Who did this to you?" Quick lowered her face next to Utley's.

The man's hand flapped against the floor. The flashlight beam followed the pointing finger and landed on the metal suitcase. The black cylinder, the trefoil symbol, and the Cyrillic script stared passively back at the scientists.

The old man's gaze returned to the ceiling, as his finger stabbed unsteadily at the concrete. Quick swept her beam at the floor. A red paste of coal dust and blood formed a ragged-but-legible word: "island."

"What island," Quick said. "La Palma?"

Droplets of fresh blood sprayed from Utley's mouth. He now saw only the Bosch painting, his gaze bouncing erratically between the images of heaven and hell. Then his tremors and his hopes finally stilled. And in the subbasement, all that remained of the old man was the gurgling reverberation: "Stop them."

Quick jumped up. The flashlight beam swept in a grid pattern around the chamber and found the three boilers and the concrete and bricks sealing off the staircase to the museum above.

She looked around once, reconfirmed Slater's absence, and silently gave thanks.

"How did he know your name? And do you really think he means La Palma?'" Hunt asked.

"I'm sure of it. But we have more pressing concerns." Quick peered down into the suitcase. The display flashed 24:19. And she looked at Hunt. "I don't suppose your phone has a signal—two stories beneath a massive stone building?"

Hunt checked his mobile. Then he shook his head.

-51-

Only lantern remained lit. Shadows crept out from the walls, enveloping the cot and the women. The occasional groans of the centenarian timbers and the uneven exit of fetid breath from the guard's mouth were the only sounds that broke the silence.

But nothing was unsteady about Slater and Amanda's gazes. Pupils fully dilated and unwavering, the women watched the Micro Uzi rise and fall with each swell of their sleeping captor's chest.

After several more minutes, Slater's silent count reached one thousand, the number of seconds since the man's chin had landed on his dirty shirtfront.

She looked at Amanda. The dreadlocked woman nodded. Slater's hands began writhing in the metal cuffs. Amanda's line of sight volleyed between the squirming hands and the guard's forward-sloping face, as the gentle jingle of Slater's cuffs joined the room's infrequent sounds.

Despite Slater tricking the guard into locking the cuffs around the bases of her hands, rather than around her narrower wrists, the metal rings still needed to travel past her hands' widest point, the line of joints at the base of her fingers.

After several minutes, Slater looked at Amanda and shook her head. *It wasn't working.*

But I will never give up.

Slater sliced her thumbnail into the meat of her palm. Blood flowed from the cut, and she rubbed her other wrist against the wound, slicking the cuff with the warm lubrication. Then she tucked her thumb against her palm and pulled as hard as she could.

It moved.

Amanda nodded vigorously. With all her might, Slater yanked her right hand, which seemed nearest freedom. Tears cut the sweat and dust on her face, but Slater did not make a sound.

The junction of her fingers and hand locked in the bloody ring. Slater drew a sharp breath. Then she pulled with all her strength. With a sickening compression of cartilage, her hand slipped free.

The empty cuff landed, clinking against the cot's metal frame. Slater and Amanda's eyes shot toward the guard, who snorted but failed to raise his head.

Slater pulled her hands from behind herself, with the remaining cuff still locked around her other wrist. She wiped away her tears. The swipes left bloody smears below each eye like war paint.

She grabbed the dangling bloodied cuff and wrapped her fingers through it. Now, the cuffs would not jangle if she moved. And Kalia Slater most certainly planned to move.

Slater crept forward. The undulations of the guard's chest remained constant, while the women's chests rose and fell like bellows, their hearts furiously pumping.

Near the wall, Slater squatted and placed her hands around a melon-sized hunk of red stone lying loose on the ground. Her mind flashed to a week ago, when she had arrived on La Palma with Dr. Quick and Eric Hunt to harvest ore samples from La Garganta del Diablo—samples of the very rock that she now held, from the very mine where she was now captive.

A few feet away, the guard slept with his head sloped forward, and his chin pressed to his chest—as if offering the back of his head for a pedestal to display the jagged stone.

Slater nodded at Amanda, who was chewing her lower lip and staring at her.

"Force equals mass times velocity squared," Slater whispered as she closed in, lifting the rock over her head with both hands.

The rock smashed down. The guard somersaulted forwarded. His face slammed into the muddy ground. Slater raised the stone, prepared to bring it down again if necessary. But the guard's body lay still, his chest unmoving.

Slater dropped the rock. She knelt, rolled the guard, slid her hand into his shirt pocket, and withdrew a key. The remaining cuff opened around her wrist, and the metal fell to the ground.

She started to stand, but then paused and knelt again. The strap slid from the dead man's shoulder. Slater's head ducked through the nylon and metal circle. The gun settled like a pageant sash.

Amanda finally released the breath she had been holding. *This chick is steel.*

. . .

Slater and Amanda ran another few yards down the shaft. Then Slater held up a hand. The women stopped moving. Slater inched forward and peered around a rotting support timber.

She found a wider tunnel stretching without apparent end, with rail tracks cutting down its middle. The opposite wall was strung with cables and lights similar to those hung by her team during their first day at La Garganta del Diablo. Except these lamps were different: the bulbs were less frequently spaced and were fluorescents, whose bluish light turned the rock's healthy red to a strangled purple. Slater stepped out onto the tracks.

"Which way now? We have to get to a fucking phone right now. I need to let my brother know what's happening," Amanda said, emerging from the side tunnel, watching Slater slowly rotate with eyes closed and face upturned as if the Hawaiian were soaking up sun. *Has she lost it?* She glanced at the Uzi.

After a moment, a smile spread across Slater's face, and she looked at Amanda.

"The air is moving this way"—Slater jacked a thumb over her shoulder—"which means an opening of some sort must be"—she pointed in the opposite direction—"that way. And if fresh air can enter, then we may be able to exit." Slater grabbed Amanda's hand, and the women pressed close to the wall and started to run.

After several minutes, Slater felt a tug on her shirt from behind and heard Amanda whisper, "What's that?"

Slater slowed. Two hundred feet ahead, something near the ground dully glowed in the fluorescent light. The Uzi slipped off her chest and moved into the lead, with Slater's finger locked on its trigger.

After a more dozen steps, the women stopped and stared. An open suitcase, made of brushed metal, sat alongside the tracks, roughly aligned with a spray-painted yellow arrow.

"But what's it doing *here*?" Amanda asked.

The Uzi muzzle traced a series of numbers, letters, circles, and tick marks painted on the stone beside the arrow. "These characters represent geographic coordinates for, presumably, this very spot on the planet," Slater said, as she crouched down. "But I'm more interested in the suitcase—not exactly Prada, but something much more special, I think."

Her finger ran over the cylinder and its inscribed Cyrillic writing and the trefoil symbol, the latter of which she had seen so many times before on labels for radioactive materials in the lab. "Whatever the reason for its presence, I don't think we want to stay around to find out. Let's keep moving."

Slater stood and slipped the Uzi's strap over her head, while Amanda just stared at the suitcase. Slater took Amanda's hand. "Come on, let's go."

The women resumed running against the incoming air.

Because Slater led, she failed to see Amanda looking back every few seconds at the suitcase—and continuing to do so long after the glistening of the luggage's innards had died.

-52-

"If mobile cannot go to the signal, the signal must come to mobile."

"Huh?" Hunt said.

He watched Quick began scraping the cellphone against the boiler's rough metal face as if it were a hunk of cheddar on a cheese grater. He looked at the suitcase display, which now read 22:47, and then again at the phone, which Quick was whipping up and down.

Hunt squinted for a moment. Then his forehead smoothed. The echo of slapped metal reverberated throughout the chamber. "Yeah, they sure don't call you Sam Quick for nothing."

"Let's just hope whoever retrofitted the Prado's heating system and entombed these old boilers down here also failed to uproot the old chimneys," Quick said. "And that their metal liners remain contiguous to the building's roofline. If so, we can expose the phone's metallic antenna by wearing down its plastic casing and then, by holding it against the iron boiler, we create one massive cellphone antenna."

Her arm continued cranking up and down. After thirty

seconds, the scraping sound changed in tone, and Quick yanked the phone from the boiler, exposing a tiny coppery star glinting along its edge.

"Here goes nothing." Quick pressed the exposed phone antenna against the boiler in the spot where the phone had scraped the old metal free of rust.

For ten seconds, Quick and Hunt held their respective breaths.

Then the mobile beeped, and four graphical bars blossomed on the display, indicating signal strength.

"YES!" Hunt yelled.

Maintaining the phone's contact with the boiler, Quick started tapping the touchpad.

Moments later, a familiar cackle issued from the speaker. "Sam, out of nowhere, your GPS signal popped back up on the tracking monitor, and my new boyfriend nearly fell off his chair. Are you really on the roof of the Prado? And did you find Kalia Slater?"

"Not exactly, Molly. Eric and I are in a subbasement under the Prado. Someone left his or her luggage behind down here, and we ain't talking Louis Vuitton. We're sitting on a Soviet suitcase bomb. And the countdown timer reads 18:32 until a thermonuclear detonation. We need some assistance with stopping the clock and finding this bag's rightful owner."

The news silenced even Matson for a moment, before she recovered and said, "Some people are so damn careless with their belongings. But I bet south Florida's videogame champion here can hack up a manual for that thing in the CIA's digital bowels."

Quick and Hunt heard Matson issue instructions and then a

stampede of keystrokes.

Matson continued, "I just got off the horn with the folks at our Madrid embassy. They were about as helpful as a burger-joint cashier who's just learned she's won the lottery. The gentleman to whom I spoke said that with the 'big guy in town,' they couldn't spare anyone to crawl through old coal tunnels to help look for lost graduate students. But with this latest development, I suspect they'll agree that *el hombre grande* would appreciate a heads-up. Hold the line, Sam, I'm going to set up one of those fancy three-way calls."

Quick and Hunt heard Matson say something and then a series of clicks and finally a weary voice. "As I told you during our previous call, Dr. Matson, we really can't help with—"

Quick cut in, "Listen, my name is Sam Quick. Right now, I'm in a subbasement below the Prado, where, I understand, the president is due imminently. And I'm staring down into a suitcase packed with a black cylinder marked with that cute little radiation symbol, which you may recall from your ninth-grade science class, and a timer with fewer than seventeen minutes on its clock. Now, I strongly suggest you scoop your balls off the floor and activate the president's evacuation protocol."

The respondent silence lasted but a second. Then they heard a thunk and shouting—first one voice, and then many. The man's voice returned to phone. "Dr. Quick, I need your exact position. A special ops team is en route to the Prado. Their ETA to the museum plaza is two minutes."

"Your special ops won't cut it," Hunt said. "By the time they arrive, the only thing your team will accomplish is its thermonuclear vaporization."

"Then God help us all. We've alerted the president's security detail. There's no time to begin an evacuation of Madrid—"

"Molly, we really need some how-to from your end," Quick cut him off.

"I know, sweetie. My young man is typing faster than a secretary on Dexedrine. Just hold tight."

. . .

Less than half a mile from the suitcase, steel-toed dress shoes smashed gas pedals. The trio of 403-hp V-8 engines roared as gasoline, air freighted from the American Gulf Coast, flooded their combustion chambers. Tires squealed, and the three Cadillac SUVs veered hard onto a narrow side street, sending several Spanish escort motorcycles careening into each other.

Ten miles away, at Barajas International Airport, Colonel Edwards immediately began reciting the sequence that she knew better than her daughter's smile.

In the adjacent seats, the copilots flipped switches, stabbed buttons, and checked gauges in a tightly choreographed call-and-response exchange with the commander. In the main cabin, the attendants ran through the plane, prepping the seats and the situation room. On the tarmac surrounding the plane, the Marines raised their weapons and began widening the exclusion perimeter around *Air Force One*.

In the middle Cadillac, the hard turn had smashed President James against the agent sitting beside him. The SUV straightened out. The agent repositioned himself and tried to right the president.

But James brushed off his hands and barked, "What the hell

is going on?"

The president listened silently, as his chief of staff replied from the front seat, and the SUVs whipped onto an expressway ramp, and their speedometer needles swept past the 100 mark.

When the man finished speaking, the car was dead quiet except for the dull whoosh of the run-flat tires.

Then President James spoke loudly and without hesitation: "Open 'em. Open every one of them. Open the silos—and make damn sure all our enemies know it."

SUNDAY, JULY 15
Island of La Palma

The women continued running for another five minutes. Then Slater looked over her shoulder and then forward again. "Did we get turned around somehow?"

Amanda followed the trajectory of Slater's finger and whispered, "WTF?"

The women ran forward and then slid to a stop.

Amanda's dreadlocks whipped back and forth. "It *can't* be."

Slater's finger traveled the wall as if it were deciphering Braille rather than tracing dried yellow paint. "These are different geo coordinates. Which means that *El Diablo* is choking on not one, but at least two of these crazy suitcases."

Slater looked at Amanda. "And that our reasons for getting the hell out of here have doubled—"

Guttural shouts echoed in the tunnel behind.

"Make that increased exponentially—move!" Slater whispered, pushing Amanda onward. The women started running as fast as they could.

Behind them, the muzzles of four Micro Uzis jagged and weaved, following the women's footprints in the red mud. Thanks to adrenaline and the hormones of aggression, pulses raced and blood was shunted to the muscles of predation. The only sounds were rough breaths and combat boots slapping mud. No words were needed: each man knew exactly what his companions thought. Their brother's death would not go answered.

But these women would not meet as fast an end. No, before drawing their last breaths, these Americans would first discover what evil really lies in a devil's stomach.

Slater and Amanda sprinted for another hundred yards. The tracks and the lighting ended at a pile of rotting wooden ties. Slater jerked out a flashlight taken from the fallen guard.

She scrambled onto the woodpile and climbed up the ties. At the top, Slater flattened herself and shimmied on her stomach between the wood and the tunnel's rock ceiling, with Amanda at her feet. After crawling five yards this way, they reached the pile's far side. They jumped down and resumed their run, now completely in the dark other than the flashlight beam.

They ran several dozen more yards. Amanda yelped. Slater whipped the beam over her. Amanda was holding her head. Blood dripped from between her fingers. Beside her, a half-fallen timber cut diagonally across the passage.

They had to keep moving. But what now motivated Slater was not the men chasing them, but rather what she felt on her own brow. She put an arm around Amanda's shoulders and guided the woman under the timber.

On the far side, Slater stood tall and inhaled a deep breath of the fresh air now moving fast enough to lift the dark hair framing her sweaty face. *We're going to make it.*

-54-

Rivulets of sweat cut flesh-colored lines in the coal dust coating Hunt's face. Quick looked away from her intern and swallowed, as a beep from the suitcase marked a red flash: 5:00.

"Molly, if for some reason we don't make it—," Quick started.

"Hush now, sweetie. No need to turn all sentimental—"

Shouting interrupted Matson. Quick and Hunt heard the geologist bark, "Send out that file, pronto!"

Then Matson said, "Sam, my little friend finally hacked Langley's database and located the disarmament instructions. No doubt, the spooks have already launched a drone squadron to take us out. But assuming these protocols are fresh, you should be in like Flynn."

The line was silent for a moment. Then Matson added, "Good luck, kiddos."

Quick replied, "Thanks a million, Molly."

"Anytime, honey. OK, here comes the file."

Quick and Hunt's eyes locked on the phone. An amoeba could have outswam the lengthening download indicator bar.

While the suitcase flashed seemingly ever faster, hitting 3:19.

. . .

Two stories above the scientists, in the Prado's main gallery, the clip of heels against marble echoed so loudly that conversations halted as everyone turned to watch the French attaché cross the room like a power-walker in an American mall.

He stopped beside his ambassador. An instant later, the champagne flute delivered by the overly friendly Spanish server crashed against the marble floor. A murmur swept the gallery. The ambassador looked wildly around, spotted his wife, and violently gesticulated toward an exit, as he began sprinting with the attaché trailing at his heels.

"I guess you won't be doing any French kissing tonight—," Delgado started to say to the other waiter when a new cascade of fast-moving heels interrupted. The Italian contingent was now racing for the exits.

Then cellphones started shrilling throughout the gallery.

"There must be rumors of better food at another reception," the other waiter said.

"Either that or—"

People began running in every direction.

A scream rang out. Then another.

Stemware crashed to the floor. Serving platters clattered against marble and bronze.

The German finance minister slipped on some fallen canapés. A chain reaction ensued, with diplomats skating and falling on colorful piles of dropped food.

A Chinese official slammed into an enormous El Greco. The

wall-sized painting crashed down onto him, trapping him and several Canadians under the old canvas.

The two waiters each grabbed a champagne flute from Delgado's tray and moved against a wall. A stream of Spanish profanity caught their attention.

They looked around and found its source: their supervisor—her face papered with squares of smoked salmon, and her uniform pissed with red wine—struggling to rise from the slick marble.

-55-

Countless times during childhood, Slater had heard her grand-mother tell the story of the star that had guided their ancestors thousands of miles across the Pacific to settle the remotest archi-pelago on earth—the Hawaiian Islands. During the summer months, Arcturus, the Hawaiian zenith star, lay directly overhead at the latitude of the Big Island of Hawaii, lighting the ancient explorers' eastward path. Its glimmer always brought Slater com-fort, as if she were hearing her grandmother's voice.

And tonight was no different. Slater gazed up the narrow ven-tilation shaft at the rectangular opening. And the photons of light that had exploded from Arcturus nearly thirty-seven years earlier reached their final destinations—the retinas of her eyes—as if on a journey ordained more than a decade before her birth.

The descending breeze was strong on her face. She smelled the island trees' piney nocturnal exhalations and almost allowed herself to smile.

Slater turned to Amanda and tapped the lowest rung of the old metal ladder running up the shaft. "We're almost there, you first."

Amanda nodded and scrambled onto the first rung. The shaft

was barely large enough to accommodate a small adult. Her dreadlocks pushed upward like a chimneysweep's brush, knocking free dirt from the unlined sides. After Amanda had cleared the first few rungs, Slater clambered after her, and the women climbed in unison.

Then they heard the low rumble of an approaching freight train. The ladder jerked hard. Amanda almost lost her footing. The metal shook. Amanda screamed, as pebbles and dirt crashed down onto her dreadlocks from above.

Slater shouted, "A tremor. Hold on."

To wedge herself more tightly against Amanda, Slater stepped up another rung. But in her haste, her shoe landed on the thinnest, middle section of the rusted bar.

Her foot crashed through the rung, as the shaking stopped. Slater shot downward. The broken rung snagged her falling arm. She screamed. Her cry echoed up the ventilation shaft and broke free into the night air.

Slater landed on the tunnel floor.

Her head cracked against rock.

The flashlight jumped from her hand.

Amanda hugged the ladder and looked downward. The stone and dirt topping her dreadlocks poured down onto Slater like soil into a fresh grave.

In the dim light of the thrown flashlight, from her position, Amanda could only see an unmoving forearm sliced from wrist to elbow.

Amanda looked upward. The star centered in the rectangle of night sky appeared brighter than ever. Amanda listened for any hint of the approaching predators and chewed her lip.

-56-

The jewel glowed. But Sokolov ignored the flashing red light on the phone and instead continued staring at the monitor. Except for the people trailing from the main building, the pixilated image of the Prado remained unchanged. Every few seconds, his eyes flicked to the screen's lower-right corner, where the timestamp ticked relentlessly onward. After a final check, a guttural roar broke from his mouth.

He lifted the handset and waited for no words from the other end. Staring at the wall map, at the circled X obliterating Washington D.C., he said, "Punish the Americans—hobble the animals so that they may never again stand tall. Russia will rise again to greatness—and with it, you and I. This changes nothing. The decapitation strike failed. But the real event happens tomorrow. This is the key to Russia's future. Now go, darling, go with the greatest of care."

The disconnect button went down slowly and evenly.

Then Sokolov ripped up the phone. It smashed into the wall map. He spun his chair and gazed out the window. The stars teased him with their twinkling hints of thermonuclear conflagration.

. . .

2120 miles away, the Beretta Bobcat landed on the tabletop lying between the sisters. The glossy wood reflected the name carved on the whalebone grip: "Nin."

Its owner snatched up a handset and growled into the mouthpiece, "Proceed to the island at maximal speed." And the Legacy 600 banked hard to the southwest.

. . .

Seven miles beneath the Legacy, Quick and Hunt slapped hands.

"Let's not get ahead of ourselves," Quick said, kneeling beside the dead man. "Like we used to say in New Mexico: with sheep to range and coyotes howling, your night has just begun."

She coaxed out the Walther P99 peering from Utley's pocket. The gun slid under her waistband at the small of her back. Then Quick squeezed the hand that had trembled for so many years, and that had ended its exertions on this boiler-room floor, scrawling the word "island" in its master's blood.

I don't know who you are, she thought. *But thank you.*

She turned to Hunt. "Does your map show a back way out of this tomb?"

"Shouldn't we wait for the special ops team?"

"I'm afraid we've no time to hang around." Quick pointed at the ramp. "We must get back to La Palma. Kalia is waiting."

-57-

For a moment longer, Amanda searched the rectangle of star-filled sky for the answer. Then, carefully negotiating the rung that had failed Slater, she scrambled down the ladder.

As quietly as she could, she jumped off the bottom rung into a crouched position beside Slater.

"Kalia . . . Kalia," she whispered, patting the Hawaiian's cheeks.

Slater coughed and sat up, nearly knocking heads with the other woman. Amanda grabbed her and held a finger to Slater's lip. "We must be quiet."

Slater caught her breath. She lifted her arm. Blood was leaking from the long cut. "What happened?"

"I'll fill you in later. Right now, we need to climb this ladder and find a phone." Amanda wrapped her arm under Slater.

The Hawaiian rose to her knees and sucked in a breath. Holding Amanda's shoulder, she hoisted herself to her full height. Then her knees buckled, and she nearly went down before Amanda caught her.

"I'll only slow you down. You have to go without me. Take

the gun. Get help."

Amanda shook her head. "Lately I've made too many cowardly choices. Now it's time for some brave ones." She pointed into the darkness beyond the ladder. "We'll hide and they'll think we escaped up the ventilation shaft."

Slater smiled at the other woman. Then she took a deep breath, causing her face to contort.

"And if worse comes to worse . . ." Amanda patted the Micro Uzi still hanging across Slater's chest. She saw that Slater's face remained scrunched, and the injured woman's chest, frozen. "Does it hurt to breath?" she whispered.

Slater shook her head. Amanda's forehead wrinkled. The dreadlocks spilled their last bits of soil, as Amanda followed Kalia Slater's gaze and looked over her shoulder.

All Amanda could see were the four red laser sights glaring at her from the darkness.

-58-

Quick and Hunt glanced at each other. Then they both looked down again. The man standing before them wore baggy shorts and a T-shirt emblazoned with the name of a heavy-metal band, a close-cut dark beard, and a purple Mohawk that split his head in half. And, as Hunt noted to himself, even with the four-inch-high blade of hair, the man barely reached his chest.

The man nodded at the office window, at the tarmac beyond. "Davies said you need an off-the-books lift to the Canary Islands. I don't need your names, but you can call me 'Zero'." A thumb jacked at a small jet sitting on the runway outside the office. "Shall we?"

Quick nodded. "By all means."

Moments later, as the scientists buckled their seatbelts, the plane started moving. It made a sharp turn. Then it accelerated, pressing Quick and Hunt back into their seats. The fuselage and the runway formed a perfect thirteen-degree angle. The Gulfstream rose only briefly and then leveled. From their respective windows, the scientists watched suburban Madrid's circuit board of lit streets and dark buildings looming large below the plane.

"Welcome ladies and gentlemen to flight triple-zero, our service from Madrid to the lovely Canary Islands," the pilot's voice boomed from the PA speakers. "Tonight, until we are well clear of the Spanish capital, we'll cruise at five thousand feet. This altitude will require some sudden maneuvers"—the plane banked hard right—"to avoid certain topographical elements"—it dove hard left—"otherwise called mountains.

"Because we understand that some passengers have tight connections on La Palma, we'll travel tonight at our G550's maximal speed, just a hair shy of Mach 0.89. Now, please sit back and enjoy our two-hour flight."

The plane banked hard again, and Quick looked at Hunt. "So, are you ready to scrap your PhD and apply to law school?"

. . .

4400 miles away, the young seaman yanked up the handset. He listened for a moment and then offered the phone to his hovering companion.

"Yes?"

"Oh, hello, Dr. Matson, I'm calling from the Madrid embassy. We spoke earlier—"

"Ah yes, the gentleman whose intransigence nearly cost thousands of lives, including that of our nation's leader. If you're calling to ask me on a date, I'm afraid my calendar is full." Matson winked at the officer.

"Um yes . . . about earlier, I do apologize. But the actual reason for this call is that we have failed to locate Dr. Quick and Mr. Hunt. They have seemingly disappeared, and we fear they might be lost in the utility tunnels. In any case, we would very much like to debrief them regarding tonight's events. And"—his voice lowered in tone—"President James would like to personally thank Dr. Quick and Mr. Hunt for their service to the nation. Has Dr. Quick contacted you since she disarmed the bomb?"

"Sam Quick's a big girl—she hardly needs check in with me." Matson glanced at the wall clock. "I haven't a clue where either Sam Quick or Eric Hunt might be. Perhaps they're following a lead on Quick's other intern, the missing Kalia Slater. Or perhaps, after saving your hairless hinny, they simply went to get some well-deserved shuteye," she said, watching a green dot steadily track to the southwest from Madrid, across Spain, on the computer screen.

"Well, Dr. Matson, if you do hear from Dr. Quick, please ask her to contact the embassy ASAP."

"I'll put your telephone number right at the top of my speed-dial list—*numero uno*. Adios."

Matson passed the handset back to the seaman. "Now, why in the hell did Sam rush back to La Palma without letting me know?"

Matson's tanned hand glowed gold against the starched white fabric covering the young man's shoulder. "Honey, you might as well make yourself comfortable, because we're in for a long night. And while you're at it, pull up everything we've got on that damn Devil's Throat. I've a feeling Sam is about to perform a doozy of a Heimlich maneuver."

-59-

The suitcase's lights winked with the regularity of a used-car sales-man. Alongside it, the men pinned down Amanda in the center of the tracks. The dreadlocked woman twisted and struggled, but the men were stronger.

Using heavy plastic ties, one of the men bound Amanda's legs and arms to the rails by squatting at each appendage and using his full weight to tighten and lock the strap. Each time, the tie's sharp edges cut deeper into Amanda's skin, eliciting a fresh scream.

Slater clenched her fists. Seeing the men overpower and hurt Amanda killed her. Her head had cleared after the fall, and she was ready to fight again. But the red laser dots playing on her chest and forehead, coming from the guns, meant she could do nothing for Amanda—*right now anyway*.

After the men had fully secured Amanda, they pushed Slater onto the tracks and forced her prone in the opposite direction from Amanda, leaving the women situated head to shoulder.

The man repeated the binding procedure. As the plastic sliced into the already torn flesh of her arm, Slater remained silent, vow-ing to never give the bastards the satisfaction of hearing her pain.

She simply pictured herself riding her board, killing a giant wave off Pohioki, her favorite beach at home on the Big Island.

The man grunted and let go of Slater's last tie. He squatted beside the women's heads and pulled out two red handkerchiefs from a pocket. Amanda's head writhed back and forth until he grabbed her dreadlocks and cranked his hand, twisting the stalks. Amanda cried out, and he shoved one of the cloth squares into her mouth. He threaded a plastic strap around her head, locking the red gag in place. The procedure was repeated on Slater.

He rose and joined the other men. To the prone women, they appeared towering giants. A knife slipped from a pocket.

The man smiled at his companions and said something in their language. Goose pimples rose on Slater's legs and arms, as he moved for her. No mental imagery could protect her from what she knew was coming.

His pants squawked. He spoke sharply, scowling at his companions. The knife withdrew. The held air escaped Slater and Amanda's lungs, as the man pulled a walkie-talkie from a pocket and pushed a button. The women heard loud and command-like barks issue from the device.

The man looked down at the women and said something that caused his companions to laugh. Slater and Amanda watched the sneering men circle like vultures.

Then they were gone.

The women craned their heads and looked at each other. They could not speak. But their locked eyes affirmed what each woman was thinking: *The men would return. It was just a matter of when.* But for now, except for the metal suitcase, Slater and Amanda were alone in the Devil's Throat.

-60-

The cabin of the Gulfstream 550 was silent. From her seat, Quick glanced over at Hunt. Since they had departed Madrid, the grad student had been typing on his smartphone with the intensity of a video-game player about to crest his lifetime high score.

Quick turned back to her window and stared out again at the predawn sky. The whirling pieces returned to her mind: *Kalia Slater. Manuelo Alcanzar. La Garganta del Diablo. The Zanin sisters. Sergei Sokolov. The dead bodies in the coal tunnel. The old man in the boiler room. The suitcase bomb.* The images twisted and swirled like fallen leaves caught in an eddy of air on a warm October day.

What are we missing—

"Sam, you need to see this," Hunt said. Quick turned and found the grad student pointing at his phone. "Way more than just the Zanins will be waiting for us when we land on La Palma."

Quick took the phone and looked at the screen. She read, rapidly swiping her thumb over the glass to keep the text scrolling. "How—"

"Using the plane's satellite connection, I revisited the Sokolov administrative network, going back over the records to see if I could find a money trail tying Sokolov to the suitcase bomb. I tried back-tracing all shipments charged to Sokolov accounts destined for Spain during the previous six months. But I came up with *nada*. Then I expanded the time range. And still nothing."

"So, you tried shipments to Prague."

"Exactly. That's when I found an air shipment from Baku that landed in Prague on the same day as Nin Zanin did, before she flew on to Madrid and our first encounter with her."

Quick stopped scrolling. "And here it shows charges for a land shipment from Prague to a warehouse in Zaragoza, Spain, which arrived last Thursday."

She looked at Hunt. "But this manifest is for a shipment of four crates, each of identical weight. Which means not one but—"

"Four suitcase bombs," Hunt completed the sentence.

"So where are the other three?"

"Keep scrolling."

Quick's thumb flicked the phone. Then she stopped and stared at the screen.

"Yeah, you read right. A shipment of three crates left Zaragoza two days ago by plane heading for—"

"La Palma." Quick handed Hunt his phone. "We need to call Florida. Now."

. . .

"Molly, Eric and I are less than one hour away from landing on La Palma, and we've got a real problem."

"I figured you were headed that way," Matson's voice replied from the speaker of the phone lying on Quick's tray table.

"What's happening?"

Quick swiftly filled in Matson on Hunt's discovery. She ended, "So Sokolov and his girls are packing three suitcase nukes on a volcanic island in the eastern Atlantic, an island that is a known catastrophic landslide risk. Are you thinking what I am?"

The geologist was quiet for a moment. Then she answered. "Well, I'll be . . . They're gonna trigger—"

"The Red Pearl Effect," Quick finished.

Hunt looked at Quick. "The what?"

Matson answered for her, "The Red Pearl Effect was a military strategy that the Soviets threatened to use during a nuke attack. They planned to lay down a strand of nuclear bombs just off the port cities of America and her allies, effectively cauterizing the flow of goods and supplies between the U.S. and Europe. They'd starve any American war effort and then roll their tanks across Western Europe—that is if we didn't nuke 'em to smithereens first."

"Yeah, but the suitcase bombs are on La Palma, nowhere near the United States," Hunt pressed.

"They're going to trick Mother Nature into doing the dirty work. Remember La Palma's eruption of 1949 and the Big Slip?" Matson said.

"Of course. Why?" Hunt said.

"Well, if La Palma collapses into the ocean, the half-trillion-ton landslide will generate the granddaddy of all tidal waves. First, the wave overruns the Canary Islands. Then it crosses the Atlantic at near supersonic speeds, barely rising a bump while traversing deep water. Then it reaches the North American continental shelf, and the wave rears like an attacking *Tyrannosaurus rex.*

Nearly simultaneously, the hungry monster blasts Miami, Washington D.C., New York, and Boston. By then, the western coasts of northern Africa and Europe are already obliterated. Think Japanese tsunami—only a thousand times worse. And the bombs don't need to be anywhere near their targets."

"And let me guess," Hunt interjected, "all you need to kick off the landslide is maybe three small nuclear suitcase bombs strategically placed along the Big Slip fault line."

"*Et voilà*," Matson replied. "Your Red Pearl Effect—the total devastation of the American and European Atlantic coastlines."

"Molly, I assume, to maximize the destruction, you would time the wave to hit at high tide?" Quick asked.

"Absolutely."

Quick and Hunt heard Matson say something off the phone and then the immediate sound of typing. A few moments later, the geologist continued, "According to our calculations, to maximize damage with the next high tide affecting the greatest area of northern Atlantic shoreline, factoring in the tsunami's travel time, the detonation will need to occur at roughly eight a.m. La Palma time. Less than two hours from now. Unless our Navy happens to have a ship in the vicinity—"

"It's up to Eric and me," Quick said. "Molly, I hate to say this: you need to call the Pentagon."

. . .

The hammer smashed against his scalp. He screamed. Blood turned the world red. He raised his hands and tried to stop Dr. Quick. But after the strike and consequent gush of blood, his strength was ebbing like the tide. The blows rained down. His consciousness was a boat on the outflowing sea. Dr. Quick smiled at him and, in preparation for the coup de grâce, raised the hammer high above her naked body. The tiny vessel carrying his consciousness slipped beyond the horizon, and all was dark.

"*¡Idiota!*" Señora Reyes smacked her husband's forehead again. "*¡El teléfono! ¡¡El teléfono!!*"

The inspector sat up, pushed away his wife's meaty hand, and then felt his head to confirm that it was actually intact. The phone on his nightstand continued ringing. He sighed and snapped on a lamp.

"*¿Sí?*"

"Inspector Reyes, it's Sam Quick. The duty officer at the Tazacorte police station gave me your home telephone number."

Reyes made a mental note to assign the man to inspect the eastern guano caves tomorrow for smugglers. "Sí, Dr. Quick, how may I be of assistance at this"—Reyes looked at his alarm clock and sighed—"early hour?"

"Inspector, Eric Hunt and I will land on La Palma in less than one hour." Reyes felt the hammer renew its assault on his head, as Quick continued, "We're trailing the Zanin sisters, who were involved with a now-aborted attack on the ICF meeting in Madrid, and who are flying approximately forty minutes ahead in their own plane. We suspect Kalia Slater is being held somewhere on La Palma, most likely in the Devil's Throat. And we believe the Zanins plan a horrific attack on the United States and Europe, and, in the process, the destruction of La Palma."

"Oh, come now, Dr. Quick—"

"Inspector, I need you to muster your subordinates and meet us at the mine. And if your arsenal includes any automatic weapons, I suggest bringing them. We will be there as soon as possible."

A click came from the handset. Reyes sighed, put down the receiver, and looked at the blanket-covered mound lying alongside him. His wife's face scrunched, as a snort broke from her mouth and echoed throughout the bedroom. He checked the time again and shook his head.

Then, his head throbbing, Inspector Reyes crawled beneath the coverlet and snuggled against his wife's warm body.

MONDAY, JULY 16
The Eastern Atlantic

The night predators had had their fill. Before morning's first light, which can turn the eater into the eaten, the nocturnia had returned to their respective lairs: some to the island's volcanic caves, some to deep burrows in the malvasia vineyards, and some to the waxy undersides of the banana tree leaves. But one creature remained on the hunt, lowering its wheels as it glided toward the airport's 7200 feet of runway.

Nin Zanin sighed and shoved her Beretta Bobcat into its thigh holster. "Sister, we are so very close: we need only finalize the detonation sequence to maximize the landfall—"

"*The landslide . . . the landslide . . .* you and Sergei never get this term right," Solta Zanin corrected.

"Yes, of course, to maximize the *landslide,* the suitcases must explode in the proper sequence with the appropriate interval between each detonation. And Dr. Quick can't interfere this time. She's probably still running about the coal tunnels looking for her missing intern—three hours away in Madrid."

The phone barked. Nin sighed and reached for it. She listened, as the thin lights of La Palma grew outside the window, and the jet glided just faster than stall speed.

Opposite, Solta watched her sister's lip curl.

"Sí. *Gracias.*" The satellite phone returned to its compartment. Nin looked at her sister. "That was our man on the island police force." She lifted the cabin phone and spoke rapidly in Azerbaijani. The Legacy's wheels bounced on the tarmac. The plane hung just above the pavement.

Then the engines roared.

In the airport tower, the solitary controller looked up from a laptop screen filled by writhing bodies to see the night predator shoot back into the sky. The Spanish controller shrugged and returned to watching her monitor and the drunken American college boys on spring break.

. . .

"OK, ladies and gentlemen, please ensure that your tray-table is stowed, that your carryon luggage is pushed fully beneath the seat in front of you, and that your seatback is in the upright, locked position. It's been our pleasure to serve you on this hop from Madrid to La Palma. We'll be on the ground shortly."

Quick looked out the window, at the emerging dark hulk of the island volcano chain. Just hold on a little longer, Kalia, she thought, picturing a scan of the mountain and Slater hidden in its throat.

A slight vibration and groan marked the wheels' descendent.

She turned from her window and looked across the aisle. The portals on the plane's east-facing side were glowing sapphire blue, with dawn's earliest light mixing with the dark sky.

The engines relaxed, and the whoosh of the ventilation

system dominated, as the Gulfstream glided into its final approach.

Hunt pocketed his smartphone and looked at Quick. "I'll be glad when we're back on terra firma—"

Suddenly the Gulfstream 550 twisted and screamed. Quick and Hunt hurtled violently sideways, as the plane banked impossibly hard toward the mountain, pushing the Gulfstream's avionics to their limits.

From the open cockpit, an electronic voice barked, "Pull up! Pull up! Pull Up!"

The control panel flashed red. A purple shark fin of hair surfaced above the captain's chair, as the little pilot pulled back on the stick with the force of his entire body, rising up from his seat.

The Gulfstream climbed so steeply that the plane threatened to roll over backwards. Hunt crushed his armrests, while Quick planted her feet and tightened her grip as if riding one of the stallions of her childhood ranch.

Just as the Gulfstream neared impact with the mountain face, the plane's wheels returned to their wells, and the craft's belly skimmed the rock wall.

Then the windows flashed orange. The sonic wave hit the tail of the Gulfstream and washed along the jet as if a giant were shaking out his laundry.

"What the hell was that?" Hunt shouted over the turbines' screeching.

In the tower, the air traffic controller ran to the window. Such a large explosion on the mountain could mean only one thing, she thought—a fatal car accident on a twisty road. She crossed herself and hoped that none of her grandchildren had gone for one of their late-night joyrides.

In the Gulfstream's cockpit, the electronic voice went quiet, and the purple Mohawk submerged below the seatback. After the near-vertical climb, now level at 6500 feet, the plane banked again, this time hard to right, putting the jet on its side again.

Photons of light, which had left Arcturus only hours after those that had beamed hope down the airshaft to Slater and Amanda, pierced Hunt's window. From her side, facing groundward, Quick watched a red line of runway lights wink as if taunting them.

The Gulfstream pulled out of the turn. No longer bothering with the PA, Zero shouted, "Reports of turbulence ahead, so I'm gonna turn on the 'Fasten Seatbelt' sign."

The Gulfstream banked again and came around hard. "If you're outgunned, there's only one way to fight an enemy aircraft." The throttle met its stop, as the pilot relaxed into his chair and completed the thought at the maximum volume that his lungs allowed, "That's head-on!"

-62-

"What does he mean head-on?" Hunt shouted.

The click of Quick's seatbelt was the only response. The scientist jumped up, scrambled into the cockpit, and climbed onto the empty seat. "I thought you might enjoy some company."

"I never turn away a pretty copilot." Zero nodded at the small jet turning in their direction, framed against the predawn stars. "Friend of yours?"

"Nah, we never really hit it off, but she just can't take a hint," Quick said, buckling herself in.

"Yeah, I've dated a few women like that. Though none have ever hunted me with air-to-air missiles."

Zero pointed to a lever on the center console. "You're in charge of the throttle. Just follow my instructions"—the volume of his voice rose to a shout for Hunt's benefit—"and everything will be just fine."

"Yeah, right," Hunt muttered, pressing himself deeper into his seat.

Quick palmed the throttle lever, while the Gulfstream jagged toward the reds and greens of the mountains. Then Zero cranked the control wheel. The plane went on its side, with its wings nearly perpendicular to a banana plantation below.

In the Legacy 600, the two Azerbaijani pilots gave each other the thumbs up. For twenty years, their killing skills—honed in the tight gorges of Afghanistan's Sanglakh Mountains, in service of the Soviet military—had lain dormant. And although the Legacy 600 was a little more than a model aircraft compared to the Soviet MiG-29s that the men had flown on attack sorties in Afghanistan, the remaining Vympel R-73 short-range missile affixed under the wing was every bit as deadly as the precision bombs that had obliterated countless Afghani fighters. Known to NATO forces as the Archer, the R-73 was a killer of both slight build—less than 10 feet long and 7 inches in diameter—and great range, effective from 1000 feet to nearly 20 miles.

Despite Nin's command—"Get it done. Now!"—echoing in the men's headphones, the pilots waited for the surest line of attack, calmly tracking their prey, now streaking on its side toward the mountain ridge in a hyperbolic arc.

In the Gulfstream, Zero said, "Ease it back a bit," as the plane's belly skimmed the mountain's bumpy face, and Quick pulled the throttle.

"OK, perfect." Zero locked his eyes on the Legacy. "Now, on my command, throttle to full." He yanked the control stalk. The plane shot away from the mountain and swept directly at the Legacy 600.

"Hit it."

Quick jammed the throttle forward. Jet fuel flooded the engines; the turbines screamed; the resultant thrust slammed all three passengers deep into their seats.

Profanities filled the Legacy's cockpit. In both aircraft and in the control tower, flashing lights and braying computers announced the imminent collision. With the planes flying head-on at maximal speeds, the gap between the jets was closing so rapidly that launching the heat-seeking Archer could only assure mutual destruction.

Quick stared glacially ahead at her onrushing opponents. While, the Azerbaijani pilots, cursing, jammed their sticks to the forward limits. The Legacy plunged. The Zanin sisters levitated, tethered only by their seatbelts, as their luxurious perches fell from beneath them. In the flight tower, the controller ran back to the window.

The leaves of the banana trees twisted and whipped as if subjected to hurricane-force winds. Overhead, at an altitude of 150 feet, the Legacy wrestled out of the dive, its avionic cables and hydraulic lines straining at their failure points. As the plane righted, red nails began clicking against burled walnut in the cabin, while the Azerbaijani pilots practically salivated up front.

The Gulfstream completed a hairpin maneuver and steeply descended. "Time to land before they have a clear shot," Zero said, snapping switches and cranking knobs with one hand, while he managed the stalk with his other one. "Thankfully, we've got a good stretch of tar, because at this airspeed, we'll need every inch."

The 550 shuddered hard, as the landing gear made an encore appearance at airspeed far higher than the equipment's engineered tolerance. The computer called the altitude in halting clips: "1200 feet . . . 900 feet . . . 700 feet . . ."

To the north, the Legacy 600 regained altitude and banked

hard, arcing out over the Atlantic, and then again to the south, toward the airport.

"300 feet . . . 100 feet . . . 50 feet . . . 25 feet . . ."

Both Quick and Zero saw the bright flash marking the Legacy's location.

The Archer wobbled for a millisecond. Then its cryogenically cooled, heat-seeking tip locked on the thermal emissions of the gliding Gulfstream, whose wheels neared touch down. The Archer raced for its target at more than twice the speed of sound.

"Plan B—brace!"

The purple-haired pilot cranked the control stalk. The Gulfstream's right wingtip dug into the runway. For an instant, the rivets and welds held, with the plane pinwheeling around an axis through the intersection of the wingtip and concrete. And had the fasteners remained true, after arcing less than 180 degrees, the plane would have smashed nose-first into pavement still warm after the tropical night. But torque forces ripped off the metal slab like a child pulling the wing off a dragonfly.

The wing, the attached engine, and its internal fuel tanks shot off in one direction. The remainder of the Gulfstream arced into the air, catapulted onward.

The discarded wing slid along the runway with a shower of sparks and burst into flame. The contents of its fuel tanks instantly oxidized into a massive thermal target. The Archer's tracking algorithms immediately redirected the missile toward the higher-intensity heat source.

The projectile slammed into the burning debris. Strings of molten aluminum and superheated chunks of concrete rose to look the air traffic controller straight in the eye—a sight far wilder than any displayed on the Spaniard's laptop screen that night.

The remainder of the Gulfstream—the fuselage, tail, and left wing—after traveling another 200 feet, crashed onto its wingless side and skidded off the runway.

The Legacy banked. Nin and Solta looked down from their windows. In the predawn blue-gray, two twisted piles burned on the airfield below, neither far from the tiny terminal building and its steeple filled with radar screens.

Nin looked at her sister. "We must make other arrangements for our journey's final leg—this airport is closed."

- 6 3 -

MONDAY, JULY 16
The Mid Atlantic

Air Force One was nearly halfway across the Atlantic. And the president's private conference room was dead silent save for the roar of the four engines relentlessly speeding the leader of the free world to his seat of power—Washington D.C.

The president looked at his top aides, each of whom were staring at him. Never before had he seen them all speechless. He was shocked himself. But nothing stopped Jasper James for long.

"Goddamn it," he thundered, slamming his hand down on the table. "What do you mean we have no military assets close enough to this island to go in and clean this up?"

"As I said, sir, the Canary Islands are not on our threat list. Our nearest strike force is already en route, but their ETA is one hour, forty-five," the secretary of defense answered, his voice issuing from the surrounding speakers, and his lips moving on the high-definition video screen affixed to the wall.

"Well, can't we just nuke the hell out of the island, vaporize the damn thing?" James pressed.

Howls rose from around the table, with the secretary of state appearing ready to leap up onto the conference table. "Mr.

President, do you realize what you are suggesting? Nothing short of the vaporization of an entire island and its population, an island territory of a sovereign power and ally, no less—"

James held up a hand. "I'd like to hear the response, if you don't mind."

"Mr. President," the secretary of defense said, "our analysts have looked very closely at exactly that option—a coordinated thermonuclear bombardment on La Palma to preempt any landslide."

James rolled his hand impatiently. "Get to the 'but,' man."

"But our best estimates for the payload required to turn the island into ash and dust range from 20,000 to 30,000 times the firepower used on Hiroshima. Obviously, we have the assets to delivery such force," the secretary continued. "But even assuming such massive bombardment, our analysts can give only a sixty percent confidence level for mission success. A significant risk would remain of residual debris generating a landslide and tsunami that would catastrophically affect the United States and her Atlantic allies, not to the mention the massive release of radiation from the bombardment—the cure may kill the patient. I'm afraid our nuclear arsenal is useless in the face of this threat."

"So, you're telling me that until our strike force arrives, our best hope is Sam Quick," James said. "We may have no choice but to accept that. But you are wrong about one thing: the nuclear arsenal of the United States of America is anything but useless." James looked around the conference table. "Because if so much as a ripple caused by this Sokolov character lands on American shores, then we hit Russia."

James looked at his chief of staff. "Now get me the Russian

president on the phone."

. . .

1000 miles away, the Legacy 600 looped around La Palma's southern tip. Above the black sands of Fuencaliente, the plane leveled at 11,000 feet and tacked northward. Nin and Solta Zanin faced each other, standing. They pulled at each other's waist straps like mothers adjusting cummerbunds before a first prom.

Both satisfied, they nodded. Nin rotated a handle. Cold air rushed the Legacy's cabin, whisking the women's silken hair from their faces. The still-shadowed western face of the volcano gazed up at them, while thinly scattered lights twinkled on the apron of ground separating the mountains and the sea.

Nin blew a kiss at her sister. Then Solta locked her thumbs beneath the nylon straps and leapt through the open doorway.

While she silently counted to twenty, Nin surveyed the lavish cabin a last time. Then she followed her sister into the darkness, spreading her arms and legs, with the rushing air growing ever warmer as she plummeted. She watched Solta's red chute flower beneath her and, below that, the beacon's rhythmic red wink at La Garganta del Diablo's entrance, as if a firefly were dancing on the tip of the devil's tongue.

Nin's chute opened. The ram-air's fabric cells filled, jerking her to her feet. The fall became a gentle drift. Nin worked her lines, tracking her sister with a paratrooper's precision. The blurred mountainside resolved into rock shards grouted with green and brown foliage. The rusted buildings marking the mine's entrance came into view. Moments later, beside Solta's collapsed chute, Nin's feet hit the gravel, her legs absorbing the landing's shock.

On the Legacy 600, the external door had been resealed after the sisters' departure. Near Nin's seat, the satellite phone blinked and rang with a La Palma telephone number flashing on its display. But in the cockpit, the two pilots failed to hear the phone. In turns, the men were recounting the Gulfstream attack. With each change of narrator, the volume of the voice rose, the distance of the missile strike lengthened, and the credit for the targeting changed.

As the senior pilot claimed that his hand had guided the Archer into the intake of the Gulfstream's engine with the same finesse that he used with his young mistress, a timer in the passenger cabin went off.

A millisecond later at the mine yard, a flash raised the heads of the sisters and the surrounding men. A sonic blast, no louder than a feeble thunderclap, arrived a fraction of a second after, as the Legacy's flaming wreckage plummeted seaward.

Nin smiled as her sister and said in English, "The aviation day on La Palma has not enjoyed a particularly auspicious start." Solta returned Nin's look, while the men furrowed their brows, unable to understand the foreign tongue. Then Nin pointed at the path leading to the mine entrance.

As they passed into the Devil's Throat, Nin handed a slip of paper to Solta and said, still in English, "Here are the arming instructions." Her head tilted toward the men. "After you've finished with your suitcase, you know what to do."

Solta nodded.

Then each sister with two men in tow started down into the mine. At the first junction, one sister and her escorts turned to the right, following the lights hung by Quick's expedition, while the other twin and her men marched off to the left.

. . .

The sweaty bond between Inspector and señora Reyes broke with the sound of separating Velcro. The inspector sat up and pushed off the blanket. Sitting on the bed's edge, Reyes sighed and shook his head. Dr. Quick would never let him rest.

He answered the phone. "¿Sí?" He sat listening for several seconds. Then a glowing iron spike rammed into his skull, and he cut the sign of a cross in front of himself.

"Was anyone killed? . . . I understand . . . A woman fled the scene?" His brow writhed. "Did this woman perhaps have dark, shoulder-length hair and a beautiful if stubborn face?"

Despite the spike poking out from his temple, Reyes smiled. "Yes, perhaps I know who she is . . . No, I cannot come. I must attend to another matter . . . Sí, sí, something more important than a plane crash. The constables from the Santa Cruz station will suffice until the Policía Nacional arrive from Gran Canaria. Adios."

Reyes disconnected the call and dialed a new number. "Sí, I know, but forget the plane crash, pick me up at my home." Recalling Dr. Quick's admonition to bring heavy weaponry, he added, "Grab two flashlights. And no sirens, understand!"

In the Tazacorte police station, the officer hung up the phone and then immediately dialed the number to the satellite phone. His brow wrinkled. The computerized voice repeated its chant: "The party you are trying to reach is unable to accept calls at this time. Please try again later."

The officer sighed and replaced the receiver. As he went to retrieve the flashlights ordered by Reyes, his hand massaged his service revolver's grip.

. . .

Soot covered her face. Her clothes were torn. Every muscle and joint ached. But Sam Quick could not have cared less. The engine of the red Jeep roared, as she slammed the transmission into first gear and cranked the wheel. A sheet of gulls rose in panicked flight, shrilling their displeasure, as the 4x4 pounded by.

With one hand on the steering wheel, Quick fished out the phone, with its disarmament instructions, from a pocket. Its interface was cracked like a shattered windshield, and one edge was deeply dented. Quick tossed it on the passenger seat. Then she reached behind her back and pulled out the Walther P99 that she had grabbed from the old man's pocket in the Prado's subbasement. The gun joined the phone on the seat.

Both hands now clamped on the steering wheel, Quick glanced at the pavement falling away in the rearview mirror. She pictured Kalia Slater during the drive to the mine exactly one week ago: the young Hawaiian laughing and chatting with Eric Hunt, as the interns sat in the back, taking in the island's sights . . . Manuelo Alcanzar, both as he sat beside her during the drive to the mine and, later that day, as he lay shot, facedown at the entrance to La Garganta del Diablo . . . the decapitated corpse in the Prague morgue . . . Zach Davies lying in his hospital bed, his arm bandaged . . . Hunt crumpled on the runway outside the burning aircraft . . . then the Zanin sisters popped into view.

Quick glanced at the heavier of her two front-seat passengers. Her execution of the plan would be as cold and methodical as her scientific training demanded. But the fire driving her forward was as raw and primal as the very forces that had created this volcanic isle and that now threatened to tear it asunder.

The Jeep careened onto the road bisecting the island into its northern and southern halves. The blacktop steadily climbed, and the Jeep's speed grew in direct proportion to the distance between the colorful houses alongside the road. On the straight stretches, the speedometer's needle flicked the triple-digit mark and then plunged as the Jeep approached the next hairpin curve. Alongside the road, the banana groves climbed in stepwise fashion up the volcanic spine.

Quick inhaled deeply, pulling in the mixed smells of the sea, soil, and volcano. The Jeep hooked into a switchback, as the first direct rays of sunlight shot from the eastern horizon and, bouncing from the vehicle's mirrors, dappled her face, while Sam Quick stared at the road ahead.

- 6 4 -

MONDAY, JULY 16
Island of La Palma

The engine died. The red Jeep rolled to a stop in the middle of the two-track, about three hundred yards below the mine, at a spot hemmed in by brush and rocks. The early morning on the mountainside was hushed, peaceful: Streaks of blue now infused the sky. The morning birds were softly chirping. The wet air, exhaled overnight by the vegetation and hills, hung close to the ground.

Quick quietly grabbed the Walther P99 and Hunt's phone, and squeezed out of the Jeep, carefully closing the door after herself. She shoved the gun under her waistband and slipped between the vehicle and a formation of jagged rock. Once past the rocks, she pressed a button on the phone. Despite the cracked interface, the screen immediately came alive, and Quick ordered 34:45 on the timer—the exact number of minutes and seconds until the likely detonation. Then she shoved it in her pocket and started running along one of the two-track's weed-strewn paths.

She sprinted but then slowed as the road turned sharply. Sixty feet before her, the awakening sky outlined the mine's dying outbuildings and rusting machinery. The structures were dark, and she saw no vehicles other than the abandoned mining equipment. But a steady hum set Quick's jaw.

She moved forward, crouched low, crossing the work yard, and flattened herself against the generator shed.

She rose and peered through a window. The light dripping from holes pocking the rusted ceiling barely illuminated a second, larger dynamo droning beside her expedition's generator. Quick figured she could switch them both off to slow whatever task occupied the Zanin sisters. *Except doing would also slow me and also might endanger Kalia.*

Instead, she moved inside and grabbed one of the flashlights lying stacked beside the generators and then started tracking the electrical cables snaking toward the mine.

Outside, the sky was now a pale blue. Half running, half crouching, she crossed the mine yard, until she stopped beside the timber-framed entrance to La Garganta del Diablo. She leaned forward and surveyed the tunnel. The mine's stale breath hit her in the face. But the shaft was empty save for the cabling and rails. She took a last gulp of fresh air and pulled out the Walther. Then the muddy gravel crunched beneath her shoes, as the mine swallowed her.

Approaching the first junction, her pace slowed. Here, the cables split into two branches. Her eyes followed the lights hung by her expedition, which led to the right, toward the site where she and Hunt had collected soil samples.

"But the other is just as fair," Quick whispered, as she and the Walther hooked hard left, shadowing the lamps that had been newly hung since her last visit.

. . .

Inspector Reyes's head still ached, but now with good reason. His junior officer drove as if he were charging atop a mainland freeway rather than laboring along an island two-track. Weeds scraped the car's sides, and stones banged against the undercarriage. And every time the compact slammed into a pothole, Reyes's head smashed against the headliner.

The car rounded a tight curve. Reyes threw up his arms and shouted, "Stop!"

The locked tires slid on the loose gravel. Reyes glared at the rear bumper of Quick's Jeep, which now lay only inches before the police car. He sighed, grabbed the flashlights, and handed one to his subordinate. "Nice driving."

In front of the Jeep and the rock formation, Reyes and the officer each silently claimed one of the worn tracks. When they reached the work yard, a now clear-blue sky backlit the old buildings. Reyes swore again. He saw no signs of new activity. Everything was as he and his men had left it after collecting the physical evidence of Manuelo Alcanzar's shooting.

"I have a good mind to leave her on the mountain and go attend to the plane crash," Reyes said, as his ears tuned into the electric hum. Of course, he thought, Dr. Quick has fired up her generator and entered the mine.

"Well, in that case," he said aloud, "I'll do exactly what draws my grandchildren from the fields after sunset—I'll flick off and on the veranda lights."

The younger officer shrugged and followed Reyes toward the generator shed.

"Yes, that's exactly what I'll do, I'll turn off and on the lights in the mine three times—" Reyes stopped in the doorway. "What do we have here?" he asked, briefly forgetting his headache as he stared at the new generator sitting beside Quick's.

The ring of metal digging beneath his scapula had no answer.

"What on earth are you doing?" Inspector Reyes barked, whirling around.

His officer answered by cracking the gun against the pink skin lying just behind the inspector's right ear.

. . .

The echoing footfalls lashed the women. Slater tried resolving the jumbled sounds into an image—of the number and intent—of their originators. But she could only determine with any certainty that the feet approached from the direction of the chamber where she and Amanda had been held captive. And that given the women's orientation on the tracks—bound heads together, in front of the suitcase—the encroaching person or persons would reach Amanda first.

The echoes grew louder, and the crunch of stone and the squish of wet mud joined in accompaniment. Slater twisted her head and found Amanda's two large eyes locked on her. Now the metal rails, to which their wrists and ankles were bound, reverberated with each new footfall, eliciting whimpers from Amanda.

Slater's eyes widened as a face appeared directly above hers. It was the first female visage that she had seen since her abduction at the hotel other than Amanda's. Beautiful, shiny black hair framed the face. Slater watched its carefully painted lips part, revealing bright teeth, white like those of the sharks at home in Hawaii.

"Hello," the woman said in English. "No, no, please don't

bother to get up. I see you are comfortable where you are. In any case, I have no time to chat. But I promise I'll be out of your hair just as soon as I attend to this lovely luggage."

Slater watched the woman turn and kneel between her and the suitcase. She heard the click of nails on plastic and metal, interspliced with a series of electronic beeps. She saw the woman pause, check her watch, and then press a final sequence of keys. Then a long beep sounded. The woman rose from the suitcase and turned toward her and Amanda.

"See, no time at all!" The woman smiled. "Now, my dears, I must go meet my sister. We have a seaplane to catch." She barked something at the men in their language and then pressed herself against the tunnel wall beside the suitcase.

In response, grinning broadly, the men jumped forward and knelt with one at each bound woman's head. Slater's stomach churned as the woman laughed. "Not to worry, I assure you they won't bother you long."

Knives sprang and moved for the plastic straps binding the women's wrists.

Slater felt Amanda's face burrow into her neck. She watched the men nudge each other and laugh at the woman's fear. But Kalia Slater was much more interested in the woman, who was smiling down on the scene from the behind the men, like a doting teacher.

Slater barely flinched as the bullet shattered the skull of the first man, slamming him down atop Amanda. She watched the Bobcat redirected its attack. Another shot rang out. The second man crashed down on her like a load of cement, blocking out all light and air.

Beside her, Amanda was thrashing and screaming. For several seconds, Slater struggled against the wet body pressing down on her face. Then she did what a life lived on the Pacific had taught her: as if a rip current had sucked her beneath the ocean's surface, she relaxed her body to conserve whatever oxygen remained within her cells and began silently counting the seconds. As Slater knew from her many close calls while surfing in Hawaii, the tally would reach no higher than two hundred before darkness fell.

MONDAY, JULY 16
North Atlantic Ocean

Alphanumeric characters popped on the dark screen like tiny, pixelated explosions of fireworks spelling a celebratory message across a night sky. Except instead of wishing a Happy July 4 or congratulations to a local sports team, the message consisted of four lines of garbled, meaningless text.

The ensign seated at the console immediately began typing the day's 32-digit authentication code. After a final entry, the four code lines instantly transmuted to a readable message.

Lt. Commander Elijah Robsen read the dispatch over the ensign's shoulder. Then he turned and calmly walked to a manned console on the room's opposite side. A message originating from a different command center, received via a different comm network, and deciphered with a different authentication code filled this screen. But down to the last character, the text was identical to the message burning on the first monitor.

Robsen read it one more time. *Sweet mother,* he thought. This mental exclamation surprised him, defying all his discipline. But the question of why never entered his mind. The countless drills, role-plays, and hours of psychological training had successfully suppressed that curiosity at least.

Robsen moved with a slow and deliberate step for a third console. Here, he pressed his thumb against a scanner and stared directly into an iris reader. A green light flashed. His voice, toneless and clear, rendered the command, "Launch depth. Prepare twenty-four. One target coordinate: 55.7500° N, 37.6167° E. Hold launch for my command."

Throughout the 560-feet length of the *U.S.S. Maryland*, amber lights silently exploded. Only those submariners performing critical tasks continued as they were. All other crew members immediately moved for their assigned stations, each sailor instantly amped by the adrenaline flood triggered by this highest call of battle.

The *Maryland*, along with the thirteen other Ohio-class submarines, formed one leg of America's three-prong air-sea-land strategic nuclear deterrence, with each sub carrying up to twenty-four Trident II missiles, and a total strike force of nearly three thousand Hiroshima events.

At any one time, the United States deployed a varying, classified number of the submarines from both its Pacific base in Bangor, Washington, and its Atlantic base in Kings Bay, Georgia. These deterrence missions silently delivered American missiles to within fast-strike distance of enemy coastlines on a constant, rotating basis. Any seaside nation considering an attack on the United States faced the possibility that nearly fifty thousand kilotons of American nuclear firepower waited at its doorstep—the ultimate "try me if you dare."

Until Robsen's command, the *Maryland* had been running at a depth of 330 feet, approximately two hundred miles south of the Icelandic coast, en route to a deployment in the Barents Sea on Russia's northern flank. But now the sub was rising fast and its forward motion, virtually halted.

Robsen calculated a rough launch-to-strike time. From this position, he figured the missiles would reach Moscow less than twelve minutes after leaving their silos. *And it wouldn't be much longer before Russia's retaliatory strike hit home.*

-66-

The sounds of gunfire arrived from two directions: two sharp shots directly ahead in the tunnel, and two distant pops behind her.

Quick stopped.

The Zanins must have split up, with one sister ahead, and one behind, both shooting their Bobcats twice in coordinated attacks.

The phone's cracked face flashed 28:02.

No time to wait for more information.

Instead, Quick shoved the Walther into the lead and continued running forward.

The shaft bent to the right in a large-diameter arc. From ahead, she heard the murmur of a familiar female voice. Her thumb quietly cocked the P99. She thought about simply killing the speaker. *But then I lose the element of surprise with the other sister. No, I must try for a quiet take.*

The voice grew louder as Quick crept further into the curve, and the murmurs resolved into comprehensible words: "You didn't think I would allow you to suffocate, did you, my dear?"

Quick paused at the final point where she would remain

invisible to the speaker. Craning forward, she watched the woman drag a man's body from the tracks twenty feet ahead: *Solta Zanin.*

The body slid free of the rails, revealing Slater lying centered and bound on the tracks, with blood smearing her face and heaving chest.

Seeing Slater, Quick reconsidered putting the bullet in Solta's head. *But I can't risk everything by alerting Nin, even for Kalia.*

Solta dropped the man's feet and turned back to Slater, continuing, "Perhaps my sister would permit such a slow death, but I'm not that sadistic. No, you'll enjoy the ultimate end: a painless death during which every atom in your pert little body is instantly consumed"—she gestured at the suitcase with her hands held palms-up like a TV game-show hostess presenting a prize—"in a thermonuclear furnace."

Then Solta bent and began hauling a second body from atop what Quick saw was another woman bound with Slater. "A rather easy death I'd say—"

Now was as good a time as any. "Step back. Now!" Quick shouted, advancing rapidly with the Walther locked on Solta.

Solta looked up, eyes wide, teeth glinting. "A cat has many lives, indeed." She released the body, slowly straightened up, and stepped away from the tracks.

Quick moved in. Her gun maintained its aim. And Solta reached for her red skirt as if to smooth it after standing.

"I wouldn't if I were you," Quick said. "Shooting you doesn't suit me just now. But my first bullet will rip into your heart before your hand slips under that pretty fabric, not to mention onto the grip of your Beretta Bobcat."

Solta shrugged and tossed up her hands. "Since you put it so graciously, Dr. Quick."

Keeping the gun on Solta, Quick grabbed some of the leftover plastic ties lying beside Amanda's feet. Then she closed in and pressed the muzzle into the exposed hollow marking Solta's breastbone. Staring into the other woman's eyes, Quick slipped her free hand under the red skirt and liberated the Bobcat, which she tossed aside.

"Turn around and cross your wrists behind your back."

Solta sighed but rotated the 180 degrees. The plastic strap bound her overlapping wrists. Quick stepped back. Then her shoe slammed the red skirt. Solta fell face-first into the arms of the corpse that she had hauled from atop Kalia Slater.

"You have a real way with the men," Quick said, as Solta glared back at her.

Then Quick turned to Slater, who was staring up at her from the tracks, her mouth still plugged by the red handkerchief. "I've never been so glad to find an intern lying down on the job."

She grabbed one of the men's dropped knives and attacked the binds securing Slater's arms. The grad student sat up with her legs still bound, and Quick pushed the knife into Slater's hand. "Finish freeing yourself and then your friend."

With the gag still in place, Slater could only nod in response.

Quick wheeled around and crouched by the suitcase. The smartphone landed beside her. She glanced at the suitcase timer and then at the countdown flashing on the phone display, confirming that the bomb's detonation was scheduled for the expected 8 a.m. *Giving me exactly 27:17.*

She pressed a button on the phone, and its cracked screen

displayed the jaggedly lettered but still readable disarming instructions. Then she firmly depressed the center button of the suitcase keypad.

Behind her, Slater was working the blade between the strap holding the gag in place and her cheek, while Amanda continued squirming against her binds, and Solta lay watching the women.

The strap broke, and Slater ripped the gag from her mouth. "And I've never been so glad to have my boss check up on me." Then she jumped to Amanda and slipped the knife under the first bind, while Quick continued working the keypad.

After several moments, a long beep sounded. The suitcase timer went black. But the phone continued its relentless countdown, flashing 25:23. Quick grabbed it and shot up. Behind her, Slater cut a final bind. Amanda spit out her gag and sprang up.

"I don't have time to explain," Quick said, reaching down, "but during the next twenty-four or so minutes, I need to disarm two more of these suitcases."

She snatched up one of the dead men's Micro Uzis and pushed it at Slater, nodding at Solta. "Tie her up and then get yourselves out of here. And if her twin shows up, shoot first and make introductions later."

Quick turned and started moving, when the words came, at first faint and strangled but then rising in volume and intent, freezing the scientist in place: "I'm so, so sorry—I really fucked everything up this time."

Quick turned and stared at the dreadlocked woman.

"I swear it was supposed to be one conventional bomb. That's what they said, I swear." Amanda looked from Slater to Quick. "You have to believe me. I didn't know. The one in Madrid was supposed to be the only one—just a little explosion to scare people into waking up, that's what Gabe said. Just one little bomb." She appeared ready to collapse as if the admission had emptied her.

"You knew about these suitcases—," Slater started.

Quick cut her off, "If I don't find the other bombs in time, none of it will matter. Just get out of here. Now." Quick turned.

"Please find them. And stop them," Amanda cried.

"Don't worry, I will—"

"Amanda. My name is Amanda—"

"Davies," Quick finished for her.

The dreadlocked woman's mouth hung open. "How—"

"Your mother is looking for you, Amanda," came the echoing words from the down tunnel, where Sam Quick was disappearing around the curve.

MONDAY, JULY 16
Island of La Palma

Con Dios 1949. Wooden crosses such as this riddled the Devil's Throat, each one crafted from two simple boards nailed at a right angle, each one marking the site where an unfortunate miner had given his life while pursuing the red ore. Running by, Quick barely caught the faded name under the epitaph, and she had no idea why it, among the countless others, stuck with her, but it did: *Poncio Díaz.*

Quick's lungs burned. Her quads screamed. Sweat dripped from her body. The second suitcase and its timer lay dark and disarmed one hundred yards behind her, bookended by two corpses with bullets in their heads, just like the men piled beside the bomb stationed by Slater and Amanda. The result, Quick assumed, of the second set of shots that she had heard earlier.

The shaft jagged left. Quick cornered. Just ahead was the junction with the main tunnel leading to the surface. A right turn would take her to sunlight. But she continued running forward without even a glance toward the outside world.

Quick entered the section where the tracks lay partially buried by the rockslides, the webs of trickling water covered the stone, and the pitch-black openings to the elevator shafts dotted the walls. She would have preferred proceeding more stealthily given that Nin Zanin surely remained somewhere in the mine. But her only chance of success was finding and disarming the third bomb as fast as possible. And that meant running forward without regard for the noise she generated.

After covering another three hundred yards, she burst into the hexagonal chamber with its rotating platform for redirecting ore carts. Fallen rocks and splintered timbers still partially covered the wooden circle as they had during Quick's last visit. But now, directly in the platform's center, beside a yellow arrow and geospatial coordinates spray painted on the planks, lay the third and final suitcase.

The chamber echoed with the thud of her boots against the old timbers. Quick knelt beside the suitcase. The Walther P99 and the smartphone landed with thunks on the wood. The phone's timer flashed 12:13.

Close. But still time.

Quick stabbed the center square of the keypad and then jagged her finger around the matrix, moving from memory, with the smartphone's instructions no longer necessary.

She had completed the first third of the disarmament sequence, when she heard it behind her—the voice she had been expecting.

"Please, Dr. Quick, don't touch another key or be so rash as to reach for your Walther."

Quick glanced at the old man's gun. Then she slowly rose and turned to face the voice. "I figured the sulfurous odor was simply the Devil Throat's off-gassing. But, of course, I should have recognized it was Eau de Nin."

"Well put yet again, Dr. Quick." The Beretta Bobcat slinked from a dark tunnel mouth, with its mistress swaying closely behind. Nin Zanin entered the chamber, while the Bobcat maintained its aim at Quick's head.

"Your tenacity is impressive," Nin said. "It's a shame that your allegiance to your nation is so clear, because otherwise, Sergei would have great use for a woman of your talents."

"A job offer about as tempting as a glass of battery acid."

Nin moved in, smiling. "However, this time, Samantha Quick, you lose." She glanced at the suitcase and the flashing timer. "And soon, your beloved country will lay wasted."

Quick returned the smile. "I'd think again if I were you." She nodded toward the tunnel beyond Nin's left shoulder.

"Really, you expect me to fall for that simple trick—"

Stone crunched behind Nin.

Her head whipped around, but the Bobcat's muzzle remained locked on Quick. A uniformed officer stepped forward with his gun aimed at Nin.

Nin's laughter filled the chamber. And the Spaniard's gun swung to Quick's chest. The police officer moved directly beside Nin, with a grin smearing his handsome face. "*Hola*, Dr. Quick."

"You see, we befriended certain members of the local authorities, anticipating just such a contingency," Nin said.

Quick shrugged. "Apparently, you've thought of everything."

"I do try." The flashing suitcase readout caught Nin's eye. She sighed. "I am afraid time precludes further banter, Dr. Quick. I must rearm the other bombs and gather my sister—"

"Let me save you the trouble." Slater marched out from a

tunnel, pulling along a stooped Solta Zanin by the hair, which was wound around Slater's arm as if it were a mountain climber's rope to safety. In the Hawaiian's other hand, a Micro Uzi drilled into Solta's temple. Behind the conjoined women, Amanda Davies quietly followed, her dreadlocks deflated, caked in red mud.

Slater stopped at the platform's edge. She glanced at the Spanish officer, who was staring at her with his jaw muscle twitching just like he had in the police station after Manuelo had been shot. *A lifetime ago.*

Slater's gaze landed on Nin. "Now lower your guns or I blow your sister's head off."

The room froze dead silent, with everyone's lines of sight locked, except for Amanda's, which flitted from weapon to weapon, stopping between each firearm on the flashing suitcase.

Finally, Nin's lips curled: "Go ahead. Kill her."

Then her Bobcat exploded at Quick, who was already diving for the Walther. Slater swung her Micro Uzi. Nin's gun locked on Quick's position.

Amanda, shrunken behind Slater until this point, rushed forward, grabbed Solta, and shoved the woman ahead of her like a battering ram aimed directly at Nin.

Another shot blasted.

Then two more.

But Amanda could not be stopped. She slammed Solta into her twin sister. Quick jumped up with the Walther. The officer aimed for her. But three rounds from Slater's Uzi demolished his pretty face. The Spaniard collapsed. Amanda, Solta, and Nin landed in a pile.

Quick and Slater had no clear shot without risking killing

Amanda. Quick jumped the suitcase, reached into the writhing mound, and hauled out the first body she grabbed: Solta's. The 110-pound frame hung limp in her hands.

From under Amanda, a strangled scream filled the chamber—Nin seeing her twin sister riddled by bullets from her own gun. The sound lasted only a second.

Until Slater's Uzi cracked against her head.

Quick lowered Solta's body to the ground, as Slater managed to say between jagged inhalations, "I know you said to go topside. But we thought we could lend a hand."

Quick nodded, gulping air and grabbing for the smartphone. "I'm glad you did." The timer pinged 4:17. *They would make it.*

Beside Quick, Slater gently turned over Amanda. The woman's face was slack, almost childlike, with the dreadlocks splayed lifelessly across the adjacent chest of the unconscious Nin Zanin. A large red stain was spreading from Amanda's right shoulder. Slater moved to clamp the wound. But Quick seized her arm.

"Leave her." She pressed the battered smartphone into Slater's hand, as the screen flashed 3:55. "Run, Kalia, run as fast as you can to the surface and use the preset number to call Molly Matson. Tell her we disarmed the bombs, and the threat is ended. And then, when help arrives, show the medics the way here. I'll take care of Amanda."

Slater nodded, took a last look at Amanda, and then jumped up and starting running, clutching the phone as if it were a baton in an Olympic relay.

Quick crouched beside the suitcase. She glanced at Amanda's lifeless body, still heaped on the unconscious Nin, with the red stain now spread twice as large across the young woman's shirtfront. Amanda would need her immediate attention when she finished with the bomb. She resumed entering the disarmament sequence, starting from the exact point where she had left off. The suitcase's electronic chirps and beeps replaced the dying echoes of Slater's retreating footfalls.

After several more taps, Quick paused, her finger tracing the embossed numeral for a split second. Then it plunged. The suitcase gave a long, final squawk. The timer display froze and then blanked out. The last bomb was neutralized.

Quick turned to attend Amanda's wound. But the young woman's body had shifted. The dreadlocks now rested on the arm of the police officer as if the dead Spaniard had gathered the young American for a kiss.

Quick lunged for the Walther. Wood exploded inches from her face. Splinters and shrapnel tore into her neck like a fusillade of tiny daggers.

Another explosion. The pistol flew from her reach with a shower of sparks. Quick scrambled forward, chasing it. She had nothing to lose.

A click sounded behind her.

She reached the gun. The stock was mangled plastic and metal. But the slide and barrel were intact.

Another click behind her.

Quick whipped around, arcing the Walther before her.

Another click. Another.

Nin's Bobcat was empty.

Sam Quick found Nin Zanin standing motionless over her dead twin, looking from her useless gun to her opponent, her lip curled in a sneer. Quick fingered the Walther's trigger. The damaged gun might explode in her face. But she did not care. She had started this expedition governed by the laws of science, rationality, cold facts. But now rage and raw emotion—so carefully and methodically channeled for all these days into finding order from violent chaos—were her masters. Her barrel synced with the beauty mark high on Nin's check, just below the almond-shaped eye.

Then from the generator shed, Inspector Reyes, his headache finally gone, summoned his grandchildren home for dinner by doing what he always did—switching off the lights.

-68-

The door of the salon exploded open. The chair rotated. Sergei Sokolov—again the harassed brothel owner: his shirtfront stained with food drippings, cheeks rough with gray stubble, hair askance—leaned forward and rested his arms on his desk.

Heavy boots clomped on polished wood. Men, none in uniform but all armed, filled the room. An array of Kalashnikovs parted. A cycling red glow led an older man into the chamber, with the smoke of his cigarette curling behind.

"Ah, the Comrade General comes to collect his due," Sokolov growled. Sokolov jumped up and pounded his fist on the desk. His face was roiling borscht—deep red, veins contorting, chin quaking.

"Does the Comrade General understand this happens with or without me? It's too late to stop the events that will raise Russia to its rightful place!"

The general responded as gently as if he were correcting a wayward child, "But Sergei, you don't understand. That is why I am here. The Americans have already stopped you."

The cigarette ground into the floor, and the voice turned to ice. "President James sends his hope that good health blesses the Falcon."

The general turned. His retreating footfalls echoed in the salon. And the Kalashnikovs closed ranks with the synchronized clack of a dozen released safeties.

Sokolov looked around the room. Then, finally, he stepped forward. He stopped before the credenza laden with the decaying remains of his nation's finest caviar. He stared at a painting hanging on the opposite wall, into the eyes of Russia's last imperial Tsar, and raised his hand in salute.

The slugs tore through his body and into the red wall behind him. Sokolov fell backward onto the hutch, his blood drenching the rotting roe.

After a moment, the Falcon reared up. He stood for several seconds, his tired cells consuming their last oxygen. Then his knees crashed to the floor. Then his gargantuan stomach. Finally, his right jowl. His stare remained fixed on the Tsar.

. . .

2000 miles away, the launch tubes closed, and the *U.S.S. Maryland* silently sank back into the deep.

ALCHEMY

Great Bear Lake
Great Slave Lake
Mackenzie
Foxe Basin
Hudson Bay
ROCKY Mountains
CANADA
Quebec
Edmonton
Calgary
Regina
Winnipeg
Vancouver
Seattle
Portland
Columbia
Lake Superior
Quebec
Ottawa
Montreal
Toronto
Lake Huron
Lake Michigan
Detroit
Lake Ontario
Lake Erie
Boston
Nova
Salt Lake City
Denver
Kansas City
St. Louis
Chicago
New York
Philadelphia
Sacramento
Washington
Baltimore
San Francisco
UNITED STATES OF AMERICA
Los Angeles
Memphis
Atlanta
San Diego
Mexicali
El Paso
Dallas
Bermuda (U.K.)
Houston
New Orleans
NRLI Headquarters
Rio Grande
San Antonio
Miami
BAHAMAS
Monterrey
Gulf of Mexico
Havana
MEXICO
Tampico
CUBA
DOMINIC
Guadalajara
Merida
Cancun
Puerto (U.S.A
Mexico
HAITI
Acapulco
BELIZE
JAMAICA
Port-au-Prince
Santo-Domingo
HONDURAS
GUATEMEALA
Caribbean Sea
ST
EL SALVADOR
GRE
NICARAGUA
Maracaibo
Merida
Car
COSTA RICA
VENEZ
PANAMA
Medellin
ECUATOR
Cali
Bogota
COLOMBIA
Quito
Galapagos (Ecuador)
ECUADOR
Guayaquil
Iquitos
A
PERU
Trujillo
B
Lima
Cusco
La Paz
B
Arica
Sucre
Iquique
TROPIC OF CAPRICORN

ALCHEMY

Wet footprints approached from the opposite direction and then turned and climbed the steps of Building B-38. Molly Matson followed the puddles down the long hall and stopped at the familiar doorway. She rapped the doorframe, provoking a chorus of "shhhhs" from inside the lab.

The geologist quietly stepped inside. Outside the wall of windows, the Atlantic was peaceful, dazzling blue with gently curling ribbons of white falling to shore. The trays of colored vials covered the lab bench to new depths. While the corner potted palm had finally admitted defeat and was now just a collection of barren stalks surrounded by crumbling fronds.

Along the far wall, a trio gathered at the ventilation hood. Kalia Slater stood at one end. Her tan had faded, and short sleeves revealed a tight scar running the length of one forearm. Beside her, Eric Hunt leaned into the hood, with cream-colored, elastic bandages peeking out from the T-shirt adorned by the red skull and crossbones, the one he had worn all those months ago while collecting samples at the mine. Beyond Hunt stood Sam Quick, with her hair dripping and uncombed from a dip at the beach outside her lab, her tank top and shorts soaked through by the underlying wet swimsuit, with a slick of ocean water gathering at her sandaled feet.

Matson approached, and Slater slid over, motioning the older scientist to squeeze in between her and Hunt. Slater nodded at Matson, while Quick and Hunt ignored her, transfixed by the simple set up under the vent hood.

A metal ring supported a large, two-neck boiling flask. A rubber stopper skewered by a thermometer plugged one neck. A sensor arm—similar in shape to what might be plugged into a car's cigarette-lighter receptacle to charge a cellphone—filled the second neck, with a curly wire tethering it to a tablet computer. Two inches of black sludge covered the flask's bottom, while a thicker band of translucent tan broth floated above this muck, like vinaigrette that had separated into strata of dark balsamic vinegar and light olive oil.

The flask's contents appeared lifeless. Then a single colorless vesicle began forming on the upper edge of the sludge layer like a blister on burnt flesh. After expanding for several moments, it broke free and rose through the pale liquid until it breached the surface, into the air space above the broth. A beep sounded from the tablet.

Then another bubble erupted and rose to the top, followed by another beep. Then another. And another. Then two at a time. Then four. Then ten, with the bubbles soon merging into a steady, frothing stream, and the beeps, into a continuous squawk.

The four scientists looked at the each other. Then Sam Quick let out a yell, followed by Molly Matson and Eric Hunt and Kalia Slater.

. . .

SATURDAY, OCTOBER 20
Key Biscayne, Florida

Citrus trees shaded the table. Dropped lemons sunned on the patio's hot bricks. In the pool, stray fruit bobbed atop the turquoise water like misshapen tennis balls. Beyond the terrace lay a low wall, then the golf course, and finally, the sea.

Matson set down the pitcher, distributed the lemonades, and lifted her drink. "Here's to 'Quick' thinking. If not for Sam and you all, then Key Biscayne would now be an empty spit of sand. And I'd be floating in the Atlantic—along with a couple million of my fellow Floridians." Her eyes twinkled. "Though that calamity might have returned the social security system to solvency!"

The glasses rose and kissed over the table.

"Eric, Kalia, and"—Quick touched Davies's wrist, just below a red jag of healing skin—"Zach were the key players. I was just along for the ride."

Slater and Davies vigorously shook their heads, while Hunt grimaced.

"Please don't make me laugh, Sam. My ribs are still killing me as it is, especially after all the yelling over yesterday's excitement," Hunt panted, pointing at his bandages.

Matson lifted her glass again. "Speaking of yesterday, here's to the Devil's Throat: if we can keep that Devil's Throat bacteria cranking out hydrogen gas using industrial waste for food, then the United States will lead the world into the Hydrogen Age—"

"*¡Hola!*"

Everyone turned.

Seeing the new arrival, Quick and Davies jumped up, while Matson and Slater rose from their seats, and Hunt struggled to push himself up from his chair. Quick and Davies hugged the man, followed by Hunt, who gingerly gave the visitor a long hug.

Matson grabbed the entrant's hand. "I'm Molly Matson, and you must be señor Delgado."

"Sí, please call me Jorge."

"A pleasure to meet you, Jorge. I trust you had a good flight from Madrid. Please sit and have some lemonade." Matson held out an arm. "I believe you know everyone present except for our young volcanologist, Kalia Slater."

The two shook hands, and then Delgado took a seat. "So nice to see you all. After such crazy times in Spain, I figured I would never see you again, that is until Dr.—"

"I may be old enough to be your *grandmadre*, but you call me Molly!"

Delgado laughed. "That is until Molly called and invited me for a visit to Florida." He sipped from his glass and raised a brow. "American lemonade is sweeter than I expected."

Today, the usual south Florida sea breezes were slack, but the customary subtropical humidity and sunshine were ever diligent in duty. By the time Quick and the others had apprised Delgado of the events since their parting outside the Madrid dance club, including the bits that had not made the media, Dolores had refreshed the lemonade pitcher three times.

"And your guide who was shot? How is he doing?" Delgado asked.

"Manuelo Alcanzar is well on his way to a complete recovery and no doubt will soon again lead tours of the hiking trails around La Garganta del Diablo, though his wife has forbidden him from ever again entering the Devil's Throat," Quick said. "We invited them to join us today at NRLI's expense, but they declined so that Manuelo can continue his physical therapy uninterrupted."

"And the headless body in Prague? Who was that?" Delgado asked.

"The decoy corpse was that of an unfortunate young woman, an involuntary worker—" Davies started.

"A sex slave," Quick interrupted.

Davies nodded. "A sex slave in Sergei Sokolov's Prague brothel—ironically, the same position that the young Nin Zanin held before Sokolov took her as his lover."

"The good news," Quick added, "is the investigation of Sokolov's business dealings has resulted in the rescue and repatriation of several hundred teenagers from his brothels and factories."

"In fact," Davies continued, "the State Department just forwarded Eric a thank-you letter from a teenage girl named Helena, who helped Eric during his visit to the Prague brothel, and who is now back home with her family in Ukraine."

"And the old man in the Prado basement?" Delgado asked.

"Turns out he was a former CIA agent whom Sokolov and the then-underage Zanin sisters discredited at the behest of the KGB during the early '80s," Davies said. "He was a man on a high-stakes mission to clear his reputation. He lost."

"I'm just glad the crazy sisters who were after you in the disco when I met you, got what they deserved," Delgado said.

"Yes, absolutely." Quick's gaze fell briefly on Slater and Hunt, and Davies. They could never share this part of the story with

Delgado or anyone else—not even Matson—lest they risk violating the terms of the national security letter that each had received during their debriefings.

But Quick pictured the moment after the sixty seconds of pure darkness in the Devil's Throat when Inspector Reyes had switched back on the power from the generator shed, and light had returned to the hexagonal chamber: Solta Zanin and the Spanish police officer crumpled on the wooden wheel. An abandoned red shoe marking the only sign of Nin Zanin. And the warmth of Amanda Davies's blood covering her hands, as she tended the young woman's wound rather than chasing Nin into the tunnels. The scientist who had arrived on La Palma, she thought, would have gone after Nin. But instead, she had stayed to help a woman whom she barely knew. *So much for logic.*

"Zach, how is your sister doing?" Slater asked.

"Thanks to Sam's remaining with her in mine"—Davies draped an arm over Quick's shoulders, eliciting glances between Matson, Hunt, and Slater—"Manny has made as complete a recovery from her physical injuries as possible, though she'll never again have full use of one arm thanks to Nin's bullet. Sam also appealed on her behalf to President James, who could little refuse after Sam had saved his life in Madrid." Davies sighed. "Even with his intercession, Manny will be an old woman when she is released from prison."

"I wonder how Inspector Reyes is doing." Hunt asked.

"I called the Tazacorte police station in the hopes of flying him in for our little pool gathering," Matson said. "But apparently the inspector retired from the police force and now volunteers for a charity providing legal aid to African asylum-seekers on the Canary Islands. Isn't that the sweetest—"

The wave raced across the beach, golf course, and pool and then crashed onto the patio. Mouths stopped moving. Heads jerked toward the water. The sound wave receded, as the noise of the outlier breaker, an ocean wave significantly larger than its companions but by no means unusual, faded.

Around the table, the six looked at each other with large eyes, and their embarrassed laughter lasted until a voice called out, "Ms. Molly?"

"Ah, there you are!" Matson shot up and across the patio to Dolores, who was flanked at each arm by a man in white—on one side, by a tanned young man in tennis shorts and a T-shirt, and at the other arm, by a tall, buzz-cut young man in a naval uniform. Matson inserted herself between the men, hooked their arms with hers, and led them toward the table.

"Everyone, this is Jake, my tennis instructor"—she turned to other man—"and this is Ensign Eddie Lewis, NRLI's tech wizard."

Everyone waved "hello," while Quick shook her head.

Matson continued, "Sam and Kalia are already suited up, and Eric is excused due to his injuries. But Zach and Jorge, I insist you follow these boys into the pool house and change into the waiting bathing suits. Then we'll have a nice swim before dinner."

Davies and Delgado looked at each other, shrugged, and rose to follow the new arrivals. As the men neared the cabana, Matson shouted, "If on the off-chance Dolores forgot to put out the suits, then don't worry, we're real casual around here!"

The tennis player looked over his shoulder and shook his head. Matson blew him a kiss.

After the men had disappeared into the pool house, Quick

turned to Matson. "You old dog—I'll wager anything that not a single swimsuit is waiting in that cabana."

Molly Matson raised her glass and looked at Eric Hunt and Kalia Slater. "No, sweetie, they sure *don't* call you Sam Quick for nothing!"

ACKNOWLEDGEMENTS

FIRST, I THANK the people of La Palma for welcoming me to your island and pointing me in the right direction as I researched this book. La Palma is truly one of the most beautiful places I've ever seen, and the islanders are some of the friendliest people on earth. I am honored to have visited.

Next, I thank geophysicists Steven N. Ward and Simon Day for their important research describing the potential threat that La Palma's western flank poses. The television program "Mega-Tsunami: Wave of Destruction" first brought my attention to this danger and set off all those nagging "what if" questions that have held me captive for all these years.

My deep thanks go to the readers who suffered through the early drafts and revisions, and whose input made this a better novel. In alphabetical order, these heroes include Paul Clark, Andrew Corlett, Kim Corlett, Joe DeMatio, Peg Kelley, Jary Larsen, and Jim Washburn. My partner in all things, Peter Rowland, endured the most rereads, and the book is far the better for his wisdom and advice.

To my other close friends and family members—Dad&Sue, Ron, A&M, BM, DC, EJ, G&G, GP, J&M, KV, M&R, and RW—I thank you for your support. And to Seven and Craig Vassau, I'm sorry I didn't finish this in time—your barks and laughter are missed.

I am in the debt of many others, including but by no means limited to John Nieto for his always excellent photography.

Finally, I am most grateful to you, the reader, for sharing this adventure with Sam Quick and me. Please tell your friends about the book. And be on the lookout—Sam Quick is already hunting for her next adventure.

SC

SCOTT CORLETT

Photo: John Nieto

SCOTT CORLETT IS the author of the Sam Quick Adventure series. He lives in San Francisco and enjoys climbing volcanic islands. Visit scottcorlett.com to learn more.

COMING SOON

SAM QUICK IS already hunting for her next adventure. The next book in the Sam Quick Adventure series will be available soon. Sign up at scottcorlett.com to receive updates.